DEADLY TASKS

GK MONÉT

MILTON & HUGO L.L.C.
4407 Park Ave., Suite 5
Union City, NJ 07087, USA

Website: *www. miltonandhugo.com*
Hotline: *1- 888-778-0033*
Email: *info@miltonandhugo.com*

Ordering Information:
Quantity sales. Special discounts are granted to corporations, associations, and other organizations. For more information on these discounts, please reach out to the publisher using the contact information provided above.

ISBN-13:	979-8-89285-713-0	[Paperback Edition]
	979-8-89285-712-3	[Hardback Edition]
	979-8-89285-711-6	[Digital Edition]

Rev. date: 10/29/2025

ONE

November 9, 1988

The detectives Bagster and Wynne weren't sure what to make of Alex Dorson.

The young man sat in their interrogation room, staring blankly at the wall, seemingly unbothered that he was detained and cuffed. What on earth had happened to him? His blond hair was in a state: stringy with sweat and clinging to his pale face. His white T-shirt and black jeans obviously weren't clean and fresh. The shirt had dried sweat stains, while the black jeans were stained with something even darker in color. Blood. Freckles of the substance also covered the kid's face and neck.

"Do you seriously think he's the one?" Wynne asked his partner. While the blood on the boy was troubling, it did not mean he was a murderer.

The murders had started quickly. There had been little evidence and no suspects. Until now. Until Alex. The kid had just strolled into the station and surrendered. All of it was a shock to those working on the cases. It didn't make sense.

Detective Bagster rubbed his face. "I don't know. Let's just see what he has to say. Are you ready?"

Bagster was older than Wynne and a little grayer in the hair, but he wore this as a badge of seniority. The two had been partners for close to a year and made a good team. So far there hadn't been a case that they couldn't solve together—except this one. While Alex Dorson did not align with their expectations, they secretly hoped he was the man they were looking for because they had nothing else.

"It's now or never," Wynne answered, uncrossing his arms. The two detectives left their side of the one-way mirror and joined the suspect in the interrogation room.

Even with the arrival of the detectives, Alex did not move a muscle. The only flicker of acknowledgment came from his eyes. They moved quickly to the gentlemen. Those eyes, dark and empty, watched the detectives as they sat down. The rest of Alex remained motionless, his face unreadable.

"You are not under arrest yet," Wynne informed the young man—to see if that would elicit any reaction from him. It did not. He continued with the procedural talk and jargon, but his words came automatically, his mind too focused on the kid's emotionless, traumatized face.

"Do you understand?" then came the words of Bagster, who gave his partner a stern look. Wynne must have trailed off, his distraction getting the best of him.

To their surprise, Alex moved at this question; he nodded in response. Bagster then explained the interview was being recorded by a wall-mounted camera and pointed at it, but Alex didn't even flinch. The camera meant nothing to him.

Wynne was again doubting that the young man in handcuffs was the one they had been searching for. He didn't strike Wynne as a killer or even a tough guy. He was just odd. "Alex," Wynne started, "they told us you have a confession to make."

Once again, Alex nodded his head, but his expression remained unchanged. After a brief period of silence, he did begin to speak: "I do have a confession. I need to confess so I can be stopped."

"Stopped? Stopped from doing what?" Bagster asked sternly as he played with the pen in his hand. He was prepared to start writing on the yellow legal pad under his hands if Alex began to share important information, although he wasn't expecting anything worth noting. "What is it you are doing that you shouldn't be doing?"

Alex lifted his head to a normal position and looked deeply into Bagster's eyes. "I murdered the four women you found."

A chill ran down Bagster's spine as he stared back into Alex's dark eyes. The confession alone wasn't enough to prove Alex was telling the truth, but the windows to his soul were starting to convince Bagster it might be true. The only word that left his mouth in response to what he had just heard was, "Why?"

"Because Jack told me to," Alex answered without hesitation or emotion.

Jack. This grabbed Wynne's attention. Could the boy mean Jack the Ripper? "Who is Jack?" Wynne asked, taking over from Bagster. "Is he your partner? Were you both involved in murdering these women?"

Alex switched his focus to Wynne, but only his eyes moved. "Jack is the one who is making me do this. If you don't stop me, you can't stop him. He is angry with me right now."

Wynne looked at him with a confused expression. "Why is Jack upset with you, Alex?"

"Because I disobeyed him last night."

"Alex, I'm having trouble following you. Are you sure you are responsible for four dead women?" It was obvious to Wynne that Alex had some sort of mental problem or situation going on in his head. He didn't want to waste valuable time talking to him if he wasn't the killer. So far he didn't seem to fit.

The question struck a nerve with Alex. He sat up straight in his chair and put both hands on the table, the cuffs clinking. Then, he inched forward and glared at Wynne. "You don't believe me?"

"I'm not sure at this point," Wynne truthfully answered. He glared back and said, "Tell me something that would convince me you are a cold-blooded killer."

The corners of Alex's mouth pulled back across his face. "There is a fifth woman you don't know anything about yet. She is dead, but I couldn't finish the job on her like Jack wanted me to. That's why he is angry with me."

The two detectives exchanged glances. They both knew that would be enough to arrest him, but only if what he said was true. Wynne decided to call Alex's bluff. He still felt Alex didn't fit the profile he had made up in his head about the killer. "The other women were discovered rather quickly, Alex. Don't you read the newspapers? If you killed this other woman, why hasn't she already been discovered?"

Alex leaned back in his metal chair and removed his hands from the table, the cuffs scraping unpleasantly. "Because she's not out in the open like the others. She's in her apartment a few blocks from here. Springdale Apartments. Number 113. Go check it out. You won't be disappointed. She's not complete, but she's worth seeing."

"Do you realize what will happen if we find something there?" Bagster tried to not get too excited about the fact that they could actually have their man. It would be horrible to have another woman dead, but she would be the last one to fall victim to Alex, and whoever Jack was.

"Yeah, I do," Alex answered. "You'll arrest me, I won't be able to kill anyone else, and Jack may finally go away. All will be well again."

Wynne asked him, "Do you know what will happen if we find nothing?"

With a stone face, Alex replied, "That won't happen. So I guess it doesn't matter, does it?"

"We will see," Wynne said. "You stay put. We will be back." He stood and left the interview room with Bagster on his heels. "Are you ready to see if he is telling the truth or not?"

"You bet I am," Bagster replied as they navigated the police station. "I think he is telling the truth."

After they made sure someone would watch Alex, the two men left the building and headed for their car. They arrived at the apartment tower in no time, as it was, in fact, only about six blocks from the police station. The two detectives immediately went to the manager's office. They'd need to get into the apartment, and a key would be their best bet. The manager had no problem going with them to the apartment in question once he saw their badges. The apartments didn't have a very good reputation, and the manager didn't want any trouble.

Detective Bagster banged on the apartment door and announced their presence loudly. When no one answered, he motioned for the manager to open the door. The man was so nervous he about dropped the key, but he finally unlocked the door and stepped back to allow the detectives to enter. Immediately, their instincts told them something wasn't right.

They made their way through the small apartment to the one and only bedroom. The door stood wide open. Cautiously, the detectives entered the room and were instantly bewildered by what they found. Neither of the men had seen anything so gruesome in all their careers.

The room wasn't completely dark. A single beam of light shone down from the gap in the curtains and highlighted a still body on a bed. Both the body and bed were soaked in the crimson of her blood. The victim's face was carved up, with flaps of skin hanging horribly, and barely looked human. Organs were possibly moved around, if not missing. Stringy muscle tissue and the white of her bones were easily visible on parts of her body.

"This is the worst one by far," Bagster said. "I think we had better call this into the station. We need people in here to process this apartment as soon as possible. The coroner is going to have a time with this one."

Wynne was still in shock as he tried to comprehend what had been done to the woman lying on the bed. "Alex said he didn't finish her. What could he possibly have meant by that?"

"I have no idea," Bagster said as he headed out of the bedroom. "There isn't much left of her to finish. I just wonder what he was trying to do."

"That's something I would like to know myself." Wynne followed his partner out of the room. "Well, now that he is in custody, maybe we can find out. Of course, we still don't know anything about this Jack person."

"No, but we will soon enough."

Bagster and Wynne waited outside until the investigators arrived at the crime scene. Wynne went back into the apartment with them to take a closer look around. As Alex had spent so much time there, he felt there had to be something left behind. The only items he found were Alex's hat, gloves, jacket, and a knife. The crime scene investigators bagged the items. Wynne knew if the gloves were left behind, then fingerprints might be left behind too.

Outside, Bagster roamed the parking lot, looking for Alex's car. He knew it had to be there, but none of them stood out to him. When the coroner arrived, he abandoned his search. An officer was put in charge of locating it as Bagster went to meet with the coroner to view the body. He tried to prepare her for what she was going to find, but there was no way to prepare anyone for such a gruesome sight.

"I guess I have my work cut out for me," was all the coroner said when she saw what Alex had left for her.

TWO

Four Months Earlier

It was a hot summer afternoon when Alex Dorson left his job at the neighborhood grocery store to drive home to his apartment. Alex was twenty-two years old, and he was enjoying life. His job as a stocker wasn't much as far as pay, but it helped pay the bills for his one-bedroom apartment while he tried to finish college. Classes for his final year were set to start in the fall. After graduation, he planned to leave Lexington, where he'd lived his whole life, to pursue a career as a journalist in New York or another large city like it.

Alex had himself a girlfriend also. Jana and Alex were high school sweethearts. She was also in college working toward a degree in business. Her future plans involved following Alex to wherever he decided to go. Marriage and a family were also in her plans, but Alex wasn't ready for any of that just yet. Jana knew with time he would be ready to settle down. She just needed to be patient and spend that time working on a career.

In addition to Jana, Alex also had two really good friends, Josh and Tony. Josh was in college at the University of Kentucky with Alex and Jana, but Tony had gone straight from high school to help his dad run the family hardware store. Someday, when Tony's dad was ready to retire, the whole store would be his. Josh was working toward a business degree just like Jana, but his plans were to stay right where he was. Lexington was a good-sized city with plenty of big businesses, and Josh figured he would start out in an entry-level position with a local business and start climbing the corporate ladder. He didn't see the point in venturing off to someplace unfamiliar to try to build a life.

Alex always knew Josh and Tony would never get too far from their families or Lexington.

As for Alex's family, his mom and dad were still married, but not happily. He suspected they only stayed together for his fifteen-year-old sister, Jessica. In his mind, the marriage would probably end the minute she left for college. Alex had told Jessica about the way he saw things with their parents, and she agreed with him completely. Part of the reason he planned to leave after college was so he wouldn't be around for the divorce, and Jessica was planning to go away to college for the same reason. Neither of them wanted to see their parents divorce, but they both could see the couple were miserable together.

On this particular day, Alex wasn't thinking about college in the fall, his parents, or his future. He drove towards home with the windows down and the music up loud. "New Sensation" by INXS was playing for the hundredth time on the radio, and Alex sang along, not caring who heard him. It was a Friday, and that meant he and Jana had a date. On Saturday nights they hung out with their individual friends. That arrangement had always worked out for both of them. Unfortunately, Alex's plans were about to change.

Without any warning, a young boy darted out in front of Alex's vehicle. His first and only reaction was to jerk the wheel left, which caused his car to cross the center line and enter oncoming traffic. A pickup truck screeched as it tried to stop, but the driver's efforts failed. The truck slammed into the passenger side of Alex's small car, spinning it sideways. Finally, his car came to a stop when it was pinned between the truck and a large tree. The loud crashes and squeals were over. There was nothing left in the air but silence.

—∞—

When Alex woke up a few hours later, he discovered he was in the hospital. His mind could barely remember the accident, but he remembered all of the people that filled the room he was occupying. The only face that mattered at the moment belonged to Jana. Her smile and warm blue eyes were all he could focus on once he started to feel pain shooting through his entire body. She seemed to bring him some peace, but she wasn't the only one there.

"How do you feel, honey?" his mom asked as she rushed to his side. She kissed him on the forehead and began to rub his hair.

"I'm fine, Mom," he groaned, wanting her to not smother him. "My body doesn't feel too well. What happened?"

His dad answered from the foot of the hospital bed. "There was a car accident. Don't you remember it?"

Alex pushed a button to raise the head part of the bed up. It caused him more pain, but only for a moment. "I remember a little boy running out in front of me. That's all though. Is the boy okay?" He really hoped he hadn't hit the child. There was no way he could live with that on his conscience.

His mom smiled at him and said, "He is fine. His mom was the one that called for help. She was here earlier checking on you because she feels horrible about what happened."

"Is my car totaled?" Alex wondered.

"It is," his dad regretfully told him. "Don't worry about that right now, son. We'll figure that out later."

Jana wanted to be alone with Alex to see if he really was all right or if he was just saying so for his parents' sake. With them there, she decided to stay quiet and be patient. Everyone knew Mr. and Mrs. Dorson didn't stay in the same room together for very long. Jana was pretty confident they would both leave once they felt Alex was indeed okay.

"Jana, dear, why don't you go see if you can find a nurse to let them know Alex is awake and in pain," Mrs. Dorson suggested to Jana. Jana smiled at the woman standing next to Alex, who was dressed in a business suit with her hair up in a bun, as she left the room without saying a word.

Alex let out a small moan as he tried to adjust himself in his bed. "Have you talked to the doctor?"

Mr. Dorson patted his son on the foot and nodded. "She told us you are in pretty good shape considering the accident. You don't have anything broken, but your body is beaten up quite a bit. She wants to keep you here overnight to keep an eye on you. One of us will be here in the morning to take you home to our house."

"I think I would rather go to my apartment," Alex stated firmly.

His mother replied, "Nonsense! You are coming to stay with us for a few days so we can take care of you. Jessica is even willing to do her part to help."

He was sure Jessica would be thrilled to just have him around again. That way she wouldn't be home alone with their parents, at least for a few days. "I guess it will be all right for a couple of days. Can one of you call the store and let them know I won't be in for a few days? I don't want to lose my job over this."

"I'll call them when I get home," his father assured him.

The door to the hospital room opened, and a female doctor entered the room with Jana behind her. The doctor looked very pleased to see her patient awake and alert. There had been some concern about possible head injuries. After she checked him out and spoke to him for a few, she was confident he would be fine. The tests she had run when he arrived didn't show anything abnormal, but she still felt better after talking to him one-on-one.

The doctor then told Alex basically the same thing his parents had said. She wanted him to stay the night in the hospital for observation, but he could probably go home in the morning. When the doctor left, Alex's parents said their good nights to him and Jana. With their departure, the couple was finally alone. Their time would be short. Visiting hours were almost over for the night.

Jana sat down on the side of the bed carefully. She moved his hair back from his face with her fingers. "Are you really okay?" she asked him softly.

Alex closed his eyes and smiled as he enjoyed the feel of her fingers on the sides of his face. "I'm much better now."

The door opened again, interrupting their private moment. It was a nurse bringing in some pain medication for Alex. She watched him take the medicine and then reminded Jana that visiting hours were almost over before she left them alone again. Jana didn't plan to stay long anyway. Alex needed his rest, and the pain pills sure wouldn't keep him awake once they started to take effect.

Once the door closed to his room, Alex asked Jana, "Will you come and stay with me at my parents' house?"

She laughed. "Alex, I love you dearly and would do anything for you, but I can't do that. I'll come to visit you though."

"I know my parents are hard to handle sometimes," Alex said, grinning. "I thought I would ask though."

"At least Jessica will be there," Jana pointed out. She leaned down and gently kissed him on the forehead. "I better get going. You need to rest, and I'm sure someone will be back to run me out of here in a few minutes."

"You're probably right," Alex said sadly. "I'll call you when I get to my parents' house tomorrow."

After Jana had left, Alex turned on the TV and tried to find something to watch. Slowly, the pain in his body started to ease up. It wasn't long before the drowsiness started to settle in him. He tried to force himself to stay awake, but as time passed he began to realize it was a losing battle. Finally, he turned off the TV, settled himself in his bed, and let his heavy lids close over his eyes.

A couple of hours later, Alex woke up to the sound of someone calling his name. The hospital room was dark, but there was a small amount of light coming in around the blinds from the street lights outside. Alex squinted into the darkness, half awake, his heart tapping away. When he found himself alone, Alex thought he had been dreaming, and he closed his eyes again.

"Alex."

His eyes popped open immediately. He knew for sure he wasn't dreaming. Alex tried to prop himself up on his arms to take a better look around the room, but he couldn't move.

His body was frozen.

Alex started to panic as he tried to move any part of his body. Pain and his racing heartbeat was all he felt. The voice whispered a couple more times. "Alex. Alex."

Alex shifted his eyes frantically around the room, but in the darkness it was hard to see. "Come on," he muttered, concentrating hard to move his fingers. The doctor had said he was fine—that he was lucky to have had no severe injuries. There was no reason for him to be paralyzed now. His body just needed to wake up.

"Alex."

Alex's eyes shot across the room, and his heart almost gave out. Someone was there. A tall and dark figure, subtle against the shadows, was there, still and watching him.

His heart and brain racing, Alex finally managed to twitch his right index finger and was overcome with relief. Finger by finger, then limb by limb, he pried his body awake. Without hesitation, he pushed the call button for the nurse. That dark patch of the room was still there, staring at him. Alex prayed it was just some illusion, but if anyone was there, they would be discovered as soon as the nurse entered.

"Turn on the overhead light," Alex instructed the nurse the second the door cracked open.

The nurse flipped the light switch on. Alex's eyes darted to the part of the room where the dark figure had been.

No one was there. Just a tall cabinet.

The nurse approached his bedside, deeply concerned. "Are you okay? What do you need?"

Maybe it was nothing after all, just the shadows in the room. But Alex swore he saw something—someone—watching him. And the voice. A man's voice had been calling *his* name. The windows were closed, the TV was off; there was no explanation. It must have all been in his head.

Not wanting to tell her about the voice, as clearly there was no one there, and he didn't want her to think he was crazy, he told her, "It still hurts when I move. Can I have another pill for the pain?"

The nurse smiled at him sympathetically and replied, "Let me go see when you last had your medication. If it's time for another pill, I'll bring one back for you."

She had left the light on when she left the room. Even though he knew it would hurt, Alex pushed the button on the bed to raise his head up. There wasn't another soul in the room anywhere. There wasn't anywhere for anyone to hide either. What he had heard and seen didn't make any sense to him, but he figured it was just his imagination. There was some comfort in the thought of being knocked out by another pain pill. Maybe he would be able to sleep until morning this time.

To his relief, the nurse returned with a pill. After he swallowed it, she left his side and turned the light off on her way out of his room. Alex kept his bed in an upright position and waited quietly to see if the voice returned. As time passed, he found it hard to stay awake. He put the bed back down and drifted off to sleep again.

—ᛘ—

"Wake up, Alex!" his mom said loudly the next morning as she entered his room. She walked to the side of his bed as he tried to open his eyes. The light pouring into the room from the morning sun made the feat hard. Mrs. Dorson kissed her son on the forehead and said, "You need to wake up. The doctor should be here soon to release you. I'm going to take you home to Jessica, and then I have to get to work."

The fact his mom had to go to her real estate office was good news to Alex. Jessica would be much easier to deal with in his condition. His mom raised his bed up and began trying to find his clothes. When she did find them, she discovered they were not fit to wear. She shoved them back in the bag they were in and put the bag in the trash.

"What are you doing?" Alex yelled at her. "What do you expect me to wear?"

Mrs. Dorson unzipped a duffle bag that was sitting in a chair at the end of the bed. "I'm surprised they even kept your clothes. I brought a pair of your father's jogging pants and a shirt for you to wear. I think they will do for now."

Time seemed to drag on forever while they waited for the doctor to arrive. When she did arrive to release him, he asked her if the pain medication had any side effects. Of course there were possible side effects, but none of the ones she mentioned explained the voice in the middle of the night. The doctor asked if he was having problems with the medications, but once again Alex didn't want to tell about his experience the previous night.

"I was just wondering what I should expect," Alex explained.

"Well, if you have any problems, just let me know. You should only be on the medicine for another three to four days," the doctor informed him. "The pain should start to subside a little more each day. You didn't have any serious injuries, but your body did take a beating. Over-the-counter pain relievers will do when the pain medication is gone, but I doubt you will need anything by then. So, if there aren't any more questions, I'll sign your release papers and let your mom take you home. If you need anything, you can call the hospital or me. Take care of yourself, Alex."

When the doctor was gone, Alex's mom helped him get dressed. He had put it off long enough. A nurse came in shortly after and gave him a prescription and a copy of his release papers. Then she pulled out a wheelchair and wheeled him to the main floor and out to his mom's car.

Alex hadn't given much thought to what he was going to do about his job or car yet. He knew his dad had probably called the grocery store and told them about the accident, but he didn't want to get fired for taking too much time off work. His dad also said they would figure out what to do about a car later, but he would need one for work soon.

He knew eventually everything would work out, and his life would get back to normal. As long as he hadn't caused any harm to anyone else, he would get through anything that came at him. If the child in the street had been harmed or even killed, Alex would have had a hard time living with himself. The boy being fine was probably the most important thing he was grateful for. It was one less thing to be worried about, and he had plenty to worry about all of a sudden.

As his mom pulled into the driveway, Alex looked at the two-story house and wondered how he would survive being back home. Jessica ran out the front door to greet her older brother. He could see the excitement on her face as she flung open his car door. Carefully, she helped him out of the seat. She rambled the whole way into the house about everything she was going to do for him to help him get better. Suddenly, he knew he would be fine with her there. He was going to be in good hands with his little sister caring for him.

THREE

The week at his parents' house seemed to drag on forever. Other than some stiffness in his body, Alex was basically returning to normal. Going back to his apartment was something he had looked forward to all week. He was actually looking forward to going back to work. He just wanted his life to return to the way it was before the accident.

Alex packed up the few personal things his mom and sister had brought him from his apartment. Luckily, he was alone and free to go at any time. After his things were gathered together, Alex carried his bag out to the car his dad had bought him the day before, which was now sitting in the driveway. He completely despised the car. It was compact and a deep maroon with a black interior. And it was definitely used. While his old car was far from new, this "new" one was even older. Though the worst part of all of this was that he had to pay his dad back for it.

After he arrived home, he noticed his apartment was clean. It wasn't ever filthy, but he was a young man that lived by himself. The apartment had a tendency to be a tad bit messy. Once he put his belongings away, he sat down on the couch and called the grocery store to speak with his boss. He wanted to make sure he still had a job.

"Mr. Jenson, it's Alex," he said when his boss answered the phone.

To his relief, Mr. Jenson sounded pleased to hear from him. "Alex! How are you? When are you coming back to work?"

"Well, that's what I was calling you about, Mr. Jenson," Alex replied. "I'm doing much better and really need to get back to work as soon as possible. When can I get back on the schedule?"

"I can probably make room for you tomorrow if that's okay," Mr. Jenson informed him. "Do you have transportation?"

Alex chuckled. "I guess you can say I do. My dad bought me a car. It's pretty old, but it runs. I need to get back to work so I can pay him back." Alex knew he couldn't complain much about the car. One day he would be able to have a nice new car like each of his parents had.

"Okay then. Be here by nine in the morning, and I'll get you on the schedule tomorrow for the next week," Mr. Jenson instructed Alex before ending the call.

The burden of money off his shoulders, Alex was ready to see Jana. She hadn't come to his parents' house. He didn't blame her either. Most of the people he knew felt uncomfortable around his parents anymore. With one quick phone call, Jana was on her way to see him. Alex put his feet up on the coffee table and laid his head against the back of the couch. He closed his eyes to rest awhile until Jana arrived.

The apartment was completely silent as Alex relaxed. While he was alone, he didn't feel alone. Someone softly called his name. Alex opened his eyes and looked around. There was no one there, just like at the hospital. He heard the voice again, but it was so quiet and soft it was hard to tell where it was coming from. When the voice came again, Alex got to his feet and began to walk around while he strained to listen. He jumped suddenly at a loud noise. It was a knock on the door.

Alex opened the door, and there Jana was on the other side. She immediately saw his paleness and asked, "Are you all right? You look like you've seen a ghost."

Alex let her in and replied, "I'm fine. My mind has been playing tricks on me since the accident. I keep thinking someone is calling my name, but I know that isn't possible."

The two sat down on the couch. Jana was concerned about Alex. She had hoped he would look better than when she saw him last. His bruises had turned an awful shade of yellow, and his face was so sickly looking. There were dark circles under his eyes that made him look like he hadn't slept in days. "Are you sure you are okay? You don't look very well."

"I feel pretty good," he responded. He did feel better. "I was in a car accident. How did you expect me to look?"

Jana had never heard such harshness in his voice. "I'm sorry. I don't know what I expected."

After realizing what he had said and how he said it, he tried to explain. "It's all right. I just need to get back to work and back to a normal routine. It wasn't much fun being at my parents' house, but I wouldn't have been able to take care of myself alone. Jessica and my mom did a lot for me. I'm glad to be home though."

She relaxed and asked, "When are you going back to work?"

"Tomorrow."

"Oh," she said, surprised. "I figured you would wait another day or two. I was hoping to be able to take care of you myself a little bit." Jana had hoped they would have some extra time together.

Alex grinned at her. "You know my back still hurts some. I could use someone to take care of me tonight. Are you interested?"

Smiling back at him, she replied, "I am. Anything I can do to help you feel better."

"A kiss would help a bunch," he suggested as he moved his mouth closer to hers. She happily obliged. It had seemed like an eternity to the couple since they had been able to share a private moment together.

The moment didn't last long. Alex heard the male voice calling his name again. He leaned away from Jana. "Did you hear that?"

With a confused look on her face, she responded, "I didn't hear anything. What did it sound like?"

He answered her with a whisper. "It sounded like a man's voice calling my name." Alex left Jana alone on the couch and started to walk around the apartment in search of the voice. When she opened her mouth to protest, he ordered her to be quiet so he could listen intently. But again, he found nothing. Alex returned to the couch.

Jana took his hand in hers. "Alex, why am I suddenly worried about you? Is there something you need to talk about? You know I'm here for you."

"There's nothing I need to talk about," he assured her.

"Are you sure? You seem a little uneasy." She couldn't quite figure out how to put it, but the thought of him hearing someone call his name when they were the only ones there wasn't normal.

Alex knew what she was getting at by asking all the questions. He knew she thought he was losing it. Maybe he was, but he didn't need her to point it out. "Everything is good!" he snapped. "There's nothing going on with me that I need to discuss with you!"

His tone completely shocked her. Alex had never raised his voice or talked to her that way before, but he had done it twice in the short time she had been there. Jana wasn't going to wait around for him to do it a third time. She picked up her purse and stood up from the couch. "I'm not sure what is going on with you, Alex, but I don't need to be talked to like that. Call me when you get back to 'normal'."

"Wait," Alex said, grabbing her arm before she could walk away from him. "I'm sorry. Please don't leave. I need you to stay with me. Sit back down."

He did look like he meant what he said. Jana sat back down. She couldn't help but smile at him as he looked at her with his big brown eyes. She brushed his hair back from his face and tucked it behind his ear. After she did the same to the other side, she said, "I love you, Alex. I always have, but something seems different about you. I haven't been here that long, and I'm already picking up on it. You don't have to tell me what it is, but I'll listen if you ever decide to."

The only response Alex gave her was a kiss on the cheek and a hug. Most times, he felt extremely lucky to have Jana. At the moment, he felt unsure. There did seem to be something different, something strange all around him, but he wasn't sure if she would understand. *He* didn't even understand it. At first, he thought it was the pain medication, but he hadn't taken any for a few days. Maybe it wasn't completely out of his system yet. The voice he was hearing sure sounded real. Maybe he should keep that to himself in the future. Jana didn't hear it, and she seemed upset about the way he had acted. He didn't want to upset her or anyone else. Maybe a few more days would be enough time for the medicine to be gone. Then hopefully the voice would be gone also. The doctor hadn't listed hearing voices as a possible side effect, but what else could have caused it?

After a moment, Alex leaned back away from Jana and said, "I think the pain medication is affecting me in strange ways. I quit taking it a few days ago, so I'm hoping it will get out of my system soon. I don't want to worry you because I really am fine, except for my back and my... hearing things."

Jana laughed. "Well, I might be able to help with one problem. Why don't I go run you a hot bath? I bet a soak in the tub will loosen up some of the muscles. And while you are soaking, I'll order us a pizza. How does that sound?"

"Great," Alex said. "A peaceful night at home with you instead of my family sounds perfect."

"Then I'll go start your bath water."

Alex watched Jana as she left the room. The main thing on his mind was what the rest of the day, and night, would hold for them. While he was at his parents' house he heard the voice a few times, but it was usually when he was asleep. He never mentioned it to anyone because he thought he could have been dreaming. Now he was hearing it when he was fully awake, and he was the only one who could hear it. He didn't want his first night alone with Jana since the accident to be ruined by his faulty imagination.

When Jana returned to the living room, she took Alex's hand and pulled him up from the couch. He followed her to the small bathroom where she helped him get undressed. Alex was completely capable of performing this task himself, but he enjoyed the help. He always enjoyed her touch, especially on his bare skin.

Once in the tub, Alex looked up at her like a child looking up at its mother, and he asked, "Are you going to bathe me too?"

Jana gave him a look that told him he was being silly. "I think you can handle that yourself."

"I could handle getting undressed by myself, also, but you helped me with that," he pointed out, laughing.

Again, she gave him the look. "You stay put. I'm going to order the pizza. I'll be in the living room watching TV when you're done." She left him alone in the tub. When he was done with his bath, Alex joined Jana in the living room, and they enjoyed the time together just relaxing in front of the TV. To his relief, his back felt much better, and he hadn't even taken any aspirin.

It was starting to get late, and Alex hated the thought of Jana leaving. He leaned into her ear and softly asked, "Will you stay with me tonight?"

Jana kept her eyes on the TV. "I will if you think you need me to."

Alex placed his hand under her chin and turned her face toward his. He kissed her passionately, taking her by surprise. He leaned back and grinned. "I know I need you to stay all night."

"What about your back?"

"My back will be fine," Alex assured her. It would take more than a backache to stop him from getting what he needed from her. She was the best medicine for him. He took the remote from her lap and turned the TV off. "Come on, Jana. I think it's bedtime."

FOUR

Alex had made it through the rest of the night without hearing the male voice. He had slept like a baby with Jana by his side. If it hadn't been for her, Alex wouldn't have made it to work on time. If it hadn't been for her, he would have definitely lost his job for not showing up. As he worked stocking cans of soup, Alex realized just how lost he would be without her. Even when they weren't together she always found a way to keep him on track.

"Alex." It was the male voice again. Alex stopped stocking the cans and looked down the long aisle of the grocery store. There was a woman with a toddler at the other end of the aisle, but he was the only man there. When he heard the voice a second time, Alex left the aisle and made his way through the store to the back employee break room. He sat at one of the tables and put his head down in his hands. Once again, the voice called him.

"What?" Alex screamed. He had finally had enough. All he could do was wonder what was going on with him. He let out a sigh when, again, he was only met with silence.

A female coworker walked into the break room and went to the pop machine. She watched Alex while she inserted money. It was obvious to her that he was distraught. After retrieving her drink, she approached Alex carefully and sat down in the open seat across from him. He glared at her but didn't say a word.

The young brunette spoke first. "I'm glad you made it back."

Alex forced a small smile. "I'm glad to be back."

After a sip, she asked him, "Are you all right? You seem like something is bothering you."

He really wished she would just leave him alone, but it didn't appear that she was going to. Alex decided it was time for him to get back to work. It wasn't his break time, and he didn't want to get into trouble. "I'm fine," he answered as he stood to leave. "I've got to get back. Thanks for your concern."

Upon returning to his position in the soup aisle, Alex found the store had quickly become very busy. Trying to ignore the customers around him, Alex went back to stocking and avoided all eye contact. This was how he spent the majority of his days at work. He didn't feel like talking with anyone. No one would understand what was going on with him. He didn't even understand it. As time passed, things began to get worse instead of better. It was obvious the pain medication wasn't the cause of his problems, but he still kept the voice to himself. He feared the people around him would abandon him.

The male voice had been calling for him more often over his first few weeks back at home. The more Alex tried to ignore it, the louder it would get. Afraid other people would start to notice his strange behavior, Alex slowly began to spend more time alone. His friends, family, and even Jana had started to worry immensely about him. That worry became worse one night when Josh and Tony decided to pay their friend a visit. The trio hadn't been together since the accident.

Josh and Tony sat on Alex's couch and watched as their friend paced around the living room. To them, Alex appeared to be overly stressed and a bit on edge. His behavior was making both of them a little nervous. As they tried to make small talk about work and going back to school, the two young men waited for Alex to explode.

Finally, Josh asked the question that would change his friendship with Alex forever. "Alex, what's going on, man? Why are you acting so crazy?"

Alex stopped pacing and glared at his so-called best friends. Someone had finally called him crazy, but it hurt that it came from them.. "Get out!" he screamed.

Tony was confused. "Are you serious? What did we do to you?"

"You don't understand. No one does! Just leave me alone!"

"All right," Josh surrendered, raising his hands. The two friends stood up and headed for the door, but Josh stopped in the doorway and turned to Alex. "Jana said you've been acting weird. We didn't believe it though. If you want to be left alone that's what you'll get. Eventually, you'll be all alone. I think you need to get some help."

"Just get out."

Josh rolled his eyes at Alex as he walked out and slammed the door.

When his friends were gone, Alex sat down on his couch and tried to calm himself while he thought about what Josh had said to him. He desperately wanted the voice to go away, but he didn't know how he could get help with that. He was convinced no one would believe him. Maybe he *was* going crazy, but it didn't feel that way. The voice was too real.

Just as he had this thought, the voice called for him yet again. Alex decided to not ignore it this time. Maybe it might go away if he found out what it wanted. Then, he would have solved his own problem. He could do this without any help from anyone.

"Who are you?" Alex asked calmly.

To Alex's surprise, the voice replied. "You can call me Jack."

He had a name to put with the voice. And an accent. Only now could Alex tell that his tormentor was British. All this was a start, but Alex needed to know more information. "Where are you, Jack? I can't see you."

"I am always nearby, but you will not see me."

Alex didn't move from the couch. "Why are you talking to me?"

"I want you to do some things for me."

"Like what?" This is what Alex really wanted to know.

"All in good time, my dear lad. I have to be sure you are capable of performing the tasks I plan to place before you."

It was just as Alex had figured. The voice wanted something from him. "If I do these 'tasks' you mention, will you go away and leave me alone?"

"Yes, if you perform all of the tasks and perform them exactly as I instruct you, I will leave, but not until then. Do we have an agreement?"

Alex chuckled nervously. "Do I have a choice?"

"Not if you want to be rid of me," Jack stated.

"Can't you tell me what I have to do first before I agree to anything?"

"As I already stated, all in good time. Now rest. We will talk more tomorrow."

Alex sat still for a moment and listened intently. Jack was gone, but Alex wanted to make sure. When he was sure he was alone again, Alex got ready for bed. Sleeping was hard for him though. His mind raced with possible tasks Jack could have for him. Then, he wondered what would happen if he couldn't perform the tasks. Would he have to live with Jack for the rest of his life? He couldn't let that happen. Jack was slowly ruining his life, and Alex needed him gone, forever. There was still the question of Jack even being real.

The next day, Alex waited to hear from Jack while he kept to himself at work. When Jack didn't speak, Alex found himself disappointed but also relieved. There would have been no way for Alex to communicate with Jack without it appearing to everyone around him that he was talking to himself. He knew they were all watching him anyway, even the customers. Everyone was waiting for him to do something to prove he was crazy. He wouldn't give them the satisfaction. There was nothing wrong with his sanity.

During the trip home, Jack paid a visit to Alex. Alex quickly demanded, "Where have you been today? You bugged me nonstop for weeks, and then you didn't even say anything at all today!"

"Now I have your full attention," Jack said. "You will hear from me when I deem it necessary. It is time for us to get to know each other. Actually, it is time for me to get to know *you* better."

"I want to know one thing, Jack," Alex started as he continued to drive toward his apartment. "Why me?"

There was a moment of silence. Alex started to wonder if Jack had left, but he hadn't. "I am hoping that now we are one you will not disappoint me in your abilities. I can stay here with you forever, or I can go. The ultimate choice will be yours."

"I want you to go," Alex said.

"Then all you have to do is follow my directions precisely."

"I will," Alex assured Jack. "What are the tasks? Tell me so I can get them done sooner rather than later for you."

Jack laughed at the young man's eagerness. "It pleases me that you want to begin so quickly, but you must have patience. I am not sure that you are capable of doing the tasks yet."

During the conversation, Alex arrived home. He parked the car but didn't leave the driver's seat. "What if I can't do the tasks? Will you leave to find someone else that can?" He doubted it would be that easy, but he had to try.

"I know you can physically perform the tasks, Alex, but I am not positive that you can stomach what I will be demanding of you. I will not leave until you can, even if you have to perform each task over and over. I'll only leave if you complete each task to my satisfaction."

Alex shook his head. "How many tasks are you going to give me?"

"I will tell you when to begin, and I will tell you when you are done. Nothing more. You have a visitor coming. We will talk more later when we are alone."

"Who's coming? How do you know that?" Alex asked, scanning the parking lot. Jack didn't answer. Alex knew silence was all he would get. After waiting a moment, he finally got out of his car and walked up to his apartment.

When he had changed out of his work clothes, Alex heard a knock on the door. It was Jana. She had dropped by to check on him. Everyone was becoming increasingly worried about Alex and his antisocial behavior.

"I talked to Tony today," Jana told him as they stood just inside the door. Her blue eyes sparked with accusation. "He told me what happened last night."

Alex glared at her. She wasn't starting the visit off very well. He knew what was coming: some interrogation on why he'd thrown Josh and Tony out of his apartment. They were supposed to be his friends, but they had forced him to defend himself. He was sure Jana was about to make him do the same to her. "So? I don't really care what he had to say. This is my home."

"Why did you make them leave? They're your best friends," she asked cautiously. She feared Alex would throw her out too if her words or tone weren't delicate.

"As I said, this is my home," Alex told her coldly. "I didn't like the way they spoke to me."

Jana had never seen Alex look at her in such an unfeeling way. He was changing for some reason, and she hoped she could stop it. Surely if anyone could, it would be her. "Okay. That makes sense. If I felt someone disrespected me, I would make them leave also." Josh or Tony didn't say they had disrespected Alex. They made it sound like Alex had disrespected them. She thought Alex would open up to her more if she agreed with him.

It had worked. Letting his guard down, Alex went to the couch to sit down. "I'm glad you understand. Come. Sit by me."

For the first time ever, Jana hesitated to go to him. Finally, she did. Alex put his hand on her leg and started to rub it. She wasn't sure why, but the gesture made her uneasy. She put her hand on top of his to stop the movement. The small physical contact with him made her feel more at ease. It was silly for her to be like that with him. She knew Alex would never do anything to hurt her or make her upset.

"Jana," Alex started as he looked at her hand touching his, "I know you don't understand what is going on with me right now, but I want you to know I'm going to take care of it. Soon, things will be back to normal."

"Can't you make me understand? Please? I want to help you. I want you back to your old self."

Finally, he looked Jana in the eye. She was close to tears. "I can't. I have to handle this by myself. Stay with me for a while and hold me. Later, I need you to leave and not come back for a long time."

Jana burst into tears and wrapped herself around him. She didn't like what he was telling her to do, but she would do it anyway, for him. He felt horrible for telling her to stay away. It was the last thing Alex wanted, but he didn't need her around, distracting him. He also didn't want to keep snapping at her. Jana was so important to him, and she didn't deserve that. But he could not tell her why he had been acting so differently and being so hateful. Her staying away was the best thing for both of them. She just couldn't see that at the moment.

For the time being, the two held each other tight. Jana's warm tears soaked into his shirt, but he didn't mind. Alex had to fight back his own tears. He knew he couldn't hold her forever, but it would be a while before they'd be able to be together again. Neither of them spoke a word; Jana's sobbing was the only noise in the room. Finally, Alex pulled her from him. He wiped her cheeks dry, but they refused to stay that way. It was time for her to go. One last time, he kissed her and told her he loved her. Then he asked her to leave and not come back.

FIVE

Tears streamed down Jana's face as she reluctantly left Alex's apartment. Alex felt horrible for making her leave and forbidding her from seeing him. It was still unclear what Jack wanted him to do, but he needed to be free to do it. Jana meant the world to him, and the only way they could be together again like before was if he got rid of Jack. If Jana knew about Jack, she would think Alex was insane. He couldn't have that. It was better for them both to hurt a little now than for him to lose her forever later.

The rest of the night passed excruciatingly slowly. Jack never made the return visit he had promised. Alex tried to keep his mind clear as he waited, but his thoughts kept returning to the look on Jana's face as she left his doorway. The pain in her eyes was causing him pain in his heart. He was already tempted to go to her but knew it wouldn't be wise. He had to take care of business. Jack wasn't making it easy though. Eventually, Alex gave up on him and went to bed.

The next morning, Alex decided not to go to work. Calling in sick was something he rarely did, but he had no motivation to go. He managed to fix himself something to eat. It was the first time he had actually put food in his body in the past two days. After breakfast, Alex put the dishes in the sink and left them. He sat in his usual spot on the couch in his boxer shorts and a T-shirt. Motionless, he sat there with his head tilted to the side and stared at nothing. The only thing going through his mind was, *Where is Jack?*

A knock at the door brought Alex out of his trance-like state. He made himself get up from the couch and answer the knock. The repeated noise coming from the door was reverberating through his brain. It was a complete shock to Alex that his mom was making the horrible noise. He definitely was not in the mood to deal with her at the moment. She was like most typical moms, always nosing where she didn't belong. And no matter what she found, she always judged.

"Aren't you going to invite me inside?" Mrs. Dorson asked her son.

"Of course, Mom," he flatly replied as he let her in. "What are you doing here?"

Mrs. Dorson proceeded to look around Alex's apartment as if it were her own. "I was on my way into the office and I saw your car parked outside. I wasn't sure if you had to work today or not, but I thought I would drop by to check on you. We haven't seen you back at the house. Is everything okay?"

A few weeks had passed since Alex had been to his parents' house. Both of his parents had been home, which was a rare occurrence. He hadn't been there long before they had begun to argue. They fought with each other as though Alex and Jessica weren't even present. Jessica eventually stormed off to her room. When Alex heard her bedroom door slam shut, he became enraged. He couldn't recall what he had said exactly to his parents, but he imagined it wasn't good. The worst part was probably the fact that he didn't care about how he reacted or what had happened. That wasn't like him at all.

"Everything's fine, Mom," Alex assured her, a small hint of dread in his tone. "Why do you ask?"

"You seemed upset the last time I saw you. And now I see that your housekeeping abilities are slipping." She stopped roaming around and asked him, "When was the last time you did the dishes or laundry? Honestly, Alex, this place is deplorable."

"I don't need this from you, Mom," Alex said with his voice raised. "I thought you were on your way to work."

She placed both of her hands on his face. "I'm only trying to help."

Alex grabbed her wrists and ripped her hands from his cheeks. "Mom," he started coldly, "I'm only going to say this nice once. Please leave."

Mrs. Dorson was shocked by his tone and the fact that he had asked her to leave. "Okay, Alex," she said, glancing away, "if you want me to go, I'll go." She looked him in the eyes again, something hurt in hers. "I love you." She side-stepped him and walked out the door without looking back. This would be the last time she saw Alex for the next few months.

After returning to his spot on the couch, Alex tried to release the stress his mom had caused during her short visit. He couldn't figure out why people just wouldn't leave him alone. They were distracting him from his tasks and were maybe even the reason Jack had stopped visiting. While it was good that Jack wasn't around talking to him when others were near, he did need to hear from Jack, so he wanted everyone to stay away. One day he would make peace with them.

As Alex started to unwind, Jack finally returned. Alex was relieved to hear his voice, which seemed strange since he had hated it for so long. Of course, talking to Jack would bring him one step closer to being rid of him. "Why didn't you come back last night?" Alex asked. "I made Jana leave so we could discuss the tasks you have for me."

"I felt it would be rude of me to talk business after what happened between you and the young lady. You were far too emotional for a serious discussion," Jack explained.

"Well, she is the last person I want to upset," Alex stated. "Right now I need to concentrate on what you want me to do. The sooner we do this, the sooner we can go our separate ways."

"I cannot help but notice that you keep bringing that up. Do you not enjoy my company? Are you in a hurry for me to go away?" Jack asked him sarcastically.

Alex laughed slightly as he leaned forward and put his arms on his knees. "No offense, Jack, but you are ruining my life. My temper is getting really short. I blow up at the most important people in my life, and then I blame them. I have no desire to do anything anymore. Look around, Jack. My place is turning into a pit, just like my mom said. I'm supposed to be at work today, but when I woke up this morning, I didn't feel like going. I can't think straight, and sometimes I have thoughts that I feel aren't mine. Where are they coming from, Jack?" Alex leaned back on the couch. "In addition to all that, I'm constantly afraid everyone will think I'm insane because of the way I'm acting. I can't seem to control all of my actions anymore though. So, forgive me if I seem to be in a hurry for you to go."

"There, there, Alex. It is not all that bad, is it? When we have finished our business together I will go, just as I promised. You will have your life back, but it will not be the same. You will not be the same," Jack forewarned him.

The comment confused Alex. "What do you mean?"

"I am going to make you a stronger person, Alex Dorson," Jack bluntly stated. "When we are done, you will be capable of doing anything you please. Your life will be better, and you will be better. If you succeed with the tasks, you will feel powerful and in control of every aspect of your life."

"And if I don't succeed? What is the outcome then?"

"That is not an option," Jack stated. "I will not go until every task is completed perfectly, even if you have to repeat each task over and over again."

"How many tasks?" Alex hoped Jack was ready to divulge this detail now.

Jack laughed. "You already asked me that, Alex. I had not planned on giving you that information as of yet, but if you must know, there will be five tasks for you to complete."

"That is a pretty low number. Why isn't there more? How long will each task take to complete?"

"Too many questions, Alex! Remember, I am the one in charge here." Jack took a moment to calm down. "I only need you to complete five, and I have certain dates for you to complete each of them. Four of the tasks should take less than an hour each. The last one will require more from you, so it will take much more time. Each task will be harder than the one before it."

"That helps me out a little, but you're still being very vague," Alex said. He would see if he could pry one more piece of information. "Can you at least tell me when the first task is to be done? I won't ask any more questions for now."

"Two weeks."

Alex got up from the couch and went to look at the calendar in his kitchen. The calendar still read July, but he knew that wasn't correct. He flipped ahead to August. It took him a moment to figure out the current date, but when he accomplished that, he looked ahead two weeks. "August 31st."

"Yes," Jack responded. "Write it down so you do not forget. Your mind seems to be a bit scrambled lately."

Ignoring that last comment, Alex rummaged through a drawer in the kitchen until he located a pen. As he wrote the word "task" on his calendar, Alex noticed he had two days left to register for classes for his senior year. School had completely escaped his mind. He realized then that he shouldn't have called off from work. To register for classes, he would have to leave work early or go in late one of the next two days. He knew his boss wouldn't like that. While there was still time to go register today, Alex took the day off thinking he'd be able to avoid everyone. Going to work or school would be risky. He didn't want to risk going off on anyone else. He'd have to register another day.

"What about the other tasks, Jack? What dates do you have picked out for those?" He'd better write those down as well.

"One at a time. After the first one I'll tell you when to expect the second."

"Why can't I do the first task sooner?"

"I thought you were not going to ask any more questions," Jack pointed out.

Alex put the pen on the counter and headed back to the couch. "I forgot I said that. Sorry." He really didn't know what to say without asking another question. There were still so many running through his mind.

"I know you want to ask more questions of me. I think we have talked enough for one day. You rest and take care of your personal business at college. Education is important. We will talk again soon," Jack said.

Alex was really getting tired of Jack knowing everything, even before it happened at times, while he remained clueless. He was starting to worry about the tasks he had to complete. There were only five, but he sensed they couldn't be very good. If they were good tasks, Jack would just tell him what they were. Regardless, Alex could see no reason why they needed to wait for two weeks to start.

There didn't appear to be any way of reasoning with Jack. Alex would have to be patient and play along. It was his only choice at the moment. Besides, there was no way Jack could drag out five tasks for too long. Right?

Jack left Alex alone the rest of the day. Alex watched a couple of movies and decided to take a long nap—all he could bring himself to do. His friends were upset with him, and he had told Jana to leave him alone. When Alex woke from his nap, he lay in his bed and began to realize he would probably be spending a lot of time alone. Jack would be his only companion. That bothered him. Maybe Alex just needed to talk to someone. Maybe he didn't have to do these tasks. Maybe Jack wasn't even real.

SIX

The next morning, Alex called his boss and informed him of his situation with his class registration. To Alex's surprise, Mr. Jenson was understanding, telling Alex to do what he had to do and come to work when he was finished. Being a good employee had paid off for Alex. His boss always trusted him to do the right thing.

At the school, Alex was going through the yearly routine of picking his classes and waiting in lines to register for them. Jodi from his political science class and Sam from his personal finance class caught up with Alex and tried to start up a conversation with him about his summer break. Alex had become friendly with many of the students and most of the faculty during his three years at the college, but today he was in no mood to socialize. As he humored the small talk with Dean from chemistry, someone else caught his attention. Jana was there signing up for her classes as well.

He desperately wanted to go to her, but it wouldn't be wise. After he quickly ended the conversation he was in, Alex ran to another line and pretended not to see her. Jana, however, had spotted him despite his efforts. She honored his request to stay away from him by not stopping as she passed by. When Alex finished his registration, he left the school and hurried to work. He was unsure of how he was going to survive at school and work while he completed the tasks for Jack. At times, all he wanted to do was isolate himself in his apartment and leave the world behind him.

When he arrived at work, he found a note attached to his time card. Mr. Jenson wanted to see him in his office before he started his shift. This wasn't what Alex wanted to do. Mr. Jenson seemed fine with him going to register for his classes that morning. It was even his idea for him to go ahead and take care of it. What could he possibly want to see

Alex about before his shift? Alex clocked in and went to Mr. Jenson's office.

Once inside, Alex took a seat in front of a concerned Mr. Jenson. "Alex," his boss began, "you have always been one of my best employees. Lately, though, there seems to be something going on with you. I've noticed it and so have some of your fellow workers. You seem to be distracted by something. I'm not sure what it is, and I'm sure it's none of my business. I want you to know I'll listen if you want to talk. Past that, you need to leave your personal problems at home. They're starting to affect your performance."

"I'm sorry, Mr. Jenson," Alex said. "I didn't realize my work was suffering. I'll try to do better." Alex really wasn't worried about how well he was stocking the shelves, or how well he was getting along with his coworkers. He was just saying the words he thought his boss would want to hear to end the meeting. Everyone had been attacking him lately, and Mr. Jenson seemed to be joining the mob. Alex was about to explode, and that would cost him his job. "May I go now?"

"Sure," Mr. Jenson answered. He had hoped for more from Alex, but he couldn't push the issue with him. Alex had worked at the store for a long time. Mr. Jenson could always tell when something was bothering him. This was different. Alex didn't even appear to be the same person anymore.

Later on, Alex walked through the store with his cart full of boxes. He suddenly stopped at the end of an aisle. As if he was being controlled by someone else, he turned and walked down the aisle, leaving his cart behind. When he reached the small section that contained various kitchen utensils, Alex stopped. His eyes immediately fixated on the kitchen knives. Without even realizing what he was doing, he reached out and took a knife from a hanging hook. He examined it closely and concluded the blade was approximately six inches in length and about one inch wide. It was a perfect size, he thought, but he didn't know what it was a perfect size for. After returning the knife to its spot, Alex left the aisle and returned to his job.

He continued to keep to himself during his shift. This was something that had become normal to his coworkers although he didn't used to be such a loner. He had been short and somewhat rude with most of them enough that they knew it was best to leave him alone. It was becoming hard for Alex to perform his job. His mind was always on something else. Other employees were picking up his slack, and even though they once thought highly of Alex, they were wishing he would quit.

When his shift was at an end, Alex clocked out and went back to the aisle he had been drawn to earlier in the day. He took the same knife from the same hook and headed for the registers. There was one register that had a new cashier working it. Alex knew she wouldn't ask any questions of him since they didn't know each other. After removing his name tag, he went to her line. The girl made casual small talk with him as she rang up his purchase. She had no idea he was a fellow employee and thought nothing of him purchasing a single knife. Alex himself wasn't even sure why he was purchasing the knife, but he felt Jack had something to do with it. It was becoming unnerving to not know if his thoughts and actions were his own or if they were Jack's.

The quiet drive home from the store was interrupted by none other than Jack. "Alex, I want you to do something for me."

"Is this one of the tasks? I thought it wasn't time yet."

"No, this is not a task. I want you to make a left turn at the next intersection," Jack instructed.

Alex made the turn. "Where are we going?"

"You will see when we get there. I promise."

"What about the knife, Jack?" Alex asked, knowing he had made him buy it. "What is it for?"

Jack answered, but not completely. "I had you purchase the knife because you will need it to complete the tasks. Don't open it until it is time."

As silence filled the car, Alex started to think about the knife. What could Jack want him to do with it? It was a question Jack obviously wasn't going to answer. However, Alex already knew it would not be good, possibly even deadly. He was beginning to question his ability to go through with the tasks, but what choice did he have? He could either do them and get his life back with Jana or spend the rest of his life alone with Jack being his only companion.

"Pull off the road here," Jack ordered. They were on a country road just outside of the city. Alex did as told, leading the car into a weed-infested open field. He stopped the engine and looked around. "Get out and walk into the trees on the other side of the field."

Alex exited his car and trudged through the thick mess of weeds, which swept against his pants right up to his knees. As soon as he entered the tree line, Alex smelled a horrible stench in the air. Nausea overcame him as the smell flowed down the back of his throat to his stomach. Pulling the neck of his shirt up over his nose, Alex asked Jack, "What is that smell? Where is it coming from?"

"Move forward about five feet. You will find the source of the odor."

Step by careful step, Alex moved forward as Jack had instructed him to do. The farther he went into the trees, the more insects he encountered in the air around him. The smell was getting stronger. It was now strong enough to pass through his shirt and into his nose. He had never smelled anything so disgusting. Just when he thought it couldn't possibly get any worse, he tripped over something on the ground.

Alex turned and looked at the ground to see what it was. The sight before him made him scamper back a few feet. He bent over quickly and vomited on a tree. It took him a few minutes to get a grip on himself, but eventually, Alex gained his composure and stood back up straight. After returning to the site, he asked, "Is this supposed to be a joke, Jack? What is this?"

Jack only answered with a question. "What do you think it is, Alex?"

Alex chuckled sarcastically. "I'm afraid to answer that. I'm hoping it's an animal. Is that what it is?" Alex inspected what he believed was a bloody, shredded animal carcass that served as a feast for the insects covering it.

Jack replied, "I will put your mind at ease. It is an animal. Study it carefully. Tell me what you see. Find out what kind of animal it was."

"Why would I want to study it? It's a dead animal. That's all I need to know," Alex said, completely repulsed by the thought of getting any closer to the rotting flesh.

"You will study it because I said so."

Without arguing, Alex grabbed a stick, covered his nose again, and squatted down by the carcass. He began to nudge the leaves and insects away from the body with the stick. His stomach was churning again, but this time he fought back his nausea. Once he found the head, Alex said, "It's a deer."

"Good. What else do you see?"

"It's a doe," Alex stated. "If you look at the neck, it seems that another animal was responsible for her death. The missing meat tells me she was food for this other animal. Now she is just food for the bugs. There is blood everywhere, but it's dried up and brown." He stood up and said, "That's what I see. Can we leave now? I realize that smell is the stench of death, and I've had enough of it."

"Is she missing any organs?" Jack inquired.

"I don't know! I'm not a vet. Can we leave now?"

"Yes. We are done here."

On the way back to the car, Alex had to ask, "What was that all about anyway? Why did you bring me out here to see a dead animal?"

Once he was back in his car, Alex asked another question. "What are you up to, Jack? You made me buy a knife, and then you dragged me out here to look at a dead animal to see if I can handle it. What do you want me to do for you? I have a feeling it isn't anything good, and I'm not leaving here until you tell me what I'm supposed to do on August 31st."

Again, Jack replied with another question, just as he had earlier. "What do you think I want you to do?"

Alex laughed hysterically. He was getting fed up with Jack. "I'm tired of the games, Jack! It's obvious you want me to kill something."

"Yes, that is correct."

"Animals?" Alex didn't want to kill animals, but he secretly hoped the answer would be yes and not something worse.

"No, Alex."

"People?" He hoped this one would be no, but it was the only alternative.

"Women."

It took a few for the realization to sink in. Once it hit him, Alex yelled back, "NO! I won't do it!"

"I will not leave if you refuse," Jack reminded him calmly. "Then we will become very close friends, and you will lose everyone in your life, even your precious Jana."

"I'll shut you out somehow!" Alex started his car and sped off down the country road. Jack continued to try to speak to him. Alex wasn't going to listen. He switched on the radio and turned the volume up until he couldn't even hear his own thoughts. After turning around on dirt the road, Alex headed home with the radio continually blaring.

There was no way Alex could hurt another person. Just the thought of the little boy being hurt accidentally when he crashed his car had been enough to worry him sick. He wouldn't be able to do it. Jack might as well forget it. As much as Alex wanted Jack gone, he just couldn't commit murder. He still couldn't believe that Jack wanted him to kill women. What was the purpose? Jack wanted him to kill five women. Why? Nothing made sense. Of course, none of it had made sense to him anyway.

As the music blasted in his car, Alex realized he would probably be stuck with Jack forever. If he was going to be stuck with him, he was at least going to drown him out the best he could. He knew Jack was trying to communicate with him, but he couldn't hear him. The loud music was working perfectly. Alex then formulated a plan to continue to drown out Jack. If he couldn't hear him, maybe he would eventually go away. It would be a long shot, but it would definitely be worth a try because there was no way Alex could hurt another human being.

SEVEN

Alex decided it was time to see someone after the little experiment with the dead deer. He started in the yellow pages and found a therapist. A phone call was made and an appointment was set. Just a couple of days later, Alex went to talk about what was going on in life and about Jack.

But therapy was no help. By the end of the session, the therapist was handing Alex a business card for a psychiatrist. He needed more than what they could offer. A therapist usually did not assist with the types of things Alex had going on with voices and such. Alex took the card and left, feeling like the whole thing was a waste of time.

The next morning, before work, Alex decided to call the psychiatrist. Jack was trying so hard to communicate with him, and he just wanted it to stop. Again, an appointment was set, and he went to see someone else. If this didn't help, he didn't know what else to do. He couldn't do what Jack wanted him to do, but maybe there was no choice. He could not spend the rest of his life living this way.

Alex sat with the psychiatrist and started to explain everything in as much detail as he could, starting with the car accident. Next, he moved to the hospital and the voice—and how it had ruined his relationship with his family, his friends, and his girlfriend. But when the psychiatrist pushed him to go deeper, Alex grew reluctant. He felt his answers sounded ridiculous, and he started to feel like he should not be there because it was all just silliness. At the end, though, the psychiatrist dropped a bomb on him: He could be schizophrenic.

From the voice he was convinced was real, the strange influence steering him, to his volatile and unsocial behavior—all of it pointed to schizophrenia. However, the only thing that kept the psychiatrist from diagnosing Alex was the fact that it all had basically just started. If it had been ongoing for several months, it would be clear. So, the doctor told Alex he needed to start coming in regularly.

Alex made another appointment before leaving, then headed to work. Some of what he had been told made sense. He later learned while spending an afternoon at the library that angry outbursts, feeling watched, and social isolation were also symptoms of schizophrenia. But what concerned him the most was that all of the books noted that the condition would worsen if not treated. It hadn't happened at the first session, but more than likely the psychiatrist would prescribe an antipsychotic drug sooner rather than later.

However, the books did indicate that other mental disorders would have to be ruled out first. After all, there were some symptoms Alex didn't have, at least not yet. He wasn't depressed or suicidal. He didn't have an alcohol or drug problem. While he didn't want to communicate with anyone, he could (and did not sound totally off his rocker). It was clear he needed to have a couple more sessions to see what the psychiatrist had to say. It was possible that Jack was all in his head and could be silenced with medication. This might be worth finding out before doing what Jack wanted him to do.

Two more sessions is all Alex attended. He wasn't believing anything the psychiatrist was telling him about himself. Even though he had read it all himself at the library, he decided that he was not suffering from any mental illness. Jack needed to be gone, but the sessions were not doing that, and Alex felt the medicine was uncalled for, so he refused it. He couldn't explain it, but he knew it would be bad for him, just as he had known that the knife in the store was the perfect one.

Alex would get rid of Jack on his own.

EIGHT

Over the next two weeks, Alex tried his best to shut Jack out of his mind. When he was at home, the TV or stereo was always turned up so loud it would give him headaches. Eventually, he had to start wearing headphones because the neighbors were complaining. The landlord was sending him letters daily about the noise and eventually threatened to evict him. So Alex bought a portable music player, and he wore headphones all the time. They made his neighbors happy, but they didn't help him with his headaches.

It was hard to escape Jack while Alex was at work. Jack usually took full advantage of the time Alex couldn't drown him out. It got so bad that Alex started taking more time off work. When he was there, he often snapped at his fellow employees, and Mr. Jenson would end up sending him home anyway. Alex knew he was close to losing his job. If that happened, he would lose his apartment also.

Alex had started to think about ending his life. Jack wasn't going to go away unless he completed these tasks. Alex wasn't a murderer though. There was no way he could take someone's life away. But even if he became a killer and got his life back, what kind of life would it be? Not to mention the chance of him getting caught. How would he explain to his family and friends why he had killed innocent women? Ending his life would be the best option. It was the *only* option. He just needed to decide how he wanted to do it.

A gun would cause a big bloody mess all over the place and probably wouldn't be a pleasant sight for the person who'd find him. Slicing his wrists would cause the same problem. Alex thought about crashing his car into a tree but then realized that was kind of what got him into this mess in the first place. He concluded the best way to end it all was to take a bunch of sleeping pills and just close his eyes forever. When his body was discovered, he would look peaceful. It seemed to be the best solution for both him and the person that would find him.

Jack, of course, knew what Alex was planning to do. The music might have kept Jack from being heard, but it didn't keep him from reading Alex's thoughts. He knew Alex wasn't a murderer. He knew Alex worried he wouldn't be able to go through with it. But Jack needed Alex to commit. He *needed* Alex to get away with it. It was possible. It had been done before in history. If Alex would only listen to him and do exactly as he said, all would be fine.

So Alex had to be stopped. There was less than a week until the first task needed to be completed.

The night Alex drove to the drug store to purchase the pills was Jack's last chance to change his mind. Jack tried endlessly to communicate with him. Alex drowned him out again with the radio. Once inside the store, Jack pleaded with him to think about the life he was throwing away. "Alex, you must realize what this would do to your family, to Jana. It would destroy them. You don't want to be the reason they crumble and fall apart, do you?"

Alex didn't want to listen. This was the only way out. It was the only way to stop Jack from controlling his actions and his mind. As Jack continued his ranting and raving, Alex read the back of the box in his hand. He suddenly caught a whiff of a familiar smell.

Alex closed his eyes as he inhaled the soft scent of lavender. A smile fluttered across his face as all his troubles fell from his tensed-up body. The scent reminded him of happier days with Jana. The lotion she wore smelled of lavender. With his eyes still closed, he could picture her beautiful smile, her blue eyes that always sparkled, and her long wavy brown hair. When he opened his eyes, the image disappeared. He looked around to find the source of the familiar scent. To his surprise, the scent was coming from Jana. She was at the other end of the same aisle.

Jana obviously felt someone watching her. She glanced down the aisle and was shocked to see Alex staring at her. As she walked toward him, he realized she hadn't seen him in weeks. No one had. She stopped in front of him and said with a smile, "How are you, Alex?"

"Fine, I guess." As much as he was relieved to see her, he still did not want to tell her how he really was at the moment.

"Are you having problems sleeping?" she asked when she noticed the sleeping pills in his hand. It would make sense if he was. Alex looked awful. He was sure he closely resembled the living dead—and probably smelled a little like them, too.

At first, Alex just looked puzzled by her question. Then, it occurred to him. "Oh, you mean the sleeping pills! Yeah, I'm having trouble sleeping at night. I just can't seem to shut my brain off," he said, trying to make a joke, but he was serious. "How are you doing?" he asked on a more serious note.

The smile faded from Jana's face as she looked deep into the eyes of the man she still cared so much about. What she saw disturbed her: Alex's eyes seemed empty, devoid of life. It hurt her to see him like this. "I'm getting by, I guess. I think about you a lot, Alex. I worry about you, and I miss you. Am I still supposed to stay away?"

Alex could see the tears starting to swell in her eyes. He desperately wanted to wrap his arms around her. Instead, he had to say, "Yes. I think that's best. You don't need to be around me right now."

As tears started down her cheeks, she asked, "When can we be together again? If not now, then when?"

"Soon, I will fix everything. I promise," he tried to assure her. "I just need more time."

Jana stood there looking like she was trying to figure out what he needed to fix. It was clear he wasn't going to tell her. There was only one thing left for her to say before she left him again. "I love you, Alex. I always will."

He watched as she left the aisle empty-handed. Quickly, he put the pills back on the shelf and left the store. Once inside his car, Alex broke down. He had not shed a tear since his childhood, but at that moment he surrendered. How could he have been so selfish to want to kill himself? That would have hurt Jana even more. They belonged together, and he needed to do what he could to make that happen again. When he finally calmed himself, he called for Jack.

"I am here, Alex. Do you finally want to talk?" Jack replied.

Alex stared out the windshield. "You win."

"What do you mean?"

"Don't play games with me right now, Jack," Alex said harshly. "Do you still promise to leave me alone if I do these things for you?"

"Yes. I have told you that from the start. I will keep my word," Jack assured him.

"I can have my life back, correct?"

"If you do exactly what I say, then all will be well."

Alex started his car and backed out of the parking space. When he started to drive away, he told Jack, "Then I guess you win. I want my life back. I don't want to end it. And most importantly, I want Jana back."

"I have not been trying to win, Alex. I am merely trying to prove a point to everyone. You do not understand what that point is yet, but you will eventually." Jack was silent for a moment. "I will say that I am most happy that you have changed your mind about causing yourself to expire. I really do not think that would have done anybody any good, especially your dear Jana."

"I want to make one thing clear," Alex started as he headed for his apartment, "Jana is the only reason I'm doing this, if I can even do this. I've never killed anything in my life except maybe some insects. What happens between us if I can't do it?"

"Alex, you have already asked that before, remember? You already know the deal." Jack's voice was calm. "We do not need to keep discussing these details. Time is growing short. We need to prepare for the first task. You need to sleep well tonight. We will start to gather supplies tomorrow."

Alex chuckled out loud. "Maybe I should have bought the sleeping pills anyway. I don't see me getting any more sleep now than I have been lately."

"Go back and retrieve them then, but only for sleeping. You do need rest to build up your strength. If the pills will help, then go back."

That was exactly what Alex planned to do. He turned the car around and went back to the drug store. Inside the store, Alex had no problem finding the pills again. But strangely, the woman at the register seemed nervous in Alex's company. He had never had that effect on anyone. He didn't dwell on it though. There were too many other things to be concerned with than what one person thought of him. She must have picked up on a strange vibe from him because of the way he looked, but that was her issue, not his.

For the first time in weeks, Alex could drive his car in peace. The radio was off, and Jack was silent. He rolled his window down and breathed in the warm August night air. All was calm and quiet. At that moment, he didn't want to think about the horrible deeds he was going to have to perform in just a matter of days. Alex only wanted to think about Jana. She was the reason he wasn't going to end his own life. She was the reason he was about to become a killer and end other lives.

Back at home, Alex stripped down to his boxer shorts. He crawled into bed, but he didn't put on his headphones like he usually did. His thoughts were still on Jana as he waited for sleep to kick in. Alex rewound his memory like an old videotape. The picture was still clear in his mind's eye: The day he realized Jana was the one. The memory then transitioned to the day he finally asked her to be his. That euphoric feeling he had when she said yes was still there also. He could see and feel everything from then as if it had just happened. Their first kiss, the first time they were completely intimate—everything up to the pain he now felt for not being with her and for what he was putting her through.

Alex only wanted to focus on the good memories, but the painful ones triumphed and haunted him. His dreams wouldn't be filled with thoughts of Jana anyway. They instead came from deep within his subconscious: visions he had seen in movies and on TV; people being murdered. The dreams were deeply disturbing nightmares filled with hate and blood. And most disturbing of all, each murderer had his face. But how could it be him? He was not a killer. When Alex forced himself awake the next day, only then did he come to a harrowing realization. He was going to be just like those people in his dreams. He was going to be one of *them*.

NINE

August 31ˢᵗ had come around quickly. Alex had been trying to prepare himself mentally the entire week. He kept a picture of Jana with him always to remind himself why he was going through with the tasks. Jack had instructed Alex to purchase some leather gloves, a hat to cover his long hair, and a form-fitting black jacket. The explanation for these items was simple. The gloves would prevent the transfer of fingerprints onto any object in the area. The hat would confine Alex's shoulder-length blond hair, which needed to stay out of his face and off the women. The jacket would be a shield for any blood. If Alex had to get away quickly, he could remove the gloves and jacket to blend in with a crowd.

On the afternoon of August 31ˢᵗ, Alex occupied his favorite spot on his couch. The TV was off. The stereo was off. The entire apartment was dead silent. He sat there with many thoughts running through his mind. In a few hours, it would be nightfall, and he would have to go complete the first task. Time was moving fast, and he still wondered if he would be able to go through with it. As the hours passed, there soon came a point when it was too late to back out.

Jack had not been around all day, but he showed up in time to have a talk with Alex before he left his apartment.

"It's about time you showed up," Alex said to Jack as he remained on the couch.

"I thought I would give you some time to yourself before tonight's events," Jack responded. "Have you changed your mind, or are you still going to do as I say?"

Alex got himself to his feet and replied, "I don't know how I'm going to make myself do this, but I'm still going to do it."

"Good. I thought you might have decided to keep me around forever after all."

"Oh, no!" Alex said with a chuckle. "I've had enough of your company. I'm just waiting for you to tell me where to go so I can get this over and done with."

"I believe it would be best to start downtown," Jack suggested.

Alex slipped on his black boots and grabbed his car keys. "Downtown it is then."

"Do you have everything?" Jack asked before Alex made it out of the door.

"Everything is in the car."

By the time Alex drove off, butterflies were beginning to flutter and multiply inside his gut. The radio was off, but his fingers kept drumming on the steering wheel. His forehead beaded up with perspiration as his heart raced. At one point he had to pull the car over to the side of the road to empty the food in his stomach outside. The night wasn't starting out too well.

When he finally reached downtown, Alex didn't know where he was supposed to go. Downtown Lexington covered a lot of area. "Now what, Jack?" he asked nervously.

"Calm yourself, Alex," Jack instructed. "Park anywhere you like. Then find a dark alley to take cover in for a while."

It took Alex a few minutes to find a place to park that was not metered and somewhat secluded. He sat in the car after he parked and worked on calming his nerves. After a few deep breaths, he put on the jacket and zipped it all the way up to his neck. Next, he pulled his hair back into a ponytail and tucked it up into his new baseball cap. He slipped on the gloves and pulled the jacket sleeves down over the tops of them. All that was left was the knife. Alex carefully slipped it up the right sleeve of the jacket.

"Are you ready?" Jack asked him.

Alex took another deep breath, held it for a brief moment, and then quickly released it. "I think so, yes."

"Good. Go find your hiding spot."

When he exited his car, Alex started walking past some small businesses and shops. Some of them were already closed, but most of them were still serving customers. As he passed a restaurant, he noticed a dark alley that ran beside it. It was the perfect hiding place since there weren't any street lights. The only light in the alley came from the restaurant's side door. Alex figured the employees used the door to access the dumpster that was across from it.

Once he felt confident he was well hidden, Alex whispered, "Is this spot okay, Jack?" There were people walking up and down the sidewalk in front of the restaurant, and he didn't want to be heard.

Jack responded without whispering, "This will do." By now Alex had figured out he was the only one that could hear Jack.

The butterflies in Alex's stomach were becoming restless. His hands were starting to sweat, and the gloves were beginning to irritate them. When Alex pulled them off so his hands could get some air, Jack screamed at him to put them back on immediately, which did very little to help his nerves.

Alex snapped back, "Don't yell at me!"

"You must keep the gloves on at all times."

"I understand that, but it is the end of August, which means it's hot. What do you want me to do? I can't keep standing here. Someone will eventually see me. How do I explain to someone why I'm hiding in the alley?"

"Be patient. No one will discover you in the cover of darkness. Soon the number of people will dwindle, and we will find the right woman."

To Alex's surprise, Jack turned out to be correct. After a while, the mass of people walking up and down the sidewalk in front of the restaurant was dwindling down to just a slim few. It wasn't long before Alex spotted a woman leaving the restaurant alone. She appeared to be older than Alex, and she was obviously an employee leaving work at the end of her shift. Her navy-blue shirt had the name of the restaurant across the back of it.

"There she is, Alex. She is the one," Jack informed him.

Alex watched the woman as she stood close to the edge of the sidewalk. "What do you think she's doing?" he asked.

"I imagine she is waiting for someone to pick her up. I suggest you move quickly before she is gone."

"Do I just go out there and grab her? Tell me what to do," Alex said, frustrated. He was new at this.

"Yes," Jack answered bluntly. "Cover her mouth and drag her back here. Make doubly sure no one is around to see first." Alex hesitated, not wanting to go after the woman. "Do it now!" Jack yelled.

Slowly, Alex peered out from the alley in both directions of the sidewalk. Once he was positive there was no one near the woman, he darted out of his hiding place. Coming up behind her fast, Alex tightly wrapped his left hand around the lower half of her face, covering her mouth entirely. With his right arm, he grabbed her forcefully around the waist and lifted her up off the ground. It only took a couple of seconds to get her from the curb to the dark alley.

As the woman frantically tried to kick herself free, he asked, "What now, Jack?"

"Get the knife and cut her throat!"

"What?!"

Jack yelled again, "Cut her throat!"

As Alex battled to keep the woman's head securely against him, he wrenched the knife from his jacket sleeve, almost dropping it. When he'd flinched to catch it, Alex's hand slipped from her mouth and she started screaming and cursing at him as loud as she could. With his adrenaline pumping higher than it ever had in his life, Alex put the blade to her neck. The woman started to fight and scream even harder when she saw the knife. Jack yelled at Alex again. Alex panicked and sliced the blade across the left side of her neck. As blood squirted out of her neck, he stopped, shocked by what he had just done. But there was no time to mourn or reflect; the blood kept pumping out the side of her neck, and Alex realized she was suffering. So he finished the job, pulling the knife the rest of the way around her neck. The woman's petite body went limp, and he let her fall to the ground. Stunned, Alex stood over her body motionless as he watched the dark shiny blood pour from her wound.

"Cut her throat again!" Jack demanded.

"Why? She's already dead! The task is done. We need to get out of here, Jack."

"No! It is not right!" Jack shouted.

Alex next discovered his fingers moving, then his arm, without his bidding. "W-what are you doing?"

Alex received no answer as his own agency was overridden by Jack. He found himself on his knees behind the woman's head. His hands lifted her up by her shoulders. As his left arm supported her weight, his right hand picked up the knife and slit her throat again. Next, Alex found himself still on his knees, but he was at her side. The right hand still held the knife while the left one pulled her shirt up and unbuttoned her pants. Alex tried to fight back to get control, but—too late—his right hand plunged the knife into her upper abdomen. The only thing Alex could do was watch in horror as the knife lacerated her stomach, blood and organs spilling out the fold.

After watching his own hand make several incisions in the woman's midsection, Alex finally regained control of his body. He was completely numb. It hadn't occurred to him that there might be more to the tasks than just killing the women. He wasn't sure how to react to what he had just witnessed and the sudden violation of his own body.

"Quick!" Jack barked. "Cover her up!"

Alex pulled the woman's shirt down to cover the cuts, but the blood was already soaking into the blue fabric. "Why do you want her covered?"

"Do not ask questions," Jack said harshly. "Pull her legs up then leave as quickly as you can!"

After doing as he was told, Alex stepped out of the darkness and headed down the empty sidewalk toward his car. When he reached the vehicle, Alex removed the gloves and jacket. He opened the trunk and placed the blood-soaked items in a plastic sack. The sack went back into the trunk along with the knife and his hat.

During the drive home, Alex tried to remain calm by not thinking about what he had done. Jack wanted to discuss the events of the evening though. "How do you feel, dear Alex?"

Suddenly Alex was flooded with several emotions at once. "How do I feel? I feel very sad for that poor woman and her family! I feel ashamed because I did something very wrong!" Alex could feel the queasiness in his stomach. He quickly pulled the car over, flew the door open, and vomited again. "I also feel very dirty because you took over my body. How and why did you do that?"

Once Alex resumed driving, Jack started to talk to him again. "It all went fine, Alex. You are being childish about it. This was your first time. I had to step in and help. Things have to be done a certain way, and I did not think you could continue at the moment."

"I don't understand," Alex told him. "Why did it have to go a certain way? What was the deal with her legs?"

"It was a minor detail... a bit of posing... for effect. I will tell you someday what all of this means, but for now you must remember to follow my directions, no matter what they are. It all has to be perfect, or as close to perfect as possible. Next time you have to be much faster though."

Alex laughed hysterically. "Faster? I don't even know what I'm doing! I must be going crazy as everyone thinks! Why am I doing this? That woman didn't deserve to lose her life!"

"Jana," Jack stated.

"What?"

"Jana is the reason you are doing this, remember? You want me gone so you can be with her again. You have completed one task, only four more to go. Then you will be rid of me," Jack reminded Alex.

"I don't want to talk right now." Alex turned on the radio to drown out Jack. The rest of the trip home Alex would remind himself of Jana. She was the reason he was now a killer with innocent blood on his hands. She was more than worth it also. But Alex wondered if he would be able to commit cold-blooded murder again. It would depend on what Jack needed him to do past the actual killing. For the other remaining tasks, Alex decided he would do whatever needed to be done. Not being able to control his own body was the worst feeling. It reminded him of the night in the hospital when he first heard Jack's voice.

The image of the woman continued to plague his mind as he tried to think about Jana. The darkness of the alley had concealed much of the graphic details from Alex's mind. He hadn't seen all of the blood that had poured from her neck, but he had seen enough. He was unable to see her face clearly after she fell to the ground. The whole event played over and over in his mind, but the images were almost monochromatic because of the darkness. The main thing he continued to come back to was the question: Would he be able to do it again?

That question would continue to haunt him. The drive home seemed to last forever. Alex pondered the cuts Jack had forced him to inflict on the woman's stomach. Nothing had been mentioned about there being more to the tasks than just murder. He kept telling himself he only had to do it four more times. As he thought about it, though, he wondered if there was going to be more to the other tasks just as there had been to this one. Alex also wondered if Jack would inform him of anything extra the next time because he was sick of being kept in the dark.

When he was back at home, Alex removed his clothes and threw them in with the tons of dirty clothes he already had in his room. Not wanting to take a shower, he decided to wash up in the sink in his bathroom. The metallic smell of blood was a clear reminder of the night's events and what he had done, and what Jack had done to him. The smell was following him, no matter how hard he thought he'd scrubbed off the blood, so he went to bed breathing only through his mouth. Once again, he replayed the events of the night in his head. He waited for Jack to say something. Jack was silent, which Alex completely enjoyed. Before long, his mind drifted to Jana. He wondered how she was doing. The pleasant thoughts didn't last long though. The guilt of what he had done and the anxiety of someone knowing it was him would make sleep impossible. If only he could push out the feeling of holding the knife and the vision of cutting the poor woman, which played in his mind like a movie stuck in a loop. And the sight and smell of the blood. He had not seen that much in his young life. There was only going to be more.

TEN

Within thirty minutes of Alex abandoning the dark alley, police cars were already filling the street in front of the restaurant. Shortly after the crime scene investigators started to process the scene, two homicide detectives arrived in the alley. Detective Bagster and Detective Wynne had been quickly assigned to the case. Both of them entered the alley and immediately began to assess the scene for themselves. Soon they were approached by one of the police officers.

Bagster asked the officer, "What is the situation so far? Who discovered her?"

The officer pointed to a woman standing by one of the police cars in the street. It appeared another officer was conducting an interview with her. "That woman over there found her. Her name is Vicky Peck. She was supposed to pick up the victim, Katie Abby, but she was running late. When she arrived, Ms. Abby wasn't waiting outside for her, so Ms. Peck went in to find her. Other employees inside informed her that Ms. Abby had already left. Ms. Peck started looking for her, and eventually caught a glimpse of something in the alley. She screamed when she realized it was Ms. Abby, and someone from the kitchen came out to see what was wrong. That person was the one that called 911."

Wynne inquired, "Are the two women friends, relatives or what?"

"Actually," the officer started as he rubbed the back of his neck, "according to Ms. Peck, they were partners."

"They were a couple?" Bagster asked.

"Yes, Detective," the officer replied.

Wynne inquired, "What else do you have for us?"

"Well, we were waiting for the coroner, but so far it appears the weapon was probably just a regular knife. Nothing special. We haven't found much as far as evidence so far, and we haven't found the weapon."

Detective Bagster approached the body to take a look at the wounds around the victim's neck. He knelt down to take a closer look but didn't disturb her body in any way. The coroner, Alicia, arrived at the scene and quickly joined him. She knelt down beside Bagster as they greeted each other.

"It looks pretty brutal," Alicia said, closely examining the neck wounds. "Both cuts are pretty deep."

"I don't think that was the only wound," Bagster said as he pointed to her abdomen. "There appears to be blood soaked into her shirt."

Alicia yelled out to make sure someone had already photographed the body before she touched the woman. When she was assured the pictures had been taken, Alicia slipped on her rubber gloves and slowly raised the woman's shirt. The long deep incisions and the other cuts could be seen clearly in the now well-lit alleyway. "These were done postmortem," Alicia stated. "There was very little blood from these wounds. What blood there was is in the shirt." Alicia then yelled for more pictures to be taken of the body.

Wynne joined the two by the victim when he had finished talking with the officer that had interviewed Ms. Peck. "Well, it seems Ms. Peck has no idea who would want to hurt Ms. Abby. She apparently had no enemies."

Alicia offered her opinion as she stood up. "Of course, I need to do an autopsy before saying for sure, but I think this was a random attack."

"I believe so, too," Bagster agreed as he stood up next to them. "It's just instinct, but I think it was random, and I think this was the perpetrator's first victim. I don't know why yet, but I'm pretty sure she won't be the last."

"What makes you say that?" Wynne asked.

"This has all of the signs of a practice killing. He obviously had a purpose for cutting her stomach like that. I hope I'm wrong, but I bet there will be other victims, and they will be in worse shape," Bagster explained to his partner.

"You said 'he'," Alicia pointed out.

"Yes. I did," Bagster admitted. "We all know most serial killers are male."

Detective Bagster was correct in his statement. Little did he know the male in question wasn't a typical serial killer. Alex was being guided by the voice he was hearing. It would be hard to find someone whose normal habits and behavior were so different from those of a person who wanted to hurt women. Not having those traits set him aside from most serial killers. Then again, most serial killers would not necessarily flaunt their true nature.

The two detectives parted company with Alicia to go interview the victim's fellow employees. They were particularly interested in the kitchen help. With the back door standing wide open all evening, it was hard for the two men to believe the only noise anyone heard was the scream from Ms. Peck. Both hoped that at least one person saw or heard something.

Unfortunately for the detectives, the restaurant employees were a dead end. As it turned out, no one in the kitchen saw or heard anything suspicious. This led the two men to believe Ms. Abby's throat had been cut as soon as her killer had her in the alley. It also seemed no one in the front part of the restaurant had seen anything either. A few waitresses had seen Ms. Abby out front on the sidewalk waiting for her ride, but none of them had seen her attacker. They all assumed she had been picked up when they noticed she was gone. All the detectives could do now was wait to see if any clues popped up from the autopsy or the crime scene. Of course, they would interview the friends and family of Ms. Abby, but Detective Bagster, with his years of experience, already felt they would lead him and his partner to yet another dead end.

The next morning found Alex at home in his apartment alone. His apartment was slowly becoming worse as far as the cleanliness of the place. Alex had been in no mood to clean, do dishes, do laundry, or even take out the trash. As a matter of fact, he barely cleaned himself. He had been neglecting his home and his personal hygiene for some time. This morning, he had taken a shower to make sure there wasn't any blood hiding in some secret place that he hadn't noticed the night before when he washed up.

Alex was amazed at how good he felt after a hot shower. For the first time in weeks, he was actually ready to tackle at least the kitchen messes. First, he fixed himself a bowl of cereal and went to his favorite spot on the couch to eat. When he turned on the TV, the first thing he saw was a news report on the woman he had killed the night before.

"Turn that off!" Jack yelled as he suddenly made his presence known.

Alex nearly jumped out of his skin and almost spilled his cereal when he heard Jack yell. "Why? I want to hear this."

"It is not a good idea. You do not need to know anything about that woman," Jack said. "Now turn it off."

"Can I at least hear her name?"

"Absolutely not. If you know her name, then her death becomes personal to you. It is best to leave it alone. The less you know about each woman, the better off you will be Alex."

By the time Alex went to turn off the TV, the reporter on the news said the woman's name. "Her name was Katie Abby," Alex said. Jack had been right. That small piece of information had suddenly changed his outlook on her. The full extent of his actions against Katie Abby hit him like a ton of bricks.

"I tried to warn you, Alex," Jack calmly said to him. "In order for you to be able to complete all the tasks, you are going to have to refrain from knowing any personal information about the women I pick for you. There is not a natural drive in you to do this. Those that have that drive, they sometimes want to know personal information about their victims. For you, though, it will only complicate matters. Please, for now, no more television and no newspapers."

A nod of his head was the only response Alex gave Jack. For a moment he listened to what Jack had to say but then slowly retreated into a trance-like state. All of the drive he had to clean was gone. All he wanted to do was continue to sit on the couch and try not to think about what he had done. He had no desire to finish his cereal or to put the bowl in the kitchen. Alex, once again, had no desire to do anything productive.

—ɯ—

While Alex was at home slipping into his own little world again, the two detectives were busy interviewing anyone that knew Katie Abby. They slowly started to add a few names to a list of suspects. One name belonged to an old boyfriend of Ms. Abby. She had left him once she realized she had no real interest in men. When Ms. Abby met Ms. Peck, she fell in love and left the man she had been living with for several years. Ms. Abby's family thought he might be involved, but Bagster still didn't believe Ms. Abby knew her attacker.

Back at their desks that evening, Bagster and Wynne reviewed what they had learned that day. Wynne stated, "I don't think any of these people on our list had anything to do with it."

Bagster, who was leaning back in his chair with his hands behind his head, agreed fully with his partner. "I don't think so either. No one has a solid motive. You mark my words, there will be another one. And if we don't catch the rotten bastard, there will be even more."

Wynne leaned across his desk, which was facing his partner's desk. "Then we need to catch him quickly. You have more experience than I do, Bagster. How do we find out who he is?"

"We pray for a good solid lead, amazing evidence, or a witness," Bagster answered. He then leaned toward his partner and said, "So far, we have nothing but a bunch of people pointing fingers at each other, and as far as I'm concerned, none of them are even worth looking into any further."

Wynne's phone rang on his desk, interrupting their conversation. "Detective Wynne," he said when he picked up the phone. There was a slight pause before he said, "You're working late. That usually means you have something for us." Another pause. "All right. We're on our way."

"What is it?" Bagster asked, hoping it was good news.

"That was Alicia," Wynne informed his partner as he stood up from his desk. "She finished the autopsy on Ms. Abby. She said there's no smoking gun, but she has some things she wants us to take a look at."

At the coroner's office, Alicia took the two men to view the body of Katie Abby. Alicia had done a thorough job examining Ms. Abby. The only thing left for her to do was to close up the incisions and type up a report. She explained to the detectives what she had concluded about the condition in which Ms. Abby had been found the night before in the alley. "Gentleman, I didn't find any hard evidence, unfortunately, but I wanted you to see what I saw." Alicia pulled the sheet that was covering the body down to the hip area. "I'll start with her neck wounds," Alicia stated. "There are two deep incisions. Both are deep, but one is deeper than the other. Each one severed the carotid artery on each side. The top one cut the artery on the left, and the bottom one cut the artery on the right. Needless to say, she bled to death fairly quickly. Both incisions also severed her windpipe and esophagus." Alicia then moved to the body's abdominal area. "The long incision that runs from the rib area down to the pelvic area is jagged, not smooth. It is pretty deep." Alicia pulled open the wound with her hands. "I don't know what the purpose of it was, but you can see the gash is deep enough to gain access to her insides. I didn't have to cut much to do the autopsy. The other cuts are nowhere near this deep."

As Alicia covered the body back up, Wynne asked, "So what kind of weapon was used?"

"Probably a regular kitchen knife I'd say, with a blade at least six inches long. Just like the one you can buy at any department store or grocery store for that matter."

ELEVEN

As the detectives focused on finding out about the evidence collected from the crime scene, Alex confined himself to his apartment. He slept through most of the first few days after the murder. Once he finally snapped out of his temporary depression it occurred to him that he had missed several phone calls. The answering machine was blinking nonstop with several messages. Even though Alex was sure he didn't want to know who had called, he pushed the play button anyway.

"Alex, this is Mr. Jenson," the first message started. "I'm not sure what has happened to you, but we haven't seen you at work for over a week. I'm sorry to have to say this, Alex, but I have to let you go. I hope you get your life straightened out. Bye."

The next message was from his father. "Alex, where are you?" His dad's voice was especially harsh. "I got a call from the dean at your school. You haven't attended any of your classes since school started last week. I don't know what planet you are hiding on, but you have responsibilities here on Earth. I also know you haven't been to work either. I advise you to get your head out of the clouds before I stop paying for college."

There were several other messages from classmates and coworkers. It seemed everyone was wondering what had happened to him. To his surprise, Josh and Tony each had called to check on him. Alex had figured they were gone from his life forever. It was nice to hear their voices, but it would have been better to hear Jana's sweet voice. She hadn't called though.

Alex assumed his normal position on the couch. He rubbed his hands over his face and started to contemplate the messages on his answering machine. It was dawning on him that he wasn't in a good spot. Without a job, he would soon lose his apartment. If his dad stopped paying for school, he would have no future. Of course, that would be the case anyway if he continued to skip class. His dad was right about Alex having responsibilities, but he couldn't work or focus in school until Jack was gone from his life. Jack had become the top priority. A knock on the door interrupted Alex's thoughts. When he opened the door, he discovered his dad standing on the other side.

"I see you're still alive," said Mr. Dorson. "Where have you been? I called you two days ago."

"I've been here," Alex said, walking away from the door.

Mr. Dorson entered the apartment and closed the door behind him. Once he saw the condition of his son's apartment, he decided to not sit down. He stood just inside the living room with his hands in his trouser pockets. Alex, on the other hand, proceeded to sit back down in his usual spot.

Mr. Dorson looked at his son with disgust. "What is going on with you?"

"What are you talking about?" Alex asked him coldly.

"Your apartment is disgusting. And when was the last time you showered or even brushed your hair?" Mr. Dorson asked. He wasn't really looking for an answer. He just wanted to point out what he observed.

Alex rolled his eyes at his dad, which was something he had never done before in his life. "I'm fine. What do you want?"

"I would like to know why you haven't been to school yet. I want to know why you haven't been going to work. I think you need some sort of help. Maybe you need to see a doctor or something. Are you depressed?"

"I'm not depressed," Alex said sharply. He had been for a few days, but now he was fine. "I just have a few personal issues I'm trying to work through right now. I'll find another job. As far as school, maybe it would be best if I take this semester off so I can get things straightened out." Alex hoped that would suffice his dad enough that he would leave.

"I don't like the thought of you taking a semester off during your senior year, but I guess it's better than you flunking out altogether," Mr. Dorson stated. "Do you want me to send Jessica over here to help you clean this place up?"

Shaking his head, Alex said, "I'll get to it. She doesn't need to come here."

"Are you sure? She probably wouldn't mind. We haven't been letting her get out too much the last few days."

"Why? Did she get in trouble or something?"

Mr. Dorson replied, "No. Didn't you hear about that poor woman they found murdered downtown in the alley?"

Alex's heart plummeted. "Uh, yeah, I did." His chest tightened suddenly, the pulse quickening in his neck, and he prayed his dad would not notice. "I-I'm sure Jessica will be okay though. You shouldn't keep her locked up." There was no way he would ever hurt his own sister.

"Well, you don't know that for sure. We think it's best to be safe and not sorry."

Alex did know for sure, but his dad didn't know that. "I suppose so."

"I've got to get going," Mr. Dorson said, reaching for the door. He stopped and turned back to Alex. "Do you need any money to get you by until you find another job?"

"Not just yet."

"All right, then," Mr. Dorson said. "I'll call you in a couple of days. Answer the phone this time, okay?"

"I will."

Once Mr. Dorson was gone, Alex glanced around at the apartment he had lived in for over a year. It became apparent to him that it was still in a horrible state. He wondered how he could possibly clean it all up alone. There was so much to do. It had to be done. Before doing anything else, he decided to make some coffee to boost his energy level. With all the sleep he had gotten, one would think he'd be full of energy, but he was lacking in that department for some reason.

As he waited for the coffee maker to produce coffee, Alex started to retrieve all the dirty dishes from the kitchen sink. He filled one side of the sink with hot soapy water, and then he put some glasses in it to soak. Even though he had missed out on the past few days by sleeping, Alex realized, as he washed the dishes, that he actually felt much better. He would have to take the whole day to get his apartment back in order, but for the first time in a long time, he actually felt like doing something. The day would be even better if Jack just left him alone.

By the time Alex had finished the pot of coffee, his apartment was looking much better. Laundry was the only chore left, and it was the one he dreaded the most. After he showered and put on clean clothes, which he hadn't done in days, Alex loaded his little car with tons of laundry. So far he hadn't heard a peep from Jack. It had been nice to have some alone time.

When Alex arrived at the laundromat, he took trash bags full of laundry inside and set them in front of a row of washers. It didn't take long for him to fill all six of them. He no sooner started closing the lids when he heard a familiar voice from behind him.

"Well, well. I haven't seen you in a while." The voice belonged to one of his best friends, Josh.

Alex started to close the lid to the last washer when he spotted his blood-splattered jeans in clear view. He quickly closed the lid and turned to face his friend, hoping he did not see anything. Alex smiled and replied, "I've been hiding out."

The two sat down in a couple of empty chairs across from the washing machines Alex was using. "Tony and I both have called you a few times. We never get an answer. Have you been hiding out at home?"

"I've been at home," Alex confessed, "but I've had some things going on that no one knows about that are kind of personal."

"I saw Jana the other day," Josh blurted out. "I don't think she's handling the breakup very well. She said the last time she saw you was at the drugstore, and you didn't look too well."

"*Breakup?*" Alex quickly became angered. "I didn't break up with Jana! Why would she tell you that?"

Josh leaned away from Alex and put his hands up. "She said you told her to stay away from you! She took it as a breakup!"

Alex thought about it for a moment and then said, "Sorry I snapped at you, Josh. It's not your fault." Josh relaxed and Alex continued to talk. "I didn't break up with her. I didn't realize she thought I had. I just haven't quite been myself the past couple of months, and I needed to be alone. I found myself getting mad and defensive all the time. She didn't need to be around me. The last thing I wanted to do is hurt her."

"I know you've been different," Josh started. "You yelled at Tony and me the last time we were at your apartment. I know you yelled at Jana, too. But the thing we all want to know is, are you better now?"

"I don't know," Alex answered. He knew he was far from being better. "I'm having a good day today, but that doesn't mean it will last. So what should I do about Jana? I don't want to lose her, but I don't want her to see me as I have been."

Josh slouched down in his plastic chair and crossed his arms over his chest. "If I were you, I would go to her and try to explain how you feel. Past that, have you thought about going into therapy or something? I don't know what problems you are having, but maybe you could talk to someone about them. It couldn't hurt, right? We all would like to have the old Alex back. I know Tony has called you a few times, but he refuses to go to your apartment after the last time we were there."

As Alex rubbed his hands over his hair, he took a deep breath and exhaled. "I'm not going into therapy. I tried that already, and the psychiatrist didn't help me at all. They all think medication is the answer. I can fix my problems myself. I just don't know how long it will take. I want my old life back. That is my goal, but I have some things to do first before that can happen. I will definitely go see Jana though. I need her there when I get through all of this. Without her, it is all pointless. Tell Tony I'm sorry for my actions, and I hope he can forgive me. I hope you can, too. I just can't be the old Alex right now."

"I wish I knew what was going on with you," Josh said as he sat back up straight in his seat, "but I'm sure you'll tell me when you're ready. What is going on with school? Is that something else that is on hold?"

"Yeah, at least for a semester," Alex answered, looking at the washing machines. "I have to find another job. I missed too many days, and I was fired."

"Maybe you could work with Tony," Josh suggested jokingly.

Alex laughed. "I don't think that would work right now. I'll find something."

Josh stood up. "Well, Alex, I have to take off. My laundry is already in the car. If you need anything, let me know. I don't have any hard feelings."

"Thanks. I'll be okay, eventually. Don't worry about me," Alex assured his friend. "I do need one favor."

"What's that?"

"I'm going to straighten things out with Jana, but can you keep an eye on her for me until I can do it myself?"

"Sure. I can do that. Especially with some maniac running loose around town," Josh said, giving Alex a pat on the back. "You did hear about the murder downtown, didn't you?"

Alex's pulse was racing again. "Yeah," he said, as nonchalantly as he was able. "I heard." Alex didn't want to talk about that news headline if he didn't have to.

"I'll keep an eye on her for you. You take care of yourself, okay?" Josh headed for the door.

Alex was relieved he didn't have to have another conversation about the murder or about his blood-stained jeans in the washer. He was also happy he had been able to make things better with at least one person in his life. He could kick himself for the way things had turned out with Jana. He never intended to end his relationship with her. She was the reason he had committed that awful act in the first place. Alex could see why she would think that was what he was doing. As long as Jack left him alone a little longer, he would finish his laundry and then go straight to Jana's apartment. He had to make sure she was still willing to be his.

TWELVE

It was obvious to Alex that he had surprised Jana by showing up at her apartment. The look on her face was priceless. As she stood there frozen, Alex smiled and asked, "Can I come in, or should I just go away?"

The question brought Jana out of her stunned state. She moved aside and replied, "I guess you can come in if you really want to."

Alex stepped inside and made his way over to her couch where he sat down. After closing the door, Jana joined him. She wondered why he was there. How could she get over him when she kept seeing him? It was pure torture to her poor heart and soul. Just the sight of Alex reopened the wounds that she was trying to heal. What could he possibly want?

"I saw Josh earlier today," Alex started as he sat on the edge of her couch with his elbows resting on his knees. He rubbed his hands together as he continued. "For some reason, he thought we had broken up. Why would he think that?"

Jana looked confused. "We did break up. Didn't we?"

He turned to her and said, "No, at least not that I knew of anyway. Do you want to be rid of me?"

"No!" she said. "You told me to stay away. Remember? I thought you didn't want me anymore."

"I always want you." Alex pulled her close and wrapped his arms around her. "I need to be alone for a while to take care of some personal problems. I want to know you will still be there when I get myself back to the way I was before the accident." He could feel her warm tears as they soaked into his shirt.

"I'll be here, but can't I help?" she asked through her sobs.

Alex lifted her away from him and took her face in his hands. "I wish you could, but I need to do this alone."

"Do what? Just what are the problems? And why do you have to take care of them alone? Tell me, Alex, please."

He knew she wouldn't understand what he was thinking. There was no point in trying to explain it. He looked deep into her eyes, then kissed her softly, tasting the salt of her tears mixed with the sweetness of her lips. When she parted her lips, Alex kissed her harder. Jana eagerly accepted him. The pain she had felt was slowly diminishing, and she just wanted him to be with her.

After a moment, Alex pulled himself away and stood up. He pulled her up by her hand and led her to her bedroom. Once inside, Alex held both of Jana's hands. He leaned down and whispered in her ear, "I need to feel you close to me. I need to feel your warmth and your touch. I need to know you still love me."

Jana wasted little time giving him what he needed. All her pain was suddenly quenched by the touch of Alex's hands on her bare skin. The passion between them had never been so intense. They both needed to show and be shown their love for one another. Jana held on to Alex with her whole body. She never wanted him to stop, but eventually, their period of intimacy came to an end.

As they both lay quietly in her bed, Alex held Jana as she rested her head on his chest. Alex wanted the moment to last forever. He knew now that she was still his, and he would do whatever he had to do in order to keep her. Unfortunately for the couple, the moment was interrupted, but only Alex was aware of the interruption.

"Alex," Jack called to him from inside his head. "It is time to prepare for your next task. You must leave her." As Alex tried to ignore Jack, he became louder. "Alex! You must leave her in order to keep her! Do you think she would still want you if she knew about me?"

Jack was right. Jana would think he was insane if she knew about Jack. That was why he had told her to stay away in the first place. He couldn't explain it to her because he would lose her forever. Once Alex realized that, he remembered why he was going along with Jack's evil tasks. He had to get rid of him so he could have her. "I have to go," Alex blurted out as he hurried out of her bed.

"Why?" Jana asked as she sat up and watched Alex frantically dress. "Did I do something wrong?"

The question made him stop. Alex sat down on the bed beside her and said, "No. You didn't do anything wrong. I just have to go."

"So all you wanted was to get me in bed," she said harshly.

Alex sighed. "No! I told you I have personal things to take care of right now. Please understand that I have to do this for us."

"I guess I still have to stay away, right? Just sit here and wait for you to come back," Jana stated.

"Please?"

Jana shook her head in disbelief. "I don't know what to think, Alex. Are you using me?"

"Jana, I have to go, but I'll be back for you, eventually. You are the only thing keeping me going right now. Please be patient with me."

She had no choice. "I'll wait for you. I wish I knew why I have to wait, but nevertheless, I will wait. All I have to ask from you is please don't hurt me anymore. I don't think my poor heart can take it."

"I never meant to hurt you in the first place," Alex said. He finished dressing and left her apartment hoping it wouldn't be long before he could be with her again.

As he drove away, Alex started to scream at Jack. "Why did you have to show up there? Why did I have to leave? And what do you mean by 'It's time to prepare for your next task'?"

"Do not yell, Alex," Jack instructed him. "I have allowed you time to yourself. I did not interrupt your fun with her. Everyone is entitled to a little recreation from time to time, but playtime is over now. The next task will be difficult for you. I want to prepare you."

"Just so you know," Alex started, calmer now, "Jana is not recreation. If it wasn't for her, I wouldn't be playing your little games."

"I am well aware of this," Jack responded. "Please accept my apologies. I didn't mean any disrespect, but the girl did provide some relief for you, did she not?"

"Yes, she did," Alex answered. He really didn't want to discuss any of it with Jack. "But not just sexually. I feel much better knowing she is willing to wait for me even though she has no idea what I'm doing. But I don't want to discuss Jana with you any further. Tell me where you want me to go."

"Do you remember where the deer was located?" Jack inquired.

"Yes."

"Proceed to that location again."

Alex drove out to the middle of nowhere once again. Everything looked the same. Unsure of the exact location of the deer carcass, he asked, "Was it around here somewhere?"

"This is close enough. Park your vehicle, get the knife, and go into the tree line," Jack instructed Alex.

Last time, Alex didn't need a knife. He started to worry about what Jack had in store for him this time. Without asking any other questions, Alex grabbed his knife from the glove box, got out of his car, and started making his way through the thick weeds in the open field. He was relieved to find no nauseating smell of rotting animals when he entered the tree line. Only the mosquitoes found him, quickly swarming and feasting on his arms. Alex ran back to his car and pulled a long-sleeved flannel from his clean laundry and put it on as fast as he could. He also grabbed the gloves from his trunk to protect his hands. When he was mostly covered, Alex returned to the trees.

Once Alex had returned, Jack instructed him on which way to walk. He led Alex step by step through the wooded area until he reached another dead deer. This one had only been dead for a couple of hours. The corpse was still intact. It had been left untouched by insects or any other animals. Alex was just relieved it didn't omit a foul stench. The last deer had smelled so bad it turned his stomach inside out. Just the thought of the odor was enough to cause his stomach to turn sour a little.

Alex looked down at the poor animal. "What do you want me to do with this one?"

"Dissect it."

"Dissect it? Why? What happened to it?"

"It is a doe," Jack started. "She was hit by a vehicle, but she did not die right away. She made it to the spot where she now lies. I want you to take your time and dissect her as I give you specific instructions."

After he knelt down beside the deer, Alex asked, "But why do you want me to cut her up? I don't get it."

"I will instruct you on this beast so you will be prepared to perform the same on your next task," Jack finally told him. "You have all the time in the world with the animal in front of you, but you will not have much time three nights from tonight."

It appeared Jack was stepping things up a notch. Last time, he only needed to kill the woman and make a few strange cuts on her, which Jack had actually done himself. If he was planning to have him cut up the next woman, what did Jack have planned for the fifth woman? Alex shuddered to even think about it. He was realizing he would have to somehow dissociate to make it through each task if each one was going to be more extreme than the last.

"Find the bottom of the breast bone," Jack said. Alex located it with his left hand. "Stab the abdomen area below that bone and cut as far down to the hind legs as you can."

He did exactly what he was told. "There's the odor," Alex stated as he covered his nose with his arm. "There isn't much blood though." He expected blood to be pouring out of the opening, but that was not what happened at all.

Jack laughed. "Of course not, lad, she is dead. The heart has stopped beating. There is a smell only because she has been here for a while. Take a moment to get used to it. Then I want you to lay her abdomen open and reach inside. Pull out the intestines, carefully."

"Basically you want me to gut her?" Alex asked. That he could do, on a deer anyway. He had never done it before himself, but he had seen Jana's dad do it after returning from his annual hunting trips.

"In a manner of speaking, yes, but with some small differences."

"Like what?"

"There are certain things you will not remove when I say to leave them intact, and there are certain places I want you to make precise cuts and take special care in removing the organs. I want everything exactly the way I tell you. This is not a butcher shop. Understand?" Jack replied sharply.

"I guess so," Alex said. He didn't fully understand what the big deal was, but he did understand that Jack was calling the shots. If he didn't follow directions, Jack would take control of him again, and he didn't like that one bit.

"Good. Let us begin."

The first cut Alex made in the doe's skin sent cold chills down his spine. The smell was horrible, but he managed to fight the sickness in his stomach. He tried not to breathe any more than he had to as he sliced open the abdomen of the deer. This was the first time Alex had seen the inside of any living thing. The pictures in books didn't even begin to prepare him for what he saw. The liver had such a dark color to it. The intestines resembled meat that had been strung out and then smashed back inside the poor animal. The blood-covered organs glistened in the sun.

Jack wasted little time directing Alex on what to do. Alex wasted no time in following his directions. Though he struggled with handling certain parts of the deer at first, his discomfort eased after a bit. Jack had to explain the names of certain body parts he wanted Alex to make incisions in, but that was the only real problem the two encountered during the process. Alex, however, still faced his inner crisis: Would he be able to do the same thing to a human? After all, a deer that had been dead for a few hours was not the same as a human who had only been dead a few minutes. One way or another, he would have to get himself together because the next task was quickly approaching.

THIRTEEN

The same day Alex was in the woods with the dead doe's body, Detective Bagster and Detective Wynne sat at their desks trying to figure out how to proceed with their case. The crime lab had thoroughly gone over everything that had been sent to them. Nothing was found. This information was disturbing to the two men. Detective Bagster was still sure there would be another victim.

Wynne asked his older partner, "Any ideas on what we should do now?"

Bagster rocked back and forth in his desk chair. "I don't know. I had hoped for at least a fiber or a partial print. I figured we wouldn't get lucky enough to get a solid lead on the killer's identity. Something would have been nice though." He stopped rocking and leaned forward onto his desk. "This may sound awful, but maybe he will leave more clues at the next crime scene."

"That does sound bad," Wynne responded with a chuckle. He thought Bagster was kidding. "I suppose we are just going to sit around and wait for someone else to lose their life. Pardon me, but that sounds cold."

Leaning back in his chair and starting to rock again, Bagster said, "That is all we can do unless you have a suggestion. We have already beefed up the patrols around the city and have asked for any tips publicly."

A moment of silence befell Wynne before he answered his partner. "I don't have any suggestions. I don't feel right about it all though."

"Would it make you feel better to go out and patrol the streets some?" Bagster asked.

"It would be better than just sitting here," Wynne answered. "At least I would feel like I'm out there trying to protect the people in this city. Isn't that what I'm supposed to do, protect the innocent?"

Bagster stood up and gathered his belongings from his desk. "That's what we get paid for I guess. Come on, let's get out of here."

—⚡—

In the woods, Alex had finished removing most of the organs from the doe. Each incision had been performed exactly as Jack had instructed. The whole process had taken over an hour, and Alex was relieved when Jack told him to stop. He sat back on the ground with his knees bent and his arms resting on top of them. He stared at what he had done without much thought about what it all meant.

"Nice work, Alex," Jack said.

"Thank you, I guess," Alex replied with a small chuckle.

"Do you think you can do the same thing faster next time? I need you to do it faster. Can you do that for me?"

Alex stood up, removed the gloves from his hands, and dusted off the seat of his pants and his knees. As he looked down at his handiwork, he replied, "I'll do my best. That is all I can promise. You were pretty precise on the cuts. Do you want them to be done exactly, or do you want them to be done fast? It's your choice."

"I want both."

"Then I can't make any promises. I'll do my best." Alex turned away from the animal at his feet and headed out of the thicket.

Once in the car, Alex started the engine and put the car in drive. After he slowly and carefully turned his vehicle around to head back to the city, he rolled down the windows. The smell from the animal's entrails were starting to fill the car.

Jack inquired of Alex, "Do you think you will be able to perform the same acts on a human being in a couple of days?"

"I hope so, but what if I can't?" Alex wondered as he noticed the sun starting to set.

Jack replied, "I will have to do it then. It is not in our agreement for me to do it though. I helped the other day because she was your first, but I do not wish to help you with the rest of the tasks."

"Yeah, well, no offense, Jack," Alex started, "but I don't really like you taking control of my body either. You might be in my mind against my will, but I would rather you stay up there and leave the rest of me alone."

"I plan to leave your body alone as long as you do it all quickly and exactly as I instruct."

"Fine," Alex agreed. "I will try to be faster, and hopefully I don't mess anything up."

Jack assured him, "You will be fine. I have confidence in you."

As Alex drove home, he was completely unaware of the two detectives he passed on the street. Bagster and Wynne were also unaware of the fact that they had passed their killer as he headed in the opposite direction. They didn't know who they were looking for, and Alex figured he was safe since no one had shown up at his apartment as of yet. He figured the police would have knocked on his door already if someone had spotted him at the crime scene. And Alex was pretty confident no clues had been left behind to identify him.

He realized he was exhausted once he arrived home. The apartment was clean and had a warm and welcoming feel to it again. He vowed to not let it get out of hand again, but that would take a great effort on his part. The laundry was left in the trunk of his car. That would have to wait until the morning. Alex undressed and put his clothes in a trash bag to contain their odor. After a quick second shower, he crawled into bed and was asleep before he knew what had happened.

—⁂—

A couple of days later, Alex awoke to the phone ringing. He grabbed the phone and groggily said hello.

"It's one o'clock in the afternoon. Don't tell me you are still in bed," Jessica said from the other end of the line.

Alex sat up in bed and rubbed his face with his one free hand. "Jessica? Why aren't you in school?"

"I need to talk to you. Can I come over?" she asked.

He could tell by the sound of her voice that it was important. He hadn't left the house since the incident in the woods, and he wasn't planning on going anywhere until nightfall. "I guess so, sis. I'll be home. How long do I have before you get here?"

"I'll be there in about ten to fifteen minutes."

"All right," Alex said into the phone, and then he hung up.

The first thing he did was start the coffee maker. Next, he dressed, brushed his teeth and hair, and washed his face. He hadn't planned to sleep so late. The day before was uneventful so he shouldn't have been so tired. Alex had spent the previous day trying to keep up on the news to see if anything had been updated on the woman he murdered or on the case itself. To his surprise, the case wasn't even mentioned. It was already old news. Jack gloated by saying, "See, Alex, I told you it would be fine if you just listened to me. Now, I said this before, no more news from here on out."

When Jessica arrived, Alex let her in and offered her some coffee. She laughed at him. She didn't like coffee, and he knew that. He went to the kitchen to fix himself a cup while she put her school bag on the floor and sat down on the couch.

"What's so important that you had to cut school and come talk to me?" Alex asked her from the kitchen.

"It's about Mom and Dad," she said.

Alex joined his sister on the couch. "What about them? Are they finally getting divorced?" he asked jokingly as he took a sip of his coffee.

"Yes, they are, as a matter of fact," she replied seriously.

The news shocked Alex. It was a common opinion that the two should divorce, but no one really thought it would happen. "Dad was just here a few days ago. He didn't say anything about it to me," Alex told her.

Jessica leaned back on the arm of the couch. "Well, they haven't officially said anything to me yet either."

"Then how do you know?"

"I overheard them talking in the kitchen last night," Jessica started. "They thought I was asleep, but I had come downstairs to get something to drink. I heard them in the kitchen, so I stayed outside the doorway and listened."

"What did they say?"

She laughed sarcastically. "Believe it or not, they weren't fighting. Dad said he had an apartment picked out close to his office. He wants Mom to keep the house. I guess I'm supposed to stay with her, but I don't know about all that. Can I stay with you instead?"

"Uh," Alex said, hesitating, "now isn't the right time to discuss that. I have a lot going on at the moment."

"I know," Jessica agreed as she sat back up, "that's why I'm here."

"What do you mean?" he wondered. How could she know anything? No one knew anything. Her comment worried him.

"You are the reason they're not telling anyone yet," Jessica started to explain. "They are worried that you may need medical attention. They talked to Jana and a couple of your friends. They think you might be depressed—that the news would send you over the edge."

His mind raced with thoughts of what his so-called friends, and so-called girlfriend, had told his parents about him. "And what do *you* think about me?" Alex asked her harshly.

Jessica noticed the change in her brother's tone. "Calm down, Alex. I don't know what to think about you. I heard them say your apartment was dirty and you were too. They discussed the fact that you were quick to snap at anyone who tried to talk to you. But I didn't know what to think because I hadn't been around you in a while. They haven't let me leave the house since that woman was killed. That is why I cut class to come to see you."

Alex didn't want to touch on the murder. He avoided that subject altogether. "Well, now that you are here and you see me, what do you believe?"

"I'm more confused now than I was last night!" Jessica said loudly as she briefly threw up her arms. "Your place is clean. You're clean and presentable. You seem fine to me. Where was all that coming from anyway?"

Alex leaned toward his sister and explained. "Jessica, I did go through a brief period where I let everything go to crap, including myself. I do have some other issues to work through before I can get back to normal, but I'm trying really hard to get to that point. I did see a doctor for a bit, but that was not what I needed. Don't let this thing with Mom and Dad get to you. In a few short years, you will be off to college, and you won't have to deal with them as much. Just make sure you go far away for college." He smiled at her.

"What about you? Will you be okay through this?" Since he had admitted to having some problems, Jessica was worried about him.

"I'll be fine. I promise," Alex said. He seemed to be saying those words a lot the past couple of months. If only everyone would believe him and leave him alone, he would be fine, eventually.

FOURTEEN

Jack made his presence known shortly after Jessica had left for home. It was time to make a plan for the night's events. Everything had to be planned out perfectly. One mistake could get Alex caught, and then Jack's long-term plans would be ruined.

"Why are you so worried about tonight? I should be the one that is nervous," Alex said as he sat on the couch. The TV was on, but he had it on mute to hear Jack clearly.

Jack replied sharply, "This time is different from the last time, and you had problems the last time!"

"It was my first time! Give me a break!"

"And this is your first time removing any organs from the victims!" Jack shouted back.

Alex sighed heavily. All of the yelling was giving him a headache. "Why do I have to do that anyway? What is that supposed to accomplish?"

"You have to do it because I said to do it," the voice in his head stated. "In order for everything to be exact, you have to do it the way I tell you to. So, stop being difficult."

"Exact? I don't get it," Alex asked.

Jack responded calmly, "It is our agreement that you will do just as I say."

The calm response from Jack worried Alex. He knew that was the agreement, but a little explanation would help the stress of the situation. After he closed his eyes tightly, Alex responded by saying, "Okay. I'll stop. Just don't yell anymore." Alex slowly opened his eyes when there was no response. "Jack? Are you still there?"

"Yes, Alex. I'm still here," a response finally came. "Now, eat some dinner and get ready. I want you downtown before nightfall."

"Yes, sir," Alex sarcastically replied. Jack didn't offer a comment back. Alex took that as a sign to stop playing around and get busy. He figured that would be the best thing to do anyway. If he continued to sit and do nothing, he would eventually start to think about what he was going to be doing later that night. Alex knew his conscience would get in the way then. And that must not happen.

After eating an early dinner, he changed into the same clothes he had worn during his previous task. He had gotten enough of the blood out of his pants when he did his laundry that no one would even notice what little bit was left. Again, he pulled his hair up into the hat, slipped on his jacket, and put the gloves in the jacket pockets. Then it was time to travel downtown to find his next victim.

This time, Jack instructed Alex to go to a different area of the city than he had the last time. Once he found a suitable place to leave his car, he got out and began to walk down a nearby sidewalk. Most of the local shops and businesses were closing up for the night, while the local bars and nightclubs were just starting to get their Monday night customers.

Alex wandered up and down the sidewalks of the same three blocks for almost an hour before Jack said anything to him. "I thought you had abandoned me, Jack."

"No. I wanted you to walk awhile. Have you taken in your surroundings? Do you know where everything is located?" Jack inquired of his subject.

"Yes, I think so," Alex told him as he continued to walk. "What now?"

"Cross the street to the building on the corner there with all the people outside of it."

Alex looked across the street. "The dance club? Is that the one you mean?"

"The one with the line of people, yes. It is starting to get darker. So find an alley close to that building. See if there is one on either side of it."

Cautiously, Alex crossed the street and started up the sidewalk toward the club. Trying to not draw attention to himself, he put his hands in his jacket pockets and kept his head down as he passed the crowd. No one in front of the club seemed to notice him as he walked by them and turned the corner. At the backside of the club, Alex finally found an alleyway. He quickly ducked into it and pressed his back against the building to be discreet.

"Very good, Alex," Jack praised him. "You found the perfect spot. I can hear the noise from inside the building out here. That will be of use to us."

"I don't like this, Jack," Alex whispered, sounding almost worried. "It's not dark enough for me to be here. Someone will find me."

"I agree. We at least know where you should be when the darkness falls. You should not stay here now and risk being discovered. You must leave the alley until the sun has completely disappeared."

Jack had no sooner said the words to Alex when he darted out of the alley. He walked away from the club, hoping he hadn't been noticed. It was hard for him to resist the urge, but Alex continued on without looking back. After a few minutes, Jack assured him no one had seen him leave the alley. Relieved, Alex entered an open coffee shop and ordered a cup of coffee before finding a table near the window. He hoped Jack wouldn't talk to him while he was there. There was no way to answer him without drawing attention to himself. And that was the last thing he needed right now. Anything could arouse suspicion.

When it was finally black outside, Alex left the coffee shop and made his way back to the alley behind the club. He could hide completely in the shadows of the alley. It was hard for Alex to even see his hand in front of his face. "How am I supposed to see what I'm doing?"

"The alley across the street has some light. That will be where you complete the task," Jack told him.

Alex didn't see how that was going to work. "That's a jewelry store. It's already closed, which means no customers. But how do I get someone from here to there without being noticed? It's impossible."

"How are you going to get someone into this alley?" Jack tested him.

"I was going to grab someone, like before, so no one would have a chance to see me," Alex answered.

"Well, that is not going to be an option either way," Jack flatly stated. "You will have to get someone to go with you to the alley over there."

"What?!" Alex burst out. When he realized he had almost yelled, he calmed down and whispered, "I can't do that. No one in their right mind will go with me to a dark alley."

"Then wait for someone who is not in their right mind."

Alex stopped and considered Jack's suggestion as he peered out of the darkness and inspected the alley across from him.

"Can you come up with a way to accomplish that?"

Laughing mischievously, Alex replied, "You know what, Jack? I believe I can. I'm going to remain here and think about it while our woman is inside enjoying her last drinks." Alex sat down on the hard pavement in the alley and let his imagination start to work. It wasn't long before he came up with a simple plan. He stood up, crossed the street, and sat down on the pavement in the other alley with his back against the jewelry store wall.

As the hours passed, Alex's thoughts wandered through the many things affecting his life at that moment. He thought about school. This was supposed to be his last year. All of his friends would be graduating without him. Jana would be graduating without him. Would she be willing to wait for him to start a new life after he was done with school? Then, there was his parents and their divorce. Alex didn't much care about that, but Jessica would be the one to suffer, not him. And, of course, there was the fact that he was unemployed and slowly running out of money.

When Alex heard the sound of footsteps coming up the sidewalk toward him, he quickly returned to the moment and got to his feet. As he peeked around the corner, he saw a woman approaching, and she was alone. It was obvious by the uneven steps that she was highly intoxicated. Alex was thrilled. He didn't expect to get so lucky as to have a woman alone, intoxicated, and on the same side of the street.

Jack, who had been quiet up to then, asked, "Are you ready, Alex?"

"This will be easier than I thought," Alex answered as he continued to peek around the corner. Quickly, he pulled the gloves from his pockets and slipped them on. He took a deep breath and slowly stepped out of the alley, then leaned up against the wall of the jewelry store.

The petite woman noticed him, but the alcohol in her system caused her to not be alarmed. She approached him and said, "Do I know you?"

As she laughed and giggled, Alex smiled down at her. "No, I don't believe so. Would you like to know me?"

She laughed again as she stumbled around some. "Only if you're nice. Are you nice? You sure are cute."

Alex couldn't believe how well it was going so far. He hated the fact that he was going to have to kill her, but he had made a deal. It also was for Jana. He buried his thoughts and emotions way down inside himself and started to pretend he was someone else. "Step inside my office, and we will get acquainted."

"I don't know," the woman said playfully. "You may not be as nice as you seem."

"There's only one way to find out," Alex said. He smiled again and pulled himself from the building. After he stepped back into the alley, he peeked around the corner at the woman and whispered, "There's no one in here. It's just me, waiting for you to come to play."

The woman walked to the corner of the jewelry store but didn't enter the alley. "I don't think I should go in there with you," she said, being a little more serious.

Unfortunately for her, she was too close to Alex. He grabbed her and pulled her into the alley. When she let out a scream, Alex quickly covered her mouth with his hand. He was having a hard time keeping control of her while trying to pull the knife out of his jacket.

"It is okay, Alex. Forget the knife. Strangle her," Jack instructed.

Doing as he was told without thinking about it, Alex wrapped one hand tightly around her throat and slammed her small body against the wall. He then removed his other hand from her mouth, and once both of his hands were around her neck, she quickly lost consciousness. "Do you want me to kill her this way?"

"No," Jack said sharply. "Cut her throat before she comes to."

Without hesitation, Alex released the hold on her neck and let her fall hard to the ground. After removing the knife from his jacket sleeve, he got down on his knees and rolled her over onto her back. He moved to the right side of her limp body, leaned over her, and cut her throat deeply. For a few seconds, he could hear the blood gurgling in her throat. The blood quickly started to drain from her neck to the pavement of the alley. He jumped up quickly as the dark shiny liquid started to flow toward him. When the sound stopped, Alex knew she was dead. Her eyes no longer possessed the twinkle of life.

"Now, there is no time to waste," Jack said excitedly. "Pull her legs up and lay them open. Get between them and pull her skirt up completely." Alex did this as fast as he could, and Jack continued to shout instructions. "Cut open her abdomen, but not too deep. Lay it open."

As Alex worked hard and fast, he tried to not think about what he was doing. She was much warmer than the deer and had more blood in her still. Jack continued to tell him step by step what to do. Alex started to remove the woman's insides as Jack instructed, but this wasn't at all like the deer. Because she hadn't been dead but for a few short minutes, her organs were still warm and soft. He could feel the warmth through his gloves.

It was a struggle for Alex to make all the necessary cuts exactly the way Jack wanted him to, but he managed to remove everything he was supposed to fairly fast. Once he was done, Alex asked Jack, "That's it. Can I go now?"

"Almost," Jack said. "Take her rings."

"Why?"

"Take her rings, and take her uterus with a portion of the bladder," Jack ordered.

"Why?" Alex asked again. He was almost repulsed by the command.

"Because I said so!" Jack yelled, making Alex's head throb again. This time, Alex obeyed him.

FIFTEEN

A few hours later, Detective Bagster and Detective Wynne arrived in the alley by the jewelry store. Once again, the crime scene was crawling with police officers and investigators. As the two men approached the woman's body, they spotted Alicia. She was already examining the corpse and recording what she saw into a small voice recorder. The first thing the detectives noticed about the victim was that they had been dissected this time.

Bagster and Wynne stood on one side of the body and looked down at Alicia, who was getting a closer look at the corpse from the other side. Bagster asked her, "How is it that you arrived at the scene before we did?"

Alicia stopped her recorder and looked up at the two men. "I just happen to live nearby."

"Do you think it's the same person that killed the waitress?" Wynne asked.

"Yes, I do," she replied. She then motioned for them to get a closer look. After they bent down, she continued. "My initial observations tell me she was attacked and murdered by the same person. Her throat only has one slice, but it is just as deep as the previous victim's. The wounds seem to be consistent with the other victim, so as of now, I'm pretty sure it was the same kind of knife."

Wynne glanced at his partner and said, "He's getting more in-depth with his victims."

"The first one was practice," Bagster replied. "I assume he either wasn't sure what he wanted to accomplish with her, or he was scared off too soon. I would guess the first."

When the men started to stand back up, Alicia stopped them by saying, "There is one more thing I want to show you." They bent back down as she pointed out the eyes of the woman. "Do you see the broken blood vessels? I believe she was strangled before her throat was cut. She has bruising on her neck that supports that theory also."

Wynne stood up. "Why would he strangle her, and then cut her throat?"

"Probably to shut her up or get her to stop fighting him," Bagster stated as he, too, stood up. He asked one last question of Alicia. "Is there anything else you need to tell us now, or do you need to do the autopsy first?"

"Well," Alicia started as she glanced around the body, "I won't know for sure until all her organs are bagged up, but so far I think she is at least missing her uterus."

"Interesting," was the only reply Bagster gave her. "Let us know when you have completed the autopsy and know for sure."

"Will do," Alicia assured him. She returned to her recorder as the two men left her to her work.

Bagster and Wynne made their way around the crime scene, gathering as much information as they could. They learned the woman's body had been discovered by a couple walking up the sidewalk to their car. They had been in the dance club. The man had felt dizzy and sat down on the pavement. When he felt a little better, he put his hands on the ground to help himself up. He had stated he felt something wet on his left hand. When he'd inspected his hand under a streetlight, he saw it was blood.

While the crime scene investigators gathered every speck of anything that could possibly be evidence, Bagster and Wynne crossed the street to start the daunting task of interviewing the club patrons and employees. It was their hope to learn whom the victim had been with that evening and if anyone had seen or heard anything. One of the police officers at the scene had discovered the woman's purse, which contained her identification. The detectives knew this information would be helpful in finding her family or someone who knew her.

The dance club was getting ready to close up. They would have to work fast. Wynne stayed at the door to ensure no one left without at least giving their name and a phone number. Bagster went in and asked the bartender to get the manager. Once the manager arrived at the bar, Bagster briefly explained the situation and asked him to make an announcement to his customers.

"Can I have everyone's attention, please?" the manager asked from the sound booth. "I know everyone is ready to go home, but the police need to gather some information from everyone concerning an incident that happened outside tonight. First, they need to know if anyone here knows a woman by the name of Megan Jones. If you do know this person, please see the detective at the bar immediately. The rest of you just sit tight until someone speaks with you. Thank you."

Bagster called over his radio for help with the interviews when he noticed there were still quite a few people inside the club. When the manager finished the announcement, two women approached Bagster and told him they had been with Ms. Jones earlier that night.

"Have a seat," Bagster said to the two young ladies. He took their names and information before asking any questions about their night. "So, how do you two know Ms. Jones?"

The first woman, who had long wavy red hair, answered, "We both work with her at the hospital. This was the first time in four months that all three of us were off at the same time. That's why we were here on a Monday night."

Bagster then asked, "What time did she leave?"

"Maybe a couple of hours ago," the second woman, a blonde, told him. "I wasn't really keeping track of the time, but that is probably close. Can I ask what is going on with Megan? Did she get into trouble or something?"

He had hoped to get more information from the women before telling them the bad news, but they wanted to know. "I'm sorry, ladies, but your friend was found murdered in an alley across the street." Just as he anticipated, the women became hysterical and started to cry. "I know this is difficult, but I need to continue. Did she leave here with anyone?"

"No," the redhead said between sobs. "She left here alone. We told her to call a cab, but she insisted she was fine to drive."

"Did she have a lot to drink?" was Bagster's next question.

The blonde responded, "She was kind of tipsy, but I think she was mostly tired. All of us were off tonight, but she had worked a double shift earlier in the day. Do you have any suspects?"

That was always the dreaded question. "Not yet, ma'am. That's why we are talking to everyone here."

The redhead leaned in close to him. "Do you think it's the same guy that killed that waitress?"

Bagster could smell the alcohol on her breath. He backed away from her and answered, "I can't say."

The officers and Bagster spent over an hour gathering information. The two friends had been of little help, and it seemed no one heard or saw a thing. Once again, the detectives were left with a body and no suspect. Bagster knew deep down the killer wasn't done. He also had a nagging feeling that there was something familiar about the way the body had been mutilated, but it wasn't coming to him. It left him wondering if he was dealing with a copycat killer. But whom was the killer copying?

On the way to the station, Bagster kept his thoughts to himself. He didn't think Wynne would be of any help figuring out the original murders. Wynne was still young and learning the ropes of being a detective. They did, however, discuss what they did know—but soon realized that wasn't much.

Wynne, who was driving, asked his partner, "How are we going to stop this guy? What kind of person would pull out someone's intestines, toss them over their shoulder, remove other parts, and toss them aside? Who would then take some of the organs?"

"I would say he has to be somewhat intelligent," Bagster replied, staring out the front windshield.

Wynne took his eyes off the road to side-eye his partner. "Are you serious?"

Bagster turned his attention to Wynne. "Do you think *you* could remove someone's organs without mutilating them? The ones he left behind looked to be in pretty good shape to me. He has to know what he's doing."

"I don't know. I just think he's crazy. Of course, sometimes being a genius and being crazy go hand in hand," Wynne pointed out.

"I suppose so. I don't know what it's going to take to find him. We really need just one piece of hard evidence to point us in the right direction."

Wynne's stomach growled. "Speaking of direction, why don't we go another direction and get some breakfast? It's already close to morning, and I'm starving."

"All right. I could use some coffee anyway," Bagster admitted.

The two men stopped at a small diner near the police station. Detective Bagster went over every detail he could remember about the crime scene while Detective Wynne shoveled food in his mouth. In his mind's eye, he could see the victim lying on her back with her knees pulled up and pushed outward. Her short shirt was pulled up over her stomach. Ms. Jones's intestines and other organs were placed, not tossed as Wynne had suggested, up by her right shoulder. Her abdomen was left wide open. The whole gruesome, staged scene bothered Bagster.

He thought long and hard about it as he sipped his coffee. It was clear to him that he had not seen anything like it before, but it still seemed familiar. Possibly something like it had occurred in another part of the country. Perhaps he had seen it on TV, maybe on the news. The waitress approached them and let Bagster know there was a call for him. He followed her to the phone and answered it. "Uh-huh," he said a few times, and finally, "We'll be right there!" He hung up the phone and returned to the table.

"What's up?" Wynne asked with a mouth full of food.

Bagster shot him a dirty look and said, "Didn't your mother ever teach you that talking with food in your mouth is rude?" Wynne shrugged his shoulders and swallowed as Bagster continued. "That was Carol from the station. The owner of the jewelry store heard about what happened already, and he came into his store early. It seems the store has a hidden camera outside. It caught something we might be interested in seeing."

Wynne's eyes grew large. He took out his wallet and pulled some money from it. After tossing the money on the table, he quickly took one last drink of coffee. "Let's go!" he said as he slid out of the booth seat.

"I'm right behind you," Bagster assured him.

At the jewelry store, the owner took the two detectives to his office at the back of the store. The short, round, bald man told the detectives,

"The club owner called me at home and filled me in on what happened in the alley." He turned on the TV and continued. "I came in to see if my camera had caught the incident. The camera is at the top corner of the front door but faces somewhat toward the end of the building at the alley entrance. It caught this." He played the video.

The three of them stood around the TV and watched as a man stepped out of the alley and appeared to start up a conversation with Ms. Jones. Then they saw him go back into the alley after a few moments. Next, the man stuck his head back out around the corner to say something else to her. She approached him. Finally, she was pulled into the alley by the stranger.

"You can't see the face of the man," the store owner said as he turned off the tape, "but I think it gives a little idea of the person who did it. He looks to be tall and is wearing a baseball cap."

"May we borrow the tape?" Bagster asked.

The man smiled. "Sure. I already made a copy for you." He handed a tape to Bagster.

Wynne said, "Thank you for your help. It is greatly appreciated."

As Bagster and Wynne left the jewelry store, they both knew the tape was probably the best clue they were going to get. They just hoped the image could be cleaned up and magnified enough to reveal some kind of detail of the person they were looking for. Anything would be better than nothing at this point.

SIXTEEN

Nightmares plagued Alex for the first few nights after the second murder. Even though he had pretended to be someone else to get through the deed, it didn't help his conscience any. He was amazed that he had been able to separate himself from the task by pretending to be someone else, at least in his mind. He remembered all the details of what happened, but as if it were a movie. The memories didn't seem to be his. Nevertheless, they were there. No matter how his mind remembered the events, he knew he was the one that had committed the horrific crime.

Alex kept close tabs on the news reports, even though Jack didn't like him to. For days he didn't leave his apartment. The couch once again became his permanent spot. The TV was on, and Alex watched it constantly, waiting to see if they had any suspects and to make sure he wasn't on the list. Just as he suspected, the two women were quickly linked to the same murderer. What he hadn't anticipated was a reporter comparing the murders to the Jack the Ripper murders from 1888, exactly one hundred years earlier.

Everyone had heard about those famous murders, but Alex didn't know any of the details. He knew the killer had never been caught. Then it occurred to him. Jack. Jack the Ripper. Surely, the namesake was no coincidence. Could it be that Jack was in some way connected to the original murders? Alex would ask now. He called out in a loud voice for Jack.

"Yes, Alex," Jack said. "I'm here. What is bothering you?"

The two hadn't spoken much since the murder, which Alex hadn't been too concerned about. "Are you listening to the news reports?"

"Yes. What about them? I wish you would not watch them."

Alex scratched his head, his fingers coming away greasy. "What does the Ripper case have to do with what I'm doing for you?"

"Whom are you referring to?" Jack asked.

"No one knows for sure," Alex stated as he turned the TV off. He had heard enough. The reports were starting to sound the same. "I don't know much about the case, but I know some women were murdered somewhere over in England in 1888. They never figured out for sure who did it."

As Alex went to the kitchen to get a drink, Jack asked, "Why would the reporter think the tasks you have completed for me are linked to those crimes? That was a hundred years ago. I do not understand."

"Exactly," Alex said, washing out a dirty glass from his kitchen sink. "It was exactly a hundred years ago. Isn't that odd?" He then remembered something Jack had said previously. "Didn't you say you wanted me to get away with these murders because it had been done before in history?"

"We have had many conversations. I do not recall."

"Are you Jack the Ripper?" Alex asked as he filled the glass with water from the faucet. He really didn't know how Jack would respond.

"My name is Jack, but I am not the person you know as the Ripper. Can we please not discuss this subject any further? The time is near for the next task. I need you to concentrate on that and not on what you hear on the news."

Alex asked one more question as he made his way back to the couch. "Can I at least read up on Jack the Ripper? I know very little about the case, and I would like to know why I'm being compared to him."

"No!" Jack snapped. "You need only to concern yourself with the next task. You are getting close to being done with them. I assume you still want to be rid of me, correct?"

"More than you know."

"Believe me, Alex, I know," Jack assured him. "Now, no more news for you. You have fallen back into a slump since the last task. I usually do not care about your style of living or your personal hygiene, but I noticed you performed the last task very well after you took care of your home and yourself. It seemed to clear your mind."

Looking around the living room at the mess that had accumulated, Alex laughed. "I hate to tell you this, Jack, but since you came into my life I don't seem to care about it much anymore."

"I understand I have upset your life, but I need you to clear your head. I am stepping up the number to two for this next event."

Alex jumped to his feet. "No way, Jack! I can't do two on the same night! One takes too much out of me. I can't sleep, I can't think, and I can't function properly after one. I'm tired of walking around like a zombie. I just can't do it!"

"Alex! Calm yourself! After this eventful night, you will only be left with one task. I will allow you a long break before that last task. Think about it, Alex. You will be that much closer to being rid of me." Jack paused while Alex stood in the middle of his living room with his hands on his hips. "You will have the rest of your life to do as you please with your beloved Jana."

"All right," Alex surrendered, throwing his arms up in the air. "What do you want me to do?"

"Get yourself back to normal, or at least close to normal," Jack started. "Clean yourself up and go visit your family and friends. Do not let them suspect anything. When you return, we will talk more."

"Fine," Alex responded as he started to look around for a place to start his cleaning. "Jack?" There was no answer. "Great. He left again."

Once Alex had finished cleaning his apartment, he gathered up the laundry and set it by the front door. He called his parents' house and asked his mom if he could come over to do his laundry. When she said yes, Alex told her he would be over after a shower. This made him happy. He would be able to complete two chores at once: laundry and spending time with his family.

The greatest challengeAlex had to tackle after his shower was shaving. It had been weeks. As he looked at himself in the bathroom mirror, Alex realized he had grown quite a beard. He could barely recognize himself. The beard would have to be trimmed down before he could even think about shaving it. The process would take longer than he had planned, but it had to be done.

For the first time in a while, he felt like a normal person. He was actually looking forward to getting out of his apartment for the day. He loaded his laundry into his car after he made sure any clothes that could have blood on them were in a sack by themselves. As he drove to his parents' house, Alex had his window down to get some fresh air. The air had finally started to cool. The leaves on the trees had started to change colors. Alex breathed in the fall air as it occurred to him that September had almost passed him by, and he hadn't even noticed until now.

He arrived at his parents' house but wasn't sure if this was the place he wanted to be for his first outing. No one had called or stopped by to check on him. Well, except Jessica. She'd skipped school to see him. It had not been his intention to leave her to deal with the divorce alone. Guilt was starting to set in as he sat in the car, looking at his sister's upstairs bedroom window. He knew he had royally messed up with her this time.

After a deep breath, Alex stepped out of his car and gathered his laundry from the trunk. He walked up the front steps and rang the doorbell. Suddenly, he felt butterflies in his stomach. He was nervous about facing his parents and his sister. It had been a while since he had seen them, and he knew the last time he had seen his mom and dad it didn't go too well. When the door opened, his mom's warm smile let him know all was well between them.

"Come in, honey," his mom said cheerfully. "You don't have to ring the bell. This is still your home, too."

Relief washed over Alex as he stepped inside his old family home. "It's been some time since I've been here. It didn't feel right to just walk in," he explained as he stood in the foyer.

She took the trash bag of clothes from him and started for the kitchen. "Alex, it doesn't matter how long you have been away. Don't ring the bell ever again. Do you understand me?"

Alex was too distracted to answer right away. The laundry. The blood. What would he say? She was walking away with the proof of his crimes.

Alex followed his mom through the kitchen to the laundry room, his heartbeat quickening. "Mom, let me do my laundry. I didn't bring it over here for you to do it."

"Nonsense," she said as she put the bag down.

Alex just stared at her—at *it*. The bag that would ruin everything. "Mom, please. I'm an adult. I can do my own laundry."

Mrs. Dorson narrowed her eyes. "What's going on with you?"

"Nothing."

Unconvinced, she eyed him up and down. "Go see your sister." Mrs. Dorson readied the washer and began to open one of the bags. "She is in the living room."

"Where's Dad?" Alex asked. It was the only thing he could think of to distract her.

"He's not here," she replied bluntly as she measured the detergent.

Alex wanted to say more but knew better. Mentioning his dad might have made things worse, judging by her snappy tone. There was no arguing with her now. Alex just hoped that the mention of his dad had agitated her enough to distract from his bloody clothes.

Without another word, he left to go find Jessica. She was in the living room lying on the couch reading a book. Alex sat down beside her as she moved her legs to make room for him. He couldn't tell if she was upset about his long absence.

"How are you, sis?" he finally got the nerve up to ask.

Jessica looked up from her book. "Truthfully, I've been better. Things have been insane around here. Of course, you would already know that if you came around more often."

The sarcasm in her voice was biting. "I'm sorry, sis. There's no excuse for me staying away. It's not fair for you to be the only one dealing with this." He turned his body toward her and whispered, "Where's Dad?"

She whispered back, "He left last week. I don't know why he left. Mom won't talk about it." The conversation ended when Mrs. Dorson joined them.

She was chipper again. Alex hated to change that, but he needed to know what was going on with his family now. "Mom, where is Dad? I want an answer."

Mrs. Dorson sighed as she sat in a chair beside the couch. "He left, Alex. He moved out. I'm not sure how to tell you this, but we're getting a divorce."

"I already know that, Mom," Alex informed her. "Where is Dad staying?"

Mrs. Dorson sighed again. "I didn't want either of you to know this, but you would have found out eventually anyway. He is staying with his girlfriend."

Silence filled the room for a moment. Girlfriend? Before Alex could interrogate this further, Mrs. Dorson furrowed her brow and began an interrogation of her own. "Alex, the second bag of clothes you had, there were little spots of what looked like blood on your pants, and the gloves were covered in something too. What on earth happened? Did you hurt yourself, or did someone else get hurt? The gloves were stiff when I took them out of the bag."

Strangely, now that his mom had asked him the dreaded question, he was calm. He quickly thought up an explanation. He'd stretch the truth, mention the deer. "I was driving the other day outside of the city when I came across a dead deer in the road. I couldn't pass it, so I stopped, got out, and had to move it. It hadn't been dead for long so things got messy." To his surprise, she seemed to accept that answer.

SEVENTEEN

During his time with his mom and sister, Alex was overwhelmed with the problems his parents had been dealing with over a period of about two years. None of the things Mrs. Dorson told her children were expected. She had kept so much from them to protect them. Alex and Jessica both were upset about the family secrets. At the same time, they both were shocked to find out this wasn't the first time their father had been unfaithful to their mother.

When the long visit finally came to an end, Alex hugged his mom and did his best to assure her everything would work out for the best, somehow. He left his childhood home knowing that things would never be the same. As he drove away, his mind raced through memories of his family from the past two years. Not a single one betrayed anything about his father's alternate life. His parents had been unhappy together for a long time, but Alex had never known the real reason why. Mrs. Dorson blamed her husband for everything. Alex felt he needed his father's side of the story to decide who was actually at fault.

After Alex arrived back home, he put away his clean clothes and called his dad. Alex asked to meet with him, and he agreed. While Alex didn't say much, he figured his dad probably already knew what he wanted. Their plan to meet for dinner was made easily.

The two men met at a locally owned burger joint. After they gave the waitress their orders, they started off with small talk. When the conversation ceased, Alex used the silence as a chance to change the topic of conversation.

"I had a long visit with Mom and Jessica today," Alex stated as he sat at the table, playing with his empty straw wrapper.

It took a few moments for Mr. Dorson to respond. "Oh? Was it a nice visit?"

Alex shot straight to the point. "Mom got a lot of things off her chest. Like two years' worth of things. I think Jessica and I learned quite a bit about you and Mom today."

Mr. Dorson looked down at the cup of coffee in his hands. "So, I suppose you know I'm staying with a friend."

"A friend?"

"All right, my girlfriend," Mr. Dorson admitted. "I guess you're old enough to handle the truth."

Sitting back in his seat, Alex asked his dad one simple question. "What is the truth, Dad?" His tone was harsh, but he felt it was necessary to make his point.

A long sigh left Mr. Dorson before he finally looked up from his coffee cup. "I know I haven't been the best husband these last few years to your mother. I'm not proud of what I've done to her. Our relationship changed long before I started having affairs. I can't pinpoint exactly when things changed, but they did change."

Alex sat quietly and listened to his dad talk about what led him to his infidelities. His dad talked about the coldness of his mom and the tension that they had between them. He tried to explain to Alex that he was happy with his new girlfriend, happy enough to finally end his marriage to be with her. There were many apologies before he let his son respond.

There was a long period of silence as Alex tried to process the new information. "Well," he eventually started as he sat up straight, "we knew eventually you and Mom would split up. I don't know how I actually expected it to happen, but I knew it would happen." Alex stopped talking when the waitress arrived with their orders. Once she was gone, he continued. "I don't know what's going to happen now. I guess I'm happy for you, but now she's all alone."

"I think in time she will discover her own happiness. She is free to find someone else she can connect with and be happy with, just like I did," Mr. Dorson tried to assure his son. "So, what has been going on in your life, Alex?"

Alex didn't want to discuss himself as a topic. On one hand, there was nothing to tell, but on the other, there was a whole bunch to tell. There was still no job, no school, and no Jana. Alex tried to come up with things to tell his dad without spilling his dark secrets. Of course, he received a long-drawn-out lecture about not working and not going to school, but after dinner, his dad gave him some money to help him get by for a while. Alex figured he did it because he felt bad for the current family situation everyone was in because of him.

As Alex drove away from the burger joint, he decided he needed to talk to someone other than his parents for a while. A quick detour led him straight to Jana's apartment. Though, once outside, Alex sat in his car. For some reason, he was nervous about going to her door. He needed to talk to someone, and he knew she would be there for him, but he also knew he would have to leave her again. After reconsidering, he decided to just leave instead of running the risk of causing her more pain. But before he could pull out of his parking spot, Jana came out of her downstairs apartment.

She motioned for him to come inside with her. Reluctantly, Alex turned his car engine off and went to meet her. "I've been wondering if you were ever going to come back," she said when he reached her.

He just smiled and hugged her tightly. "I said I would be back."

Jana led him inside her apartment. They sat on the couch and stared at each other for what seemed like an eternity. "Where have you been lately?" Jana finally asked.

"At home hiding out," Alex answered. "I probably should have stayed there, too."

Jana looked at him strangely. "What makes you say that?'

He laughed insanely at her question. "I went to visit my family today. As it turns out, my parents are getting divorced, and my dad is living with his new girlfriend."

"I guess it wasn't a good visit then, huh?" Jana said sarcastically, but not meaning any harm.

"Not exactly," Alex stated. "I called my dad after the visit. We just had dinner together. I don't know what to think about the whole thing. I came by to have someone to talk to, but I really didn't want to bother you with this."

She moved closer to him on the couch. "Alex, I'm always here for you. I hope someday you can be there for me again, too."

"I'm getting there," he said as he wrapped his arms around her and pulled her even closer to him. "Are you still willing to wait for me?"

"Always," Jana replied. "I just hope it doesn't take forever."

The couple spent several hours talking about Alex's parents. Jana listened and offered some input, but there was nothing either of them could do about the situation. Jessica was more of a concern to Alex than either of his parents was. He needed to be there for her, but he had other things to take care of first. No one understood what he was going through, but they were finally leaving him alone. Even Jana wasn't pressing him for answers. To his relief, she did offer to help keep an eye on Jessica.

The last subject the two of them discussed late in the night was their future together. Alex expressed his concerns about them ending up like his parents.

"I don't think that will happen to us, Alex," Jana said. "When we are together, we are perfect."

"I just don't want to end up being bad for you."

"You won't. You're not a bad person."

Inside, Alex wanted to scream as loud as he could. If she knew the things he had done, and the things he was going to do, she wouldn't say that. It occurred to him that he was doing what his father had been doing. He was deceiving everyone. He had become a cold-blooded killer. He was leading a double life. What he was doing was much worse, and he was still portraying himself as two different people. The time was close for the dark side of him to once again go on the prowl for not just one victim, but two.

The upcoming events started to weigh heavily on his mind. He found himself mentally trying to predict how Jack might want the night to go. Silence had fallen between him and Jana. This allowed him to consider his plans. There would have to be a precise plan in order for him to accomplish two tasks in one night and not get caught. He wondered what Jack would want him to do to the bodies this time. Time would be so important. He would have to work fast. Could he do that? Of course he could.

The type of victims was the next thing to consider. The first two women hadn't been very tall. They didn't present much of a problem as far as controlling them, but the second one, who was very petite, didn't offer much space to work inside her abdomen. Alex wondered if the dissection process would go smoother with a taller woman that had a longer abdominal cavity. It was a theory he planned to discuss with Jack. He also wanted to see if Jack would be okay with him sneaking up behind the victims and cutting their throats first thing. If he didn't have to grab them, he wouldn't have to worry about a struggle.

Once Alex had compiled a list of things to discuss with Jack, he realized Jana had fallen asleep while leaning on him. He smiled to himself at how peaceful she looked. Carefully, he slid himself out from under her and scooped her up in his arms. He carried her to the bedroom and placed her gently on her bed.

"Stay with me," she quietly requested as she awoke briefly.

"Okay. I will," Alex whispered to her. He removed his shoes and climbed into the bed next to her. She snuggled up to him, and they both drifted off to sleep.

EIGHTEEN

"Alex, wake up."

Alex opened his eyes and saw Jana sitting next to him with a coffee cup in her hand. Smiling up at her, he said, "Good morning. What time is it?"

"It's about seven o'clock," Jana answered as she watched him stretch out his long body in her bed. "I didn't want to wake you, but I have to go to work. I brought you some coffee."

"Thank you," he replied, sitting up in bed. He took the cup from her and had a drink. "I'm glad you woke me up. I have some things to do today."

"Like what?"

The question temporarily stunned him. He had no job and wasn't going to school. What answer could he possibly give her? "Nothing important," he finally replied as he rubbed the back of his neck with his free hand.

Jana took a sip of her coffee and casually asked, "Will I see you later?" She already knew the answer.

Alex sighed heavily. "No." Quickly, he finished his coffee. As he stood up, he looked down at her and said, "I'll get out of here so you can go to work. I'll get in touch with you sometime in the next few days."

Without taking her eyes off his, Jana stood up in front of him. "Are you sure it won't be sometime in the next few weeks?"

It was definitely time to go. Another guilt trip was not on his agenda for the day. "A few days, I promise." Alex reached down and retrieved his shoes from the floor. He left her bedroom and headed for the front door.

Jana followed close behind him, watching as he put his shoes on by the door. When he was finished, Alex motioned for her to come to him.

Tightly, he wrapped his arms around her, then kissed her on the top of her head before letting go. Jana looked up at him and smiled.

"A few days, I promise," Alex repeated with a smile. Then he opened the door and left.

During his drive home, Alex barely gave a second thought to Jana. All he could think about was the two tasks that faced him that night. The first two tasks had seemed to eat away at his consciousness, and his stomach, but these two seemed to try his patience. It was as though he couldn't wait until it was nightfall. Originally, Alex worried about Jack raising the bar to two in one night. At the moment, he viewed it as a challenge. One he was determined to conquer.

Once home, Alex made some coffee, and then he took his usual spot on the couch. He called out to Jack a few times. When Jack responded, Alex explained he felt it was time to make a game plan for the night's events. Jack readily agreed. He quickly inquired about Alex's eagerness.

A laugh came from deep within Alex. "I thought you knew all my thoughts. How is it you don't know that I've thought long and hard about tonight?"

"I was trying to be gracious by leaving you completely alone while you visited your family and friends," Jack explained. "By the way, how were your visits?"

"Well, let's see," Alex started sarcastically, "my parents are getting a divorce, and my dad is living with his girlfriend. That is how my family is doing right now. Then there's Jana. I'm beginning to wonder if she is close to hating me because I'm never around anymore. The kicker of that is I'm doing what you want me to do so I can be there for her again, without you. Now that you have made me realize just how bad my life is falling apart, can we get down to business?"

After a brief period of silence, Jack said, "I am truly sorry about how things are going for you, Alex. I know I am to blame for the problems with Jana, but I think your parents' situation would have happened without my presence."

"I realize that, Jack," Alex asked calmly. "Can we move on to the next subject, please?"

"Of course," Jack replied. "Tell me, Alex, what have you been thinking about as far as your next tasks?"

An almost evil grin crept across Alex's face. "You know what, Jack? I think I'm actually looking forward to tonight. I've tried to plan both incidents out in my head."

"Good. I am glad you have gotten past the awkwardness of these tasks. Please, tell me what you have in mind."

Alex got to his feet and started to pace around his living room. "I think, if it's okay, I'm not going to mess with them as much this time. Grabbing them and getting them out of sight is too much work. I figure cutting their throats first when I come up behind them will make things faster." Alex demonstrated his plan as he continued. "I'll sneak up quietly. Then quickly I'll wrap my hand around the forehead area and slice through the neck. If I do it that way they won't be able to scream or fight. It will leave more time for whatever else you need me to do. What do you think?"

"I think your plan is brilliant, Alex. Of course, you will have to be more careful. Before, you completed everything under the cover of darkness. You must not be seen," Jack warned him.

"I'll be careful," Alex assured Jack as he stood with his hands on his hips. "I assume you want me to remove certain organs and such."

"Yes."

"Do I need to go practice on another dead animal this time?" he asked as he went to the kitchen. He opened the refrigerator door and peered inside. The gurgling in his stomach reminded him that he hadn't eaten since the day before when he met with his dad.

"I do not think that will be necessary this time. You just need to follow my directions when the time comes."

The refrigerator was mostly empty. Alex hadn't grocery shopped in a while. He was able to find some lunch meat that was still good and some ketchup to put on it. "I don't think following your directions will be any problem this time," he said as he dug through a bread bag for two pieces without mold. When he found two suitable pieces, Alex pulled a plate out of his cabinet and began to make his sandwich. "So when and where is this going to take place? How long of a wait do I have?"

"It is still morning, Alex," Jack reminded him as he smeared ketchup over both pieces of bread with his finger. "We will leave after nightfall. Tonight will be your night. I will instruct you, but you must decide where to go and whom to pick. You seem very excited about performing these two tasks, so I will give you some degree of control."

"I am excited," Alex replied. He stuck his ketchup-covered finger in his mouth. When he pulled it out clean, he asked, "Do you know why I'm excited?"

"I do have to say I am curious."

Taking his completed sandwich to the couch, Alex explained, "I discovered yesterday that nothing in life is guaranteed and nothing is ever perfect. My plan was to start a great career, marry Jana, have a couple of kids, and live happily ever after. In less than twenty-four hours, I realized there is no such thing. My parents' marriage is over. All these years they spent together are gone. They can't get them back. My sister's life is being turned upside down. And I can't fix it. I'm angry at them for what they have done to each other and for what they are doing to her." Alex paused to take a bite of his sandwich. After he swallowed, he started talking again. "After I completed the first two tasks, I shut everything out and worried about no one. At least for a while, I want to get back to that again. I want something to take my frustrations out on, and then I don't want to feel anything."

There was a long period of silence as Alex ate his sandwich. Jack finally broke through it by asking, "Do you feel two women's lives are worth you getting what you want?"

Alex laughed hysterically. "What, are you trying to be my conscience now? You got me into this, remember?"

"I remember. Do you remember why you agreed to do all of this in the first place?"

Laying his head back on the couch cushion, Alex knew exactly what Jack was referring to. "Jana. She is the reason I went along with you. I don't think you were listening to me. Look at what happened with my family. That could happen to Jana and me. Is it even worth taking the risk? I don't want to think about it right now. I need to do this tonight to make myself curl up into my own little shell. You told me I have to do this in order for you to leave, even though you are all I have anymore. If I have to do it anyway, then I might as well benefit from it."

"Well, my boy," Jack started as Alex forced himself to take his plate to the kitchen sink, "I am not here to give advice on your life problems.

I am here to make sure you do what I want you to do by any means necessary. After tonight, you will have enough time to contemplate what you plan to do with the rest of your life. You will have thirty-nine days to think before you perform the last tasks for me. I will be gone after that night. You will be free to do as you wish."

"So that's it?" he asked as he stood in front of the kitchen sink with his hands on the counter. "When this is over, my life will be back in my control? You have helped mess it up, to a certain degree, and then you are going to just hand it back to me."

"Yes. That is how it is going to be in the end. Now, get some rest today. You will not perform well if you are tired." With that being said, Jack vanished from Alex's mind, leaving him alone for the rest of the long day with nothing but his thoughts.

Thinking was all he could do. Alex hoped he wouldn't be able to think much after performing two tasks on the same night. He desperately wanted to shove all of his problems into a corner and leave them there forever. The rest of his life had been planned out at one point. Finishing school was the only thing standing in his way back then. Once school was over, he would be ready to start the next chapter of his life with Jana. It never occurred to him that his life would take a drastic turn for the worse after one little incident. That one incident led to so many chain reactions, some related to Jack, some not.

Alex lounged around his apartment until he couldn't take the boredom any longer. He retreated to his bed to take a short nap. Jack's advice to rest up seemed like a good way to waste some time. As Alex tried to force himself to sleep, he tried not to dwell on his parents and how their fate could possibly be his one day. He knew it would be if he didn't finish the tasks as soon as possible. Eventually, Alex gave up on sleep. He would have to suffer the long wait for nightfall conscious and all alone.

NINETEEN

There were still traces of indigo in the sky when Alex left his apartment and drove downtown. Sitting and waiting alone in his apartment was more than he could stand. Of course, he would need total darkness before starting his first task, but Jack had left the location up to him. He would need extra time to pick the right place.

When he reached the downtown area, Alex realized he definitely needed to go elsewhere. As he drove along the one-way streets, he saw that the police had taken over. The last two tasks had been completed at opposite ends of the city, but it was obvious the police department wasn't taking any chances. They had most of the streets under patrol. With this newfound information, Alex left downtown and drove to the local mall. He needed to think of another suitable area to find his targets. The mall would be crawling with potential subjects, but it would be too public to carry out such deeds.

After parking by one of the mall's main entrances, Alex walked across the parking lot toward the doors. He zipped up his jacket and put his hands in the jacket pockets. The wind had a chill to it that was only growing colder as the dark of the night devoured the last remnants of daylight. He could feel his gloves and folded baseball cap in his pockets. As he got closer to the doors, Alex stopped and surveyed the building, then his surroundings. It occurred to him that the outside of the mall had plenty of dark private areas in which he could hide and carry out his tasks. After a quick glance at his watch, he headed in to start watching the mall shoppers.

The first place Alex hit once inside was the food court. There he acquired a cup of coffee from one of the small fast food stations. He took a seat at a vacant table and began to take in the people around him. A woman by herself would be the perfect subject. Surely he would find one on a Tuesday night. As he sat and waited for that one woman to appear, Alex found himself drawn to a young woman working behind the counter at the pizza parlor across from his table. He wasn't sure what it was about her, but he couldn't keep his attention on the mall patrons.

Though she was pretty, it wasn't attraction that captured his attention. He couldn't quite put his finger on it. She seemed perfect—just the right height for the initial attack. Someone short would make the attack awkward since he was so tall, and most women were short compared to him. This woman was close enough to his height that he would be able to grab her head and slice through her pretty neck without bending over. Her slender frame would also be easier to carry off to a secluded place where Jack would give his final instructions.

"What are you doing here, Alex?" Jack inquired as he made his presence known.

Alex whispered, "I'm observing the people, primarily the women."

"It's still early. Why did you leave your apartment without me?"

"I wanted to get an early start," he replied, taking a drink from his Styrofoam coffee cup. "I didn't know I could do anything without you knowing."

Jack's tone made his dissatisfaction with Alex clear. "There are times that I am not with you. That does not mean I am out of reach," Jack somewhat explained. "This is not what I expected of you this evening, Alex. Why are you here and not in the downtown area? I prefer that location."

Alex continued to watch the woman. "Downtown was crawling with cops. I figured you would know that since you seem to know everything. Besides, I've already picked out someone for one of my tasks."

"I do not know everything," Jack said sharply. "Who is this creature you have chosen? Point her out to me so I may evaluate her."

Evaluate her. Alex couldn't figure out what Jack meant by that statement. It didn't matter what he meant by it. The woman he had been watching would be his. Alex sighed and pointed in the woman's direction. It was a quick motion. He didn't want to be noticed. "She is over there behind that food counter."

"Ah, I see her. She will do just fine. I still wish we were closer to the downtown area. I do not like straying so far."

"It will be fine, Jack," Alex assured him. "I've already spotted a couple of dark areas outside where I won't be spotted. Now, help me find a second target. I have to complete two tasks tonight, right?"

"Correct."

"Then we need to pick another one. I'll keep a close eye on this one, but I want her to be the second one."

For over an hour, Alex watched every woman that came close to the food court. Jack offered his opinion on each and every one. The two couldn't seem to agree on any of them. When the crowd of people started to dwindle, Alex glanced at a clock hanging inside one of the food shops. It was near closing time for the mall. They needed to pick someone quickly. Alex would have to work fast on the first one in order to get to the one he wanted before she left the mall.

"Which one, Jack?" Alex asked as he stood and started to pace around the food court.

Jack replied, "Go to the nearest exit. We will pick one on the way out. All you have to do is look for a woman by herself. Follow her outside, and she is yours."

Doing as he was told, Alex hurried to the doors where he had entered the mall. He didn't stand directly by the doors. He chose a spot in front of a nearby store to try to be somewhat inconspicuous. It was only a few minutes before Jack yelled, "Right there! The woman in the high heels!"

Of course, Alex was the only one to hear Jack's outburst, but it startled him just the same. "High heels? Won't that make it more difficult for me?"

"No," Jack answered. "She will not be able to run or fight as well. Go after her."

As he started to follow the woman, Alex knew the high heels would make no difference in the woman's ability to fight. If everything went according to his plan, the woman would be dead before she even knew she needed to protect herself. A quick kill was what this hunter was looking for in this victim. Alex's only worry was what he would find on the other side of the glass doors to the parking lot. He desperately needed the parking lot to be empty. If it wasn't, everything could be ruined.

The woman exited the mall through the glass doors with Alex directly behind her. He slipped on his hat and gloves as he walked. It seemed strange that the woman hadn't even noticed his presence, but then it occurred to him she might be ignoring him. Whichever the case may have been, Alex wasn't going to waste time trying to figure it out. With a quick glance around the parking lot, he noticed they were indeed alone.

Alex continued to stay a distance behind the woman until he noticed she had reached her car and was fumbling with her keys to get the door unlocked. Once he was positive they were still alone, Alex charged after her. Just as she stuck her key in the lock, Alex wrapped his left hand around her forehead and pulled her head back against his shoulder. Her neck was then fully exposed, and Alex ran the blade of his knife through it. As soon as he heard the gurgling noises he let her fall to the pavement beside her car.

Alex bent down and scooped the woman up in his arms. Once he was back on his feet, he was relieved to see he was still alone in the parking lot. That wouldn't last long with closing time quickly approaching, so he bounded with the woman in his arms toward a dark corner of the building obscured by bushes. It was one of the spots he had noticed earlier. The dead weight of the woman slowed him down a bit, but eventually, he reached his hiding place.

After dropping the woman to the ground, Alex noticed she had left blood all down the left side of his jacket and pants. He could see the blood shimmer when a faint glow of light hit his arm. The wetness of the blood on his pants had started to soak in, cooling on his upper thigh. It was the first time he had gotten that much on him. Now wasn't the time to think about it. He had a job to do, and he needed to work quickly. The woman of his choice would be leaving work soon. He couldn't let her get away.

Alex went to the woman's feet and got down on his knees just like Jack always had him do. Then, as he had previously been instructed to, he stuck his hands under the woman's knees and lifted them up. After putting his hands on his own legs, Alex let out a breath and said, "Okay, Jack. Tell me what you want me to do this time."

There was no response.

"Jack? Are you there? You better be there!"

"Shh," Jack finally replied. "Be very still for a moment."

"What's going on, Jack?" Alex whispered as he felt his heartbeat quicken. Jack didn't answer. "Come on, Jack. This isn't funny."

"Hush, Alex," Jack demanded.

Alex sat still and stayed quiet while he waited for Jack to elaborate. His stomach was beginning to turn into one big knot. The longer the silence went on, the more convinced Alex became that he was about to be caught. He was so close to completing the tasks. This couldn't happen to him now.

"Alex," Jack finally whispered. "There are too many people leaving this place right now. It is not a good idea to continue this."

"No one knows I'm here," Alex said. He didn't want to be caught, but he didn't want to leave without having one more task out of the way. "Tell me what to do so I can finish this. I'll work quickly."

"No, Alex. You must sneak away without being seen. The woman you want will be leaving soon. Make your way to the doors so you will be waiting for her departure."

"But, Jack—"

"Go, now!"

Alex got to his feet. He was confused, but he knew he had better listen. If Jack said there were too many people, then he had better not push his luck. While he watched the parking lot closely, Alex made his way along the outside wall of the mall, leaving his victim's body behind on the cold asphalt. Once he reached the same doors he had exited from earlier, he tried to blend in with the shadows since he was covered in blood. Eventually, the number of people coming out of the doors diminished. It wasn't long before the woman Alex had wanted the whole night came out of the doors. She wasn't alone though.

"Are you sure you don't want me to walk you to your car?" the older man asked her. He appeared to be her manager.

The woman smiled and said, "I'll be fine. I do this every night."

"I'll watch you from inside the doors until you reach your car," he told her.

"Okay, if that will make you feel better," she said, still smiling. "I'll see you tomorrow."

The man stepped back inside the doors. Alex didn't know what to do. He hadn't anticipated someone watching out for her. Alex watched as she reached her car and got in the driver's side door. The manager left the doors once she was inside her car. Disappointment filled Alex, but soon that was replaced by hope. The woman had forgotten something and was getting back out of her car. As she approached the doors, Alex knew she was his.

This was the one. This was who he had been waiting for all night. She couldn't get away. Alex couldn't believe how his luck had changed. If she would have just driven off, all of his plans would have been ruined. He had no clue what he would have done for a replacement. The mall was close to empty. Only a few employees remained inside the building. Jack may have demanded that he start over at a new location. That wasn't going to be the case though. She was coming back toward the doors, back toward him.

"She is returning, Alex," Jack stated.

Alex smiled and whispered, "I know."

"Be ready," Jack ordered. "There is not much time. If you want her, you have to move with speed."

"Shh," Alex ordered Jack. "She is getting closer."

TWENTY

The woman strolled quickly toward the mall doors as she twiddled her keys around her index finger. Alex could feel his heartbeat race inside his chest. Excitement grew from deep within him. She was the one he wanted, and now he would have her all to himself. He wouldn't be able to sneak up on her as he had planned. The attack would have to be sudden, but he would have to carry her off instead of killing her first.

There was no time for Alex to formulate an exact plan. She was getting close. When he felt the moment was right, he leapt from the shadows and grabbed her. With one hand around her mouth, Alex wrapped his other arm around her tiny waist. He lifted her up and ran to a dark area away from the doors, opposite where he left his last victim. Alex was unaware of the fact that the woman had dropped her keys when he grabbed her.

Once he had her in the darkness, she started to fight him. He struggled to hold her as he reached for the knife that was inside his jacket sleeve. While the woman's persistent fighting made things difficult for Alex, her desire to escape made him want to keep her here all the more. At last, Alex was able to free the knife from his sleeve, but he was still having problems controlling the woman. The harder he tried to force her into a position to slice through her neck and end the struggle, the harder she seemed to fight, especially after seeing the knife he had produced. After several missed attempts, which resulted in a few slashes to her face, Alex finally hit his mark. The fighting ceased as the woman's body went limp in his arms. He let her gently slide down his body and come to rest on the ground.

"Very good, Alex," Jack congratulated him. "For a moment I thought she might get away. I guess you really wanted this one."

Alex moved the woman's body into a position where he could do his work on her. "Yes. I definitely wanted this one. I wasn't going to let her get away." He stood over her for a moment and looked at the damage that had been done to her face. "It's a shame that had to happen though. She was very pretty."

"Do not concern yourself with that now," Jack stated. "Time is growing short. You must hurry."

Quickly, Alex took his position between the woman's legs and prepared her for the dissection. In the dim light, Alex was captivated by the woman's smooth abdominal skin. He felt compelled to touch it. Slowly he ran his gloved hand over her stomach. It reminded him of Jana's skin. It was flawless. His mind started to drift to the last time he had touched her bare skin.

"Alex!" Jack shouted. Alex snapped his attention back to the moment. "You must work quickly before the other woman is found."

"Okay, I'm ready." Alex stuck the knife into the woman's skin just below her breast bone. Slowly, he dragged the knife down to her pelvic bone. With a few more incisions, her abdomen was laid wide open. He was now ready to receive directions from Jack.

Jack quickly and precisely gave Alex directions on what to do. Alex made the perfect cuts to remove the woman's large intestines. This was always the worst part for him. They were so slippery he could barely keep them together in his hands. His gloves didn't seem to help either. It amazed him that the heat from organs always penetrated through the gloves to his hands. He had never considered how warm 98.6 degrees could feel. It was something he never noticed with the last victim he dissected.

Next, Jack directed Alex to remove part of the woman's colon. Jack also wanted the womb removed, but he wanted the cervix and vagina left unharmed. Alex had done this with the second victim, so this didn't strike him as unusual. The final organs Jack wanted removed were the kidneys. Carefully, Alex excised the left one exactly where Jack instructed him to.

Just as Alex started to repeat the same procedure on the right kidney, Jack yelled, "No, Alex! Someone is coming."

Alex jumped to his feet. "Okay! I guess that's it."

"Wait!" Jack yelled before Alex ran off. "Cut off her right earlobe."

"What? Why?"

"Just do it!"

Alex shrugged and bent down next to the woman. He grabbed her earlobe with one hand and cut it off with the knife in his other. It didn't make sense to him why Jack would insist on the earlobe, but then again, nothing made sense about Jack. As Alex fled toward another shadowy area, he felt a sudden rush of adrenaline pulse through his veins. His breathing was heavy by the time he reached his new hiding spot. Only as he started to calm himself from the run did he realize he had just taken the lives of two women. But instead of being shocked or disgusted by himself, he felt empowered.

"Wait a few moments here, Alex," Jack said to him. "I will let you know when to go to your vehicle. You did very well."

Alex was concerned though. "What about the first one? I didn't get to do anything to her. Does that mean I still need another one tonight?" Secretly, he hoped the answer would be yes. He didn't feel satisfied with the first woman. He didn't think Jack would be satisfied either.

"No, Alex, she is fine. You are done with these two. Now, casually make your way to your vehicle and leave."

During the drive home, Alex felt full of energy. By this time he should have felt numb or even a little guilty, but he didn't. He'd turned the radio up, and he sang along and danced around in his seat. When he reached home, Alex took the plastic bag containing his blood-soaked gloves and jacket and went straight to the kitchen to wash them. Before, he had always let them sit until he forced himself to go to the laundromat, but this time there was far too much blood.

As Alex laid his keys on the counter and started the water in the sink, he whistled. Jack inquired about Alex's good mood. "You seem to be in good spirits. Why the change?"

He shrugged as he pulled the gloves from the plastic bag and placed them under the running water. "I'm not sure, Jack. I just feel like I accomplished something tonight. Lately, I've been feeling rather worthless. I feel like I have failed at everything. I have let everyone down. Tonight, you presented me with two tasks to complete, and although one was left still intact, I completed what you wanted me to do."

"I see. You feel good that you managed to follow through with something. Good. But why are you cleaning up your clothes now?"

"I'm doing it now so they will be ready for the last task," Alex said as he took his jacket from the bag and placed it in the sink. The gloves were put in his dish drainer to dry.

"Well, that is fine, but do not forget about your pants and shoes. They require a good cleaning as well," Jack pointed out.

Looking down at his pants and shoes, Alex realized Jack was right. He pulled off his boots and then removed his pants. The blood had soaked through his pants and dried on the skin of his legs. Everything, including himself, smelled sickeningly metallic. It occurred to him that he could kill two birds with one stone by taking a shower to clean himself, and by putting his clothes in there with him. "Jack, I will be back shortly," Alex said as he placed everything in the plastic bag. "I'm going to go clean up, and then I want to know about the last task you have for me."

After a long shower, Alex wrung out his wet pants and jacket. He hung them over a towel rack and left his boots in the tub. He dressed in a pair of shorts and a shirt and then returned to the kitchen. It was getting late, but Alex had been gone since dusk. The pains coming from his stomach told him he was hungry. Unfortunately, the cabinets and refrigerator were empty. The only food available was an almost empty bag of stale potato chips.

Alex took the bag to the couch anyway. Sitting in his usual spot, he called for Jack as he shoved a handful of chips into his mouth.

"I am here, Alex," Jack replied.

Alex swallowed the chips. "Tell me about the last task you have for me."

"I would rather discuss it at a later date," Jack said. "As I said before, you have over a month to get your situation under control. There is no need to talk about the last task tonight. You need to rest for now. Tomorrow, you need to work on your own tasks."

"What tasks?" Alex asked, nearly spitting potato chips everywhere. "What do I need to do for myself? Come on, Jack. I'm ready to do this last thing for you. I'm revved up to do it. Once you're gone, I can work on myself."

"You said yourself that everything in your life is falling apart," Jack reminded him. "When I am gone, it may be too late to fix things with your family and friends. You have performed the tasks that I have requested of you thus far. Tonight you did very well. My tasks did not seem to bother you as the previous ones did. That pleases me. The last one will be a true work of art. It will take everything you have deep inside you to complete it and make it perfect. You need to get your life sorted for when we part company. This is the best way for you to deal with what I will be asking of you."

"So there's no way to get this over with sooner?" Alex asked. The gaps in time between the tasks didn't make much sense to him. Neither did the fact that Jack wanted him to get his life back on track before completing the last task. Jack was the reason for the mess in his life still. The situation with his parents was the only thing Jack couldn't be blamed for, but Alex not being there for Jessica was something Jack *could* be blamed for. "I've grown used to you, Jack, but I feel it would be better to do this now and be rid of you sooner. I don't care what it is you want me to do. Just let me do it."

"No," Jack responded sharply. "Now is not the time. I think you are starting to develop a liking for this. I do not intend for that to happen. You have one month to regain what you have lost. You will not hear from me during that time. I will return after one month to help you prepare for the final task. Do not call for me because I will not respond. Do not believe I am gone forever, for I will return. Until then, Alex, I must go. Farewell."

Alex sat in his spot on the couch, stunned. He called out for Jack a couple of times, but, just as Jack had promised, there was no response. What was he supposed to do now? Jack was suddenly gone, but he was supposed to return. Nothing made sense. The only thing left for Alex to do was wait for Jack's return and try to repair his relationships with those who had occupied his life before Jack. He would start on his to-do list after a good night's sleep. Maybe things would be clearer to him as time passed.

TWENTY-ONE

The mall parking lot was crawling with police officers when Bagster and Wynne arrived to investigate the newest crime scene. The two men were finding it hard to believe that two victims had been found at the same location and in such a public place, no less. The city mall was a far cry from a dark alley. As the detectives exited their vehicles, they were approached by a uniformed officer.

"Detective Wynne. Detective Bagster," the officer said, greeting them with his right hand. "We have two female bodies. Both have had their throats cut, but only one has been mutilated."

As the detectives walked with the officer, Bagster started asking questions. "Who found the women?"

"The older gentleman over there found one of the victims," the officer replied, pointing to the pizza shop manager who was being questioned by another detective. The poor man appeared very distressed, almost in tears. "The other woman was located by a fellow officer when he arrived here at the scene."

"Which one should we address first?" Wynne inquired of his partner.

Bagster stopped in his tracks and looked around the parking lot. There were police cars everywhere, but he was more interested in the other cars present. One of the cars he recognized. It belonged to one of his fellow homicide detectives. Three of the cars, however, were unfamiliar. "Officer Davis, do we know who the three vehicles belong to?"

"Which ones?" the officer asked, scanning the parking lot.

The vehicles were spread out, but Bagster clearly pointed them out. "Do we know which vehicle belongs to which person?" It was obvious they belonged to the two victims and the manager. He was hoping someone had already addressed which car belonged to which person.

"I believe Detective Brown is working on that as we speak. The pizza manager knows the victim he found. She was one of his employees. He claims he walked her out, but she didn't want him to escort her to her car. Supposedly, he watched from inside the glass doors to make sure she made it into her car safely. Once he saw she was inside, he said he went back to finish closing up the pizza counter."

"So how did he stumble upon her body?" Bagster asked.

"When he came back out of the same doors to go home, he found her keys lying on the ground," Officer Davis explained. "He noticed her car was still in the parking lot, so he started looking around for her."

Wynne scratched the back of his head. "What about the other victim? Anything on her identity?"

"Yes, but I don't know all the details. Detective Brown should be able to fill you in on the rest."

"Okay. Thanks, Officer Davis," Bagster said as they parted company.

Bagster and Wynne walked across the parking lot to Detective Brown. Neither man spoke a word, but they both knew the same person who was responsible for their two new victims was the same person responsible for the others. The same unspoken questions plagued both their minds: Why two victims all of the sudden? Was the killer becoming more confident? And why was one mutilated while the other one was left intact? They both hoped to have some clue to these questions before they left the scene.

"Detective Brown," Wynne called out to get his attention.

The plump man turned to face his fellow detectives with a pen in one hand and a small notepad in the other. He smiled at the men as they approached him. "Well, well, gentlemen. I was beginning to wonder if you were planning on joining us tonight."

"Cut the sarcasm, Brown," Bagster said. He had never cared much for Detective Brown. The man was lazy, in his opinion. The only cases he usually worked on were the ones he could handle from his desk. Nonetheless, Brown was part of the team, and they needed the info he had gathered in their absence. "What do you have so far?"

"Let me finish up with this gentleman, and I'll fill you in," Brown requested as he turned to acknowledge the pizza manager that stood just beside him.

Wynne replied this time, his tone a little nicer than Bagster's, "We'll take a look around and come back later." Wynne gently nudged his partner away from Brown. Once they were out of Brown's hearing range, Wynne said, "I know you two don't get along, but he made it here first. I don't know how, but he did. Now we need him."

"I know," Bagster replied in a sharp tone. "I'll deal with him later. Let's take a look at the bodies."

It wasn't long before they noticed Brown wasn't the only one to get to the scene before them. Alicia was doing her preliminary work on the young woman that had been dissected. The dark area, where the body lay, was being lit up by several officers and CSI techs holding flashlights for her. The flash of the bulb from a camera helped some with the darkness also. The detectives approached the area but didn't speak. They just watched Alicia work while they made their own assessment of the scene in their minds.

Once Alicia was done with the young woman, she joined the two men as the body was placed in a bag to be taken away for a more thorough check later. "Well, I'm sure you two would like to know about my initial observations, and whether I have checked out the other woman yet."

"It would be helpful," Wynne said, smiling at her while he stood with his hands inside his coat on his hips.

She smiled back, and then replied, "Yes, I have already seen the other woman. Her body has already been removed. She was found over toward the other end of the building."

"What kind of condition was she in?" Bagster asked. "We were told her throat had been cut, but that was it."

"That was it," Alicia confirmed, sounding surprised about that information. "Of course, you two are the detectives, not me, but there was very little blood near her body. I think she was killed elsewhere and brought to that location. I'm pretty sure she was either dead or very close to death when she was placed there."

"How was she positioned?" Bagster asked, knowing this would indicate whether the two murders were linked, or if the murders just happened to take place on the same night at the same location with two separate killers, which was highly unlikely. Anything was possible though.

"Same as all the others, including the one I just looked at. Her legs were pushed up with the knees pushed out to the sides," Alicia stated, confirming what both detectives already figured. Before she could say another word, her face lit up with amusement, and she had to cover her mouth to keep herself from laughing.

Bagster and Wynne turned quickly to see what had changed her mood so fast. Wynne began to grin and snicker, whereas Bagster hung his head down and shook it in disappointment. Detective Brown was making his way toward the small group. He was moving as fast as he could, but his sheer bulk, shifting from side to side, made it hard for him to cover much ground quickly. His waddling was very amusing to Alicia and Wynne. It was just pitiful to Bagster.

Brown was completely out of breath when he reached the others. Beads of sweat glistened on his forehead while the bigger droplets ran down his temples. He ignored the joy Alicia and Wynne were obviously experiencing at his expense. Pulling a hanky from his pocket, Brown wiped his face, and then he addressed the one person who was being serious. "Well, Bagster," he started as he caught his breath, "I'll brief you on what I know so far and then I'm going back home. This case, I believe, fits in with the other two you have so it doesn't concern me."

"I agree. Just tell me what you got, and then you can go," Bagster snapped.

They walked away from Alicia and Wynne to cover the information Brown had gathered. While Bagster was dealing with Brown, Wynne continued with Alicia—once they were able to compose themselves. Alicia's initial examination of the two victims led her to believe the same type of instrument had been used on the necks of both women. She also concluded that the organs from the young woman were removed exactly the same way as one of the previous victims. Nothing appeared to be missing this time though. The big difference between this victim and all the others was the fact her face had been cut up and part of one ear was gone.

Wynne made a mental note of that bit of information, and then he thanked Alicia for her time. "Be sure to let us know when you're done with your examinations of the two."

"You know I will," she assured him with a warm smile. "I'll be in touch in a few days."

Shortly after Alicia left Wynne, Bagster returned to share what he had learned from Brown. It was now clear which car belonged to which person. The manager from the pizza counter left in the little silver car. The old blue car belonged to the young woman that worked at the pizza counter. And the red sports car belonged to the woman that only had her throat cut. Her purse with her identification inside had been found near the car. Her name was Clair Morgan. The other victim's purse was located inside her car. She was identified as Stephanie Lindel.

"Now we have to watch hours of security video from the mall cameras," Bagster informed Wynne. "Hopefully, we can pinpoint a suspect in one of the videos."

"It would be nice to find something to compare to the jewelry store video," Wynne added.

"That's what I'm hoping for."

TWENTY-TWO

The beginning of October turned immediately cold. The temperatures had been fairly mild throughout September. Alex had been able to get by with only a sweatshirt or a jacket, but suddenly that wouldn't be enough. He had spent the first week in his apartment after Jack deserted him. Alex tried to make sense of things during this time. It was still unclear why Jack had left so suddenly, and why he wanted Alex to fix things in his life before the last task.

Alex shivered as he sat in his car outside his apartment. It was the first time he had been outside the warm confines of his home in a long time. This made the cold temperatures even more bitter. Alex flipped the heat on, and as his car slowly warmed, he started to formulate a plan for the day. If he was to have his life back in order by the time the last task was to take place, the first thing he needed to do was get a job.

It was still fairly early when Alex arrived at his old job, the grocery store. He actually missed the place. Well, he missed having a paycheck more. The money his dad had given him a couple of times had helped but didn't go far enough. Bills were piling up, and he was in danger of being evicted. Maybe if Mr. Jenson could find it in his heart to give Alex one more chance, he could borrow a little more money from his dad to get by until he started receiving paychecks again. Surely his dad would help him out one more time if he was working.

New and old faces stared at Alex as he made his way through the store. One employee informed Alex that Mr. Jenson was indeed in his office. He stopped just outside the office door and took a deep breath. Quickly, he exhaled, then rolled his head around in a circle to loosen his neck muscles. He knocked and waited for a response, which came quicker than he had expected.

"Come in," a manly voice called from the other side of the door.

Slowly, Alex turned the doorknob and entered. As his stomach filled with knots, he managed to smile at his old boss. To his immediate relief, Mr. Jenson's face lit up at the sight of his former employee. The two men greeted each other cheerfully, and Mr. Jenson offered Alex a seat in front of his desk.

"How have you been, Alex?" Mr. Jenson asked as he sat back down in his desk chair.

Alex tucked his hair behind his ears. "I've been good, for the most part anyway."

Mr. Jenson didn't waste much time with small talk. He had been in enough managerial positions to know old employees rarely stopped by just to chat. "I'm glad to see you, Alex, but I'm wondering what the purpose of your visit might be."

"You don't waste time do you," Alex remarked.

As he folded his hands on his desk and leaned forward, Mr. Jenson shrugged at Alex. "It's instinct to know when someone has an ulterior motive for a visit to an old boss. So, what is your motive today?"

With a slight laugh and a glance at the floor, Alex answered him. "All right, I'll fess up. I wanted to see what my chances are of getting my old job back."

"Well, that depends, Alex," Mr. Jenson told him.

"On what?" Alex asked, though he knew what Mr. Jenson was getting at.

Mr. Jenson sighed. "You were always one of my best employees. I could depend on you to be here and to do your job well. Do you remember why I had to let you go?"

He remembered, clearly. "Yes. I remember. Things are better with me now." That was partially true. A lot of things still didn't make sense to him, but he didn't feel like he was losing his mind anymore.

"I'm glad to hear that," Mr. Jenson stated. "Do you think I should give you another chance? Would you give someone like you another chance?"

Alex thought about what the best answer would be for a minute. Then he opened his mouth and said, "I think everyone deserves a second chance. I would give me a second chance."

"Okay then," Mr. Jenson said, leaning back in his chair. "Be here at nine in the morning, and we'll do your paperwork."

"Thank you, Mr. Jenson. You won't regret this." Alex stood and extended his hand to him.

"I hope not." Mr. Jenson shook Alex's hand. "I'll see you in the morning."

Alex shoved his hands in his coat pockets as he exited the store and braved the cold wind. He cranked up the heat in his car as he thought about meeting his dad for lunch. Getting his job back went easier than he had planned. Mr. Jenson had always been a reasonable man, but Alex thought he would have to fight harder to get what he wanted. Of course, he probably would have to with his dad. It could be to his advantage that his dad still felt guilty for tearing the family apart. He still sounded like he did, at least, when Alex talked to him that morning on the phone. He had given Alex money during their last get-together for that very reason.

As Alex sat in his car, he started watching the customers coming and going. Without even realizing it, he had narrowed his attention to the females. His mind slowly drifted from what he was going to say to his dad to the women he was watching. Then it occurred to him. He was observing these women the same way he had been at the mall. He was picking each of them apart as he decided which ones would be easy targets.

Alex tried desperately to get his thoughts back on his father, but every time another woman would pass in front of his car, his mind would race back to figure out her weak points. With each woman he watched, his heart would pound a little harder. It wasn't long before he started to take in his surroundings and look for hiding places. He knew there had to be someplace he could hide to be able to attack his prey. There had to be a perfect place he could take them to perform his deadly task, just as Jack would want him to.

Suddenly, Alex was brought back to the reality that Jack was gone. It was only temporary, but he was still gone. It was hard for Alex to comprehend how he could be so happy to have a break from Jack, yet find himself feeling so alone. Jack was nothing more than that annoying, British voice inside his head that convinced him to do horrible things. He wasn't an actual physical human being that he could see or touch.

Nevertheless, Jack had become a strange part of his life, and Alex didn't know how to readjust to life without him.

Once Alex glanced at his watch, he realized it was still early. The meeting with Mr. Jenson took less time than he had originally planned, so he had time to kill, in a manner of speaking. Of course, he couldn't fight the urge to scope out potential victims. It was something he very recently discovered he enjoyed doing, but he needed something else to help him pass the time for a while. After all, he knew it could be hard to resist the temptation to attack if someone seemed perfect. Jack probably wouldn't be happy with him if he did that on his own. He needed to be distracted to avoid the temptation.

Many options of how to pass the time raced through his mind. Since he was supposed to be getting his life back in order, Alex figured it was time to make amends with some old friends. He knew Josh was probably in class since it was a school day, so he put his little car in drive to head to the hardware store where Tony worked with his dad. Alex didn't know if he would be there, but he had nothing else to do anyway. The trip itself would use up some time.

Tony's old pickup truck was parked next to his dad's when Alex pulled into the parking lot next to the store. Alex was somewhat nervous about what kind of reaction he would get from Tony. The two hadn't spoken since Alex exploded and kicked his friends out of his apartment. Josh had seemed to accept Alex's apology when they talked at the laundromat a few months earlier, but that felt like so long ago. He had never made the attempt to apologize to Tony. It could go either way. Tony could accept it or tell him he never wanted to see him again.

When the door to the store was pushed open, it hit a bell placed above it. The sound caused Alex to jump slightly. The bell hadn't been there before, and he didn't need it drawing everyone's attention to him. He was nervous enough without all the customers staring at him. One glaring set of eyes stood out in particular. Tony's. With an apologetic smile, Alex walked to the counter to greet his old buddy. Tony didn't return the smile. His face was blank.

Alex tried to be upbeat. "Hey, Tony, how are you?"

"Good, I suppose," Tony replied flatly. "What do you want, Alex?"

"Can we talk for a minute? I won't take up too much of your time. I promise," Alex pleaded.

Tony glared at Alex for another moment before he called to his dad, who was at the other end of the store. "I'm taking a short break, Dad. I'll be back in a minute." When his dad answered back, Tony emerged from behind the counter and motioned for Alex to step outside.

"Okay, Alex, what do you want from me?" Tony shoved his hands deep into his jeans pockets as he and Alex faced the biting wind outside.

Alex looked at the ground. "I know things ended badly the last time we hung out together. I just wanted to apologize for the way I behaved." He looked up to try to read Tony's facial expression. Unfortunately, it hadn't changed.

"Apology accepted. Is that it?" Tony asked.

"No, that's not it," Alex said harshly. Tony's cold response upset him. "We've been friends for years, Tony. I would like to continue our friendship. I was wrong, and I'm saying I'm sorry. Can we get past this and be friends again?"

Tony sighed heavily. "I want to be friends again, Alex, but you haven't been the same person for the past couple of months. Everyone knows that. You quit school. You hide out in your apartment all the time, alone, and you talk to no one."

"That's not entirely true!" Alex snapped. The problem was he couldn't explain what was true or why things were the way they were.

"Then what is true, Alex? Why haven't I heard from you until now? Why do you only go around Jana long enough to hurt her more? We all care about you and worry about you, but you have shut us all out. Why?"

Alex hung his head again. The look in Tony's eyes was more than he could bear. Tony was absolutely right. "I can't give a good enough explanation for my actions for the last couple of months. All I can do is ask for forgiveness and try to make things right. I won't waste any more of your time." Alex stepped around his friend to walk to his car.

"Wait," Tony quickly said. Alex turned back to look at him. "Let's get together tonight. Maybe go have a couple of beers with Josh or something."

A smile crept across Alex's face. "I was planning on spending time with Jana tonight if she wanted me to. I have a lot of work cut out for me with her."

"I know you do," Tony stated with a slight laugh. "Bring her along. It'll be like old times."

"Sounds good," Alex agreed. "A new start."

"A new start," Tony repeated as he opened the door to step back inside.

Alex felt good about his short visit with Tony. It had gone better than he had anticipated. Tony could have made Alex's apology worthless, but he didn't do that. Alex, Josh, and Tony had been friends for so long. He missed them. He wanted them back in his life. Josh and Alex had already talked a while back. He felt things would be okay with Josh, but Josh was generally more understanding than Tony. Alex felt he was on the right track with getting his life and friends back. There were only a few things left on his list.

So far, Alex had a job and had made amends with Tony. He was on his way to meet with his dad, and then he needed to visit his mom and Jessica. And last but not least, he had to fix things with Jana. Of everything left for him to do, Jana was the one he looked forward to the most. He knew she would be thrilled to see him. He just hoped she would be as thrilled to forgive him for his behavior over the last several weeks. The first thing was first though, and that first thing was lunch with his dad.

TWENTY-THREE

The same day Alex was working to get back what he had lost, Wynne and Bagster were busy still trying to fit together all the pieces of the messes he had made. Bagster had been called to the forensics lab to review some of the evidence gathered at the mall. Even though there had only been a few clues that looked promising, the crime scene investigators had been ordered to collect absolutely everything they could. Potential evidence had been collected from both areas where the women were found, their cars, and also from the security cameras, inside and out.

While Bagster went to meet with one of the forensic techs, Wynne met with another fellow detective. Detective Owens had been placed in charge of reviewing the security videos. It had been days since Owens had started watching the tapes, but Wynne knew there were several hours of video to watch. It didn't help much that they weren't sure what Owens was supposed to be looking for in the videos. He had watched the footage from the jewelry store, which gave him a small idea, but it was only of minimal assistance.

"Well, Wynne," Owens started when the two sat in front of the small TV the department owned. "I think I may have found your guy."

"Seriously?" Wynne asked, leaning forward to see better.

Owens turned on the TV and VCR. "I found him in the food court. It looks like he watched the young woman at the pizza counter for quite a long time." He pushed the play button on the remote. "See him sitting at the table? He's wearing the same type of jacket as the man in the video from the jewelry store."

"Are you sure this is the same guy?" Wynne asked, leaning toward the TV screen.

"Well, the jewelry store video is of horrible quality, but I can still make out that same jacket. Here, I'll speed up the tape some. He sits there for a long time." Owens fast-forwarded the tape. He stopped it when the man stood and left the table. "Another tape shows him by the front doors. There you see him around the other woman, but he doesn't do anything to her inside the mall."

"Please tell me you have him on camera outside the mall?" Wynne's eyes were pleading with Owens for even a glimmer of hope.

With a huge grin stretching across his face, Owens answered, "Yes. There isn't much footage of the slightly older woman, but there is a camera pointed at the doors. Hold on and I'll show you." Owens took the first tape out of the VCR and replaced it with a second tape.

The air was silent as they watched the events of the night play out on the screen in front of them. The girl from the pizza counter walked out with her manager. They talked briefly. Then, the girl walked away from the doors as the manager walked back in the mall. The area remained vacant for a moment. Suddenly, the girl appeared back in front of the camera. She was grabbed and taken away, her keys falling, before she could make it safely inside the doors. This time, the man was wearing the baseball cap, just like on the jewelry store tape.

Wynne leaned back in his chair, speechless, as Owens stopped the tape. This was more than he or his partner had hoped for in the beginning. "Is there anything else?"

"There are videos of him entering the mall and making his way to the food court, but that's about it. I can show them to you if you want to see them. I personally didn't see anything important in them."

Wynne sighed. He was glad to have something on video, but he desperately wanted more. "Are there any clear shots of his face?"

"No," Owens responded flatly. "With the camera angles and the bill of his hat, it was impossible to make out anything above his mouth. A good part of the time he had that covered too."

"Can you do me one more favor?" Wynne asked his fellow detective as they both stood up.

"Sure, if I can."

"Try to find a good shot of him that we can put on the news. Maybe someone can tell us something by looking at just a little bit of his face."

"I'll see what I can do," Owens said.

Once in his car, Wynne called Bagster to see what he had learned and to share his newfound information. Bagster wasn't done. He told Wynne to grab them both some lunch and meet him back at their desks. Wynne had hoped they would meet for lunch somewhere, but he didn't mind being the gofer for the day. Loud noises were coming from the pit of his stomach. As long as he was able to eat, it didn't really matter if he was sitting at his desk to do it. He decided to hit a Mexican restaurant that was up the road. There he would order two lunch specials to go and would be back at the office before Bagster.

The restaurant had a large lunch crowd. Wynne sat at the bar, which was separate from the family dining area, and waited for his order. He carefully studied every male face he could see in the mirror behind the bar. Would someone be able to recognize the killer with only his mouth and jaw visible? It would be difficult, he knew, but if someone was very close to the killer, it might be possible.

"Would you like something to drink while you wait?"

Wynne was snapped out of his private thoughts by a pretty waitress standing in front of him on the opposite side of the bar. "No, thank you, I'm fine," he replied with a smile.

"Okay. Let me know if you change your mind." She returned his smile before she walked away.

The first victim of the case came rushing into his mind as he watched her walk away. The first victim had been a waitress in a restaurant only a few blocks from where he was sitting. He now carefully watched the waitress in the mirror. Who could say she wouldn't be the killer's next victim? Did the killer seek out particular types of women, or did he just look for easy targets? This was just one thing to consider. There were so many other things. Wynne decided to think about it back at his desk when a different waitress sat two paper bags on the bar in front of him. He paid for the lunches and headed for the door. As he passed a table in the bar area, he noticed a young man sitting alone with shoulder-length blond hair and a familiar jawline. Distracted, Wynne failed to see the waiter crossing his path and bumped into him, causing a tray of chips and salsa to fall to the floor. Wynne apologized and helped clean up some of the chips. When he stood up again, he looked back at the blond-haired young man. There was something dark in his eyes—something tense and accusing—that made Wynne have to glance away. He shrugged off the young man's hostility. He had just spilled his lunch, after all. With another apology, Wynne sidestepped the mess he had made and headed for the door.

Bagster was already at his desk when Wynne arrived back at the office. "I figured I would have to start eating without you."

"I was almost done when you called," Bagster said as he stopped reading the papers on his desk. He took one of the sacks and stated, "I take it we're having Mexican."

"Yeah. I hope you don't mind," Wynne replied as he grabbed the other sack.

The two partners emptied the contents of their sacks as Bagster asked about the videotapes from the mall. Wynne gave him all the details of what he observed from the videos. He also relayed to his partner that it did appear to be the same man from the jewelry store video, but they still didn't have a clear shot of his face. That's also when he mentioned the plan to release a picture from the video to the news stations. Bagster agreed it was worth a shot. Anything was worth a shot.

"So, how did you make out at the forensics lab?" Wynne asked before taking a bite of his Spanish rice.

Bagster swallowed the food in his mouth. "About the same as you did. There are a few things, but nothing to lead us to him."

"What are the few things?" Wynne inquired.

"Well…" Bagster paused to chew up another bite. "We now have almost a full boot impression that was left in the blood of the older woman. It's pretty clear the boot is a work boot, but they are trying to narrow in on the brand right now. It'll help when we do find him, but it doesn't do much as far as pointing us in the right direction."

"Do they think it's a pretty common boot?"

"Yes. That is the problem with that," Bagster answered. "Once we have him, there will be no problem matching the boot print to the boot, but we have to have the boot first."

Nodding his head, Wynne said, "I know. Hopefully, we get the boot at some point. What else did they have for you?"

"Let's see," Bagster said as he moved his lunch and began looking through the papers on his desk again. "There was a bloody handprint on the wall next to the younger victim, but it was determined he was wearing gloves. Past that, they tested numerous fiber and hair samples. They found nothing with those. They are working on some different blood samples from both crime scenes, but so far they don't look very promising. I just don't understand how a man could kill two women, one right after the other, and leave nothing behind to tell us who he is. How does that happen?"

Wynne shrugged. It was odd to them both. "I don't know, Bagster. He has left nothing significant at any of the crime scenes. I was wondering earlier at the restaurant about a lot of things."

"What were you wondering about?"

"I was wondering about things like, how does he pick his victims? Why does he mutilate some of them, but not all of them? Why is he even doing this in the first place? Now I'm wondering how he could be so clever."

"In my opinion," Bagster started after he swallowed another bite, "I don't think he has a method of choosing his victims. I think he just picks the ones that are convenient at the time."

"That's what I was thinking, but he was clearly watching the pizza counter girl in the video," Wynne pointed out.

"What about the other one?"

Wynne shook his head. "No. I don't think he was watching her."

"Then maybe the pizza counter girl just caught his attention for some odd reason. I just don't see a common link between these women," Bagster said firmly.

"So what about all the stuff on the news about Jack the Ripper?" They hadn't discussed the media's take on the cases, but Wynne really wanted to know what his older, more experienced partner thought about it. "Do you think they are onto something?"

Bagster stared at Wynne blankly for a moment before answering his question. "I've said for a while that these murders reminded me of something I've seen before, right?" Wynne nodded yes. "I do have to say they bear a strong resemblance to those murders. I don't like that the media has brought that up, but we can't keep them from voicing their opinions and thoughts. I don't know why someone would decide to copycat those murders though. It does appear that's what's happening, especially with these last two. Do you know any details about the Jack the Ripper murders?"

"Not that much. I know he was never caught."

"I suggest you do a little research, Wynne," Bagster offered. "Jack the Ripper was never captured. At the rate this case is going, we will never capture this guy either. I can't have that."

Wynne agreed with that statement. He didn't quite understand what research on Jack the Ripper would accomplish, but he was willing to try anything. They couldn't let the women's deaths go unpunished. They couldn't let the killer get away with his horrible deeds. Wynne became a homicide detective to catch the bad guys and make sure they were put away for taking the lives of innocent people. With Bagster's help, Wynne had been able to do just that. The two of them had helped many families get justice, as well as closure, during their partnership. For the first time since becoming partners, Wynne and Bagster were close to not catching the guilty person.

The two detectives parted ways after lunch. Bagster had a few things to check out that pertained to a case a fellow detective was working through. While he was alone, Wynne went back through the files on the victims and tried to find any other similarities to give him further insight into the killer's mind. After a few hours of scouring page after page, and picture after picture, he came up empty-handed. He decided he might have to take Bagster's advice and research Jack the Ripper. If the cases were similar, he needed to know how. He couldn't let his cases end up like the Ripper cases.

TWENTY-FOUR

The Mexican restaurant Alex was supposed to meet his dad at was busy. He ended up at a table in the bar area because the family dining area was full. Alex usually didn't eat Mexican food. It didn't agree with his stomach much. He knew it would probably cause him problems, especially with the butterflies he was already dealing with over having to ask his dad for more money so soon.

Even though Mexican food could make Alex miserable from time to time, he had purposely picked it for lunch because it was his dad's favorite. This particular downtown restaurant also happened to be his dad's favorite place to eat Mexican food. Alex was hoping to make him happy with the restaurant, the food, and the fact he had a job again. He secretly hoped his dad still felt guilty about the breakup with his mom. All these things could play to his advantage, which could make asking for money a whole lot easier.

As Alex bounced his leg nervously, he observed the other people seated around him. One person at the bar caught his attention. This person was also observing the other people in their area. The man seemed to be deep in thought, but not nervous like Alex. Curious, Alex followed the man's gaze. Nothing seemed out of the ordinary with any of his targets. Alex returned his focus to the man, who was now flinching as a waitress started talking to him. When the waitress walked away, the man started watching her. This puzzled Alex. He couldn't tell what the stranger was up to, but he was sure it was no good.

After a bit, he noticed the man walking in his direction with a bag of food. The man seemed to go out of his way to make eye contact with Alex, but as he did so, he bumped into the waiter who was bringing Alex his chips and salsa. The inquisitive man apologized and bent down to help clean up the mess, but he kept eyeing Alex. There was something accusatory in the man's eyes, but Alex, not wanting to draw even more attention to himself, could only glare and wonder what he had done to warrant such attention from this stranger. At the last moment, though, the reason became clear: When the man stood up, Alex glimpsed a badge on the man's belt under his jacket. For a split second, Alex stopped breathing.

Luckily, a familiar voice swept in to rescue him from the officer's scrutiny. "Have you been waiting long?"

Alex quickly turned his head to see his dad sitting down across the booth from him. "Uh, no, not really."

Mr. Dorson looked toward the bar. "What were you staring at?"

Alex glanced back toward the bar in time to see the man heading out the door with his sacks of food. "Nothing really. I was just passing the time watching people."

The same waitress the man had been watching approached their table. Alex couldn't help but look the waitress up and down and size her up for a kill. "I see your company has arrived. Are you ready to order, or do you need a few minutes?"

"I'm ready. How about you, Alex?" Mr. Dorson said cheerfully.

"Yes. I'm ready," Alex agreed, wondering if he should just stick to having something to drink. He knew that wouldn't go over too well with his dad though.

After ordering, Mr. Dorson skipped the small talk and got to the point. "So, Alex, what is the point of our little lunch date today?"

"What do you mean?" Alex responded, trying to look surprised by his dad's accusation that something else was on his agenda besides lunch.

Mr. Dorson gave Alex a stern look as he said, "Last time we met for a meal you had just found out about your mom and me splitting up. That wasn't very long ago. Has something else happened that I'm not aware of that you need to discuss with me?"

"No, not that I know of anyway. I haven't talked to Mom or Jessica since I last saw you. I'm assuming everything is the same," Alex told him.

"Then what is it you need?" Mr. Dorson pushed.

Alex looked down at the table. He started running his finger along a scratch in the table's surface. "I need a little more money," he finally stated. Then he waited for a response.

"Okay. Is that all?'

Alex looked up at his dad. It wasn't supposed to be that easy, but he was relieved it had been that easy. "Yes. I just need to borrow a little bit of money until I get my first paycheck." He slipped that last bit in, hoping his dad would catch it.

He did. "Paycheck? Does that mean you finally have a job?"

"Yes, Dad. I start back at the grocery store tomorrow morning," Alex informed him. "I went to talk to Mr. Jenson this morning. He has agreed to give me another chance."

"What about school?"

With a sigh, Alex responded, "I already told you I would start back next semester. I'll graduate late, but that doesn't matter. We'll talk about that later, okay?"

Sensing he was starting to push too hard, Mr. Dorson lifted his hands, leaned back in his chair, and said, "All right! Another time then. How much money do you need?"

"I don't know."

"It will be a couple of weeks before you get paid, right?" Mr. Dorson remembered the grocery store only paid their employees on a biweekly basis.

"It will be two or three weeks. I'm not sure," Alex confirmed.

Mr. Dorson reached into his back pocket and pulled out his wallet. He counted what was in it. Alex tried not to watch his dad count his money. He didn't want to seem overly eager to get his hands on it. After a moment, Mr. Dorson pulled out all the money he had in his wallet, folded it up, and handed it over to Alex. Then he motioned for Alex to put it away. Alex shoved the money into his back pocket while he thanked his dad.

"I'll pay you back," Alex promised.

"Don't worry about it. I'm just happy to see you're finally getting your life back on track," Mr. Dorson said. "So, how is Jana these days? Are you two still a couple?"

"I think so," he replied sheepishly.

Confused by the response, Mr. Dorson asked, "You don't know for sure? Have you two been having problems?"

"Just me, Dad. I've been the problem. She's on my list next."

"What list is that?"

Alex chuckled slightly. "My 'make amends' list. I'm trying to fix everything I've screwed up in the last few months. She tried to stick by me, but I haven't been there for her. I'm just trying to make things right again."

The waitress approached their table with two plates of food. After she had them all situated, she left them to their meals. Mr. Dorson appeared to be more than pleased with how good the food on his plate looked. Alex just viewed the food in front of him as guaranteed heartburn, indigestion, and a possible delay in his plans for the evening. He would eat it anyway. It would please his dad, even though it would make him miserable.

During lunch, Mr. Dorson tried to find out what had been going on with his son for the last few months. Of course, Alex wasn't eager to talk about it with anyone, especially his dad. The only thing he could come up with to explain his erratic behavior, and the fact he had completely messed up his life, was a lie about suffering from depression. To his amazement, his dad actually believed it. Of course, he had suffered from brief bouts of depression after the first two tasks, so it wasn't a complete lie. He just left out the nagging voice in his head that was making him complete horrible deeds. Since his dad believed the whole depression story, Alex now had an excuse to give everyone else.

When silence fell between them at one point during their lunch, Alex seized the opportunity to change the subject. The topic had been eating at him for long enough. It was time to talk about his dad and his new girlfriend. Even though Alex couldn't be sure if he really wanted to hear all the details, he knew he needed to. His parents had been having problems for years. Everyone basically knew the couple had split for good. Alex just wanted to hear more about his dad's new life before he went to hear about his mom's new life. He was sure hers would be less exciting.

Alex hurried and asked his dad a question to avoid the conversation drifting back to his life. "So, Dad, tell me about the new girlfriend. Last time we talked, we never made it that far in our conversation."

Shock sprang to the surface of Mr. Dorson's face. He wiped the food from his mouth and asked, "Do you really want to know about her?" Alex nodded yes. "What do you want to know?"

"Everything you're willing to share," Alex said, hoping there wouldn't be much for him to share.

"All right, then," Mr. Dorson agreed. "Her name is Joanne, and she is twenty-five."

Alex started to choke on his food. He dropped his fork and started coughing and wheezing. His dad tried to help by telling him to take a drink. Finally, Alex did take a drink from his glass. It helped wash the food down, and that, in turn, helped him breathe again.

"Are you all right?" Mr. Dorson asked, his voice full of concern as he watched Alex slowly return to normal.

Alex was still coughing some as he asked, "She's twenty-five? You have to be kidding!" This news just seemed to make things worse.

"I'm not kidding, Alex. She's twenty-five. Why does that appear to be a problem for you?" His tone let Alex know he wasn't happy with his reaction.

"How did you expect me to react?" Alex asked his dad harshly. "She's not much older than I am! Are you having a midlife crisis? Is that what's going on here?"

"NO! I know this isn't the typical relationship for someone my age. She isn't bothered by my age, and I'm not bothered by hers. Age is just a number."

"Well, in your case, those two numbers seem to have a difference of about twenty years!"

"Okay, Alex. That's enough," he snapped back at his son. "You wanted to know about her, so I'm trying to tell you."

Alex sank down in his seat. "Sorry. It was just a shock to my system. Go on. Tell me more about her." At this point, he really didn't care to hear anything else about Joanne, but he didn't want to go back to talking about himself. He would just have to grin and bear it.

"Well, she's a nurse at the hospital," Mr. Dorson started.

"I suppose you're going to say you met her while I was there after my accident," Alex interrupted, sounding very sarcastic.

"No. As a matter of fact, I met her a couple of months before your accident through a mutual friend. We just seemed to hit it off right away."

"So what makes her different from the other girlfriends you've had? Why did this make you decide to leave Mom?" Alex asked. He knew these would be the tough questions. He sat up in his seat and crossed his arms as he waited for the answer.

Mr. Dorson was silent for a moment. Finally, he opened his mouth and said, "I really don't know, Alex. As scary as it sounds, she kind of reminds me of your mother when she was that age. Joanne seems to have a little something extra that your mom never had though. I can't quite put my finger on it, but it's there, and I like it. The girlfriends I had before didn't mean anything to me. They were all the same."

Alex leaned in to look into his dad's eyes. There was a little sparkle there when he talked about Joanne. It was never there before when he talked about his mom. He knew his dad was being honest. She did make him happy, for whatever reason. "Well, Dad, I guess all I can say is I'm happy for you. I don't know what to do with Mom now, but I'm happy for you."

They finished their lunches and parted ways. Alex had planned on visiting his mom and sister, but he had spent enough time with family for one day. So far he had managed to get his job back, rekindle a friendship with Tony, and somewhat reconnect with his dad while getting money from him. Lunch wasn't bothering him yet, which was a good thing. While he didn't plan to visit his mom and sister now, his day wasn't over by far. There were still plans with his friends, and Jana to deal with before that. In his mind, Alex rescheduled his mom and sister for the next day after work as he drove toward Jana's apartment.

TWENTY-FIVE

The shock was written all over Jana's face when she opened her front door. "Alex," she finally said, trying to hide the surprised state she was in. "I wasn't expecting you. Come in."

Alex stepped inside the threshold of her apartment, but for the first time ever he felt like he wasn't welcome there. "Were you expecting someone else?"

"No, but it's been more than a few days," she replied, closing the door. "I thought you were gone again. I really didn't think I would see you for a while since you didn't come back like you said you would."

She stepped around him and went to sit in a chair. Once again, things didn't seem right. Jana was acting strange. She seemed nervous and obviously wanted to keep her distance from him. It had only been about a week or so since she had pleaded with him to spend the night by her side. What could have possibly changed in that short time period? He took a seat on the couch, alone.

Painful silence filled the room before Alex finally spoke. "Are you at least happy to see me? If not, I can go."

"Of course I'm happy to see you. Just a little surprised. That's all."

"Then come sit next to me." He patted the cushion next to his.

"Okay," Jana replied as she joined him on the couch.

"I saw Tony this morning," Alex said. Jana was beside him now, but she was still keeping her distance. He tried to ignore that little fact by starting a conversation.

She smiled meekly. "Are you two talking again?"

"I think so. He invited me to go out with him and Josh tonight, but I said I wanted you to come too," he told her with a smile on his face. "Will you go with me tonight?"

Jana shrugged. "I don't know. It might be better if I didn't."

That was it. Alex knew something wasn't right. All she had complained about for months was the fact that he kept disappearing. She was always telling him he wasn't around enough. She said she felt like he was pushing her away. He wanted her to come along tonight. He wanted to spend time with her and have her near him, but she thought it might be better if she didn't go.

Alex tried to control the temper that was building inside him. "What is going on that I'm missing here?"

"Nothing," she responded without hesitation.

"Then go with me tonight. Let's spend some time together."

Jana crossed her arms and sighed heavily as she looked away. "Why? So you can disappear again tomorrow morning, if not tonight?"

Alex gently held her chin and turned her face toward his as he leaned into her. "I'm not going anywhere this time. I'm trying to make amends to those I've done wrong. That is why I saw Tony this morning. That is why I had lunch with my dad earlier. That is why I'm here now with you." He let go of her chin and leaned back. He smiled and said, "On second thought, I will be leaving in the morning. I start back at the grocery store tomorrow morning at nine o'clock."

Jana's eyes lit up. "Really?"

With a slight laugh, he answered her. "I'm trying to get back to where I was before I turned everyone away from me." His tone turned serious. "Tonight is an important step for me. I want you with me. Please come with me."

"Okay. I will," she answered as she reached over and took his hand in hers.

There was still something not right. Alex felt she was keeping something from him, but the time wasn't right for him to push the issue. If he was going to have a good night with his friends, he would have to leave it alone. There would be plenty of time to dig for more information later on down the road. He only wanted to accomplish what Jack had instructed him to do in his absence. Things were finally falling into place. His life was coming back together, and unknown issues with Jana didn't need to stop his progress. Alex wrapped his arms around her as they leaned back against the couch.

Around four o'clock that afternoon, Alex left Jana's to go home for a while before meeting Tony and Josh. He told Jana he would return in a couple of hours to pick her up. She assured him she would be ready and waiting. Back at his apartment, Alex set his alarm clock and climbed into his bed. He needed to shut down his mind and body for a little bit. There had been a lot going on since he woke up early that morning. If he was going to make it through a night with his friends and Jana, he had to get some sleep.

A few hours later, Alex picked up Jana and went to a small tavern near the college. It was a place that was always full of college students drinking, playing pool, and even a few dancing in an area set aside by the jukebox. During warmer weather, the tavern would have local bands play live in an outside field behind the building. The stage had been fenced in to allow the tavern to charge the students a cover to get in to see the show. Since it was well into the month of October, the backfield was closed up, and everyone was inside staying warm.

As Alex and Jana entered the front door, they both heard several voices calling out and greeting them. Alex recognized most of the people occupying seats throughout the tavern. He assumed some of the new faces belonged to the new freshmen at the school that year. One voice calling out to the couple caught their attention more than the others. It belonged to Tony, who was at one of the pool tables in the back corner of the tavern with Josh.

The couple slowly made their way to the back corner. Alex was stopped by several people he knew but hadn't seen for a long time. Some of them he hadn't seen since the previous spring before school let out. They were the ones that had family elsewhere, and they would leave to be with their families over the summer months. The others were locals he had grown up with and had known his whole life. Still, everyone here had one thing in common: They all wanted to know where he had been hiding. To their dissatisfaction, the only response Alex would give was, "I've been around."

When they finally reached Tony and Josh, the friends all exchanged hugs. Jana went off and joined a group of three young women that had been watching Tony and Josh play pool at a table. Jana knew all three of them from school. The men started with small talk while Josh racked up the pool balls for another game. The small talk didn't last long.

"So, Alex." Josh started casually switching the balls in the plastic triangle. "You seem like your old self. I'm happy to see it. But what has been going on with you the past few months?"

Alex knew that question would keep coming up. Luckily, he had an excuse ready to go. "I was depressed for a long time. It started shortly after the wreck. I was constantly up and down."

"So I guess you're up now, but what about tomorrow?" Tony asked as he rubbed the little square blue chalk on his pool stick.

"I think I'll be fine," Alex proudly announced. He watched Tony hit the cue ball. "Nice shot, Tony. Too bad nothing went in any of the pockets."

Tony walked around the pool table to Alex and said, "Let's see if you can do any better."

With the first shot, Alex knocked in a solid color ball. Then he sank two more. He missed on the fourth attempt. "I think I did okay. Your turn."

Josh wasn't in on the game, but he tried to stay in the conversation while he sat at the table with the women. "Tell me something, Alex. What makes you so sure you'll be okay now? Are you on medication or something?"

Alex could see Josh was sitting next to Jana. He could also see she was paying close attention to what was being said. As he answered Josh's question he tried to be cheerful, but he already wanted the topic of their conversation to change. "No, I'm not on any medication. I just decided to pull myself up out of the hole I was in and get my life back. That's what I'm trying to do right now. I got my old job back, and I'm working on getting back to school next semester."

"So you are going back," Tony stated as he missed the ball he was aiming at. "Your turn again."

"Yeah. I'll be a semester behind, but I've come too far in school to not finish," Alex said as he examined the balls on the table. After he planned out the next shot, he leaned over and took it. The ball slammed into the corner pocket. Alex smiled at his good aim. "After school, I plan to get away from here. I want to leave everything behind me."

Jana spoke up from the table. "Even me?"

Smiling, he responded by saying, "That is your choice to make. You'll be out of school before I am. You have to decide if you're going to wait on me or start a career here." He took another shot, but this time he missed. "I think we need to talk about it some other time though."

She nodded, but Alex could tell she really didn't like his response. A better one probably would have been him saying he couldn't live without her and would never leave her behind, never. Maybe she would have liked that better. Even though that was true, he didn't want her to think he expected her to wait around for him. The plan had always been for him to leave after graduation. Alex just always assumed she would follow. Since things had changed—since *he* had changed—nothing could be assumed anymore.

The group of friends enjoyed themselves well into the night. Alex was on a roll. He won more games of pool than he lost. When it began to get late, everyone agreed it was time to go home. Jana was standing at the bar talking to the bartender. He was a local they all had grown up with, but, just like Tony, he had decided to work in the family business instead of attending college. Alex didn't want to interrupt the conversation, but he did want to let her know it was time to go.

Quietly, he came up behind her and placed his hands on her hips. He then bent down and put his chin on her shoulder.

"Is it about time to go?" she asked, giggling about his face being right beside hers.

"I think everyone is getting ready to leave," he answered.

The bartender asked, "How have you been, Alex?"

Alex grinned and said, "It's a long story. I'll just say things are looking up for me now."

"That's good to hear. It was good seeing you again. Hopefully, I'll see you both soon. We always appreciate the business." The bartender nodded his head to the couple and left them alone.

Alex stood up straight and spun Jana around, placing his hands on the bar behind her and locking her in. Then he leaned down and kissed her. Slowly, he moved his mouth to her neck. As her breathing intensified, he moved his lips to her ear and whispered, "Your place or mine?"

Unexpectedly, she pushed him away. "Not tonight, Alex." Then she walked away from him.

Alex stood there, stunned by her reaction. Why was she acting so strange? Something still wasn't sitting right. He again chose not to pursue it right then. It had been a good night. It wouldn't end the way he had planned with Jana, but he was going to leave on a good note. The situation with Jana would have to be resolved soon though.

TWENTY-SIX

The sound of the alarm clock startled Alex the next morning. He wasn't accustomed to waking up to its loud buzzing anymore. It had hardly been used since he lost his job and was something he would have to get used to again. The biggest thing Alex needed in his life was money. In order to get money, he needed to have a job. Mr. Jenson had been nice enough to give him another chance. He couldn't afford to blow it this time. He would need this job to last until he could finally graduate. Considering he still had a few months before he could even start back at school, the job would have to last for more than a year.

Alex arrived at the grocery store a little early. Mr. Jenson already had everything set for him to begin work. After signing all his paperwork and clocking in, Mr. Jenson took him around to introduce him to some of the new people that had started to work there while he was gone. There weren't too many new faces. The ones Alex did encounter were friendly enough. One new employee was someone Alex already knew. Her name was Stacy.

Stacy had graduated earlier in the spring. Alex was surprised to see her. Obviously, she hadn't put her degree in business management to good use just yet. The two employees greeted each other, but it wasn't long before Mr. Jenson rushed Alex to the back store room. There he let Alex know he was still going to be a stocker.

"Now, there have been a few changes," Mr. Jenson started to explain. "Some things have been moved to different areas. I'll send someone with you today so you can figure out where everything belongs. For now, I want you to load these boxes of canned soup on that flat cart. Someone will be with you shortly."

"I think I can handle that, Mr. Jenson," Alex said cheerfully.

"Good. It's nice to have you back," Mr. Jenson stated as he patted Alex on his back.

Loading the boxes wasn't as easy as Alex had remembered. The first few didn't seem to bother him, but the rest seemed to just get heavier and heavier. He realized he hadn't really lifted anything since he'd stopped working, except for a few women when he was completing a task for Jack. That didn't really count for much though. None of them seemed as heavy as the boxes were. He was sure they had been, though. His adrenaline had kept him from noticing how much each woman actually weighed. At least the job would help him get back in shape.

When he was about done, Stacy entered the storage area. "Mr. Jenson sent me to work with you today. I guess I'm supposed to show you where everything is now," she told him in a happy little way.

"I thought you were new here?" Alex pointed out with a confused look on his face. It didn't make much sense for Mr. Jenson to send a new employee to work with him on finding where everything was located.

Stacy laughed. "I'm not that new. I've been here for about a month. I helped move most of this stuff around. I know where everything is in the store."

"And you sound very proud of that little fact," he responded with a hint of sarcasm. "Okay, then show me where the soup aisle is located."

"Right this way," Stacy said as she turned on one heel and started for the double doors. Alex followed her while he pulled the cart filled with boxes.

They worked together emptying the boxes and stocking the shelves. The soup was still in the same aisle. It hadn't been moved at all. Stacy tried to tell Alex what items had been moved and where their new location was, but he wasn't following too well. Stacy was of average height and blonde. She seemed very smart, but her bubbly personality was almost too much for Alex to bear. How could anyone be that chipper all the time? Alex thought maybe a conversation about something serious might tone her down a notch or two. If not, then he might just have to add her to a list of possible victims for the final task. There was no way he could spend the next year working with her.

"So, how did you end up working here?" Alex asked her. "I figured most people that graduated from the college moved away from this place."

Her tone did change, slightly. "I planned to leave, but then my dad got sick. I can't leave my family right now."

"I'm sorry to hear that," Alex said, trying to sound sympathetic. Her dad and his illness might have just saved her. Alex would keep her off the list for now. He would just have to deal with working with her.

"Besides," she continued, getting chipper again, "if I'm here long enough, I may end up in Mr. Jenson's position. You know I have a degree in business management. Well, this is a business, and Mr. Jenson is the manager!"

Alex opened the last box of soup cans and said, "I don't think Mr. Jenson will give up his position too easily to you."

"Probably not, but he's old. I figure he's not far from retiring. When he does, I'll be right there!"

The subject was dropped. Stacy bounced right back from her sick dad to her bubbly self. Alex couldn't believe she was actually after Mr. Jenson's job. Maybe he should put her back on the list. There was no way he could stay here if she did become the boss. He made a mental note to start looking for another job if she did end up being the manager. Killing her wouldn't be a good idea, even though he was sure he wouldn't mind it. They were already linked to each other, and that wouldn't be a good situation for him. The thought of putting her out of her misery made him smile though.

Once the soup cans were stocked, Stacy escorted Alex up and down every aisle of the store. She pointed out what items had been moved and gave a brief explanation on the reason the items had been moved. They spent the whole day together. They even took their breaks at the same time. At the end of his long shift, Alex made his way alone to the office area to clock out. Mr. Jenson was standing outside his office, waiting.

"How was your first day back, Alex?" Mr. Jenson was leaning one shoulder against the wall with his arms crossed, smiling.

Alex gave him a stern look as he punched his employee number into the time clock. "This has been the longest day of my life."

Laughter poured from Mr. Jenson and filled the hallway. "What makes you say that?"

"Something tells me that since you're laughing, you know why." He turned to his boss and asked him, "Why did you put me with her today?"

As he continued to smile at his employee, Mr. Jenson told Alex, "It was my way of making you suffer for making me fire you. Besides, she may be your boss one day. You know she's planning to take my job, eventually."

"You know about that?"

"Of course I do," he assured Alex. "I have a few very loyal employees that tell me everything. Don't you worry about that though. I still have a few good years left in me." He pushed himself off the wall and put his hand on Alex's shoulder. "Now, you go home, and I'll see you tomorrow."

With that, Alex left work for the day. First, he went home and changed clothes. Next, he called his mom and told her he was coming for a visit. Mrs. Dorson was thrilled. She told him she would fix dinner for the three of them. Then, Alex left his apartment and drove to what was now his mom's house instead of his parents' house. The trip took longer than usual. He drove slowly because he was dreading the visit. When he finally arrived, he took a deep breath, put on a fake smile, and walked through the front door.

"Mom, I'm here," he shouted as he closed the door behind him. There was no one around in the living room.

A voice called from the kitchen. "I'm in the kitchen, honey!"

Alex could smell something wonderful as he approached the kitchen. It was something new, something unfamiliar. It didn't smell anything like a normal meal his mom would make, but it made his mouth water just the same. It had been a long time since he had eaten a home-cooked meal. He would probably eat pencil shavings as long as they were home-cooked.

It was a familiar sight to see his mom in the kitchen. She glanced up from the stove to smile at him. "Are you hungry?" she asked her son.

"Sure. What is it that you're cooking? I don't recognize the smell."

"It's a new recipe a friend of mine gave to me. It still has a few minutes left to simmer. Why don't you go see your sister? She's up in her room."

He sighed. "I guess I could go see what she's up to."

The initial contact with his mom went better than expected, but visiting with Jessica would be another story. She had been unpleasant during his last visit. He expected the same during this visit. Gently, he knocked on her door. At first, he received no response. After tapping again, the door finally opened. Jessica said nothing as she left the door and returned to her bed. Alex assumed it was okay for him to at least enter the room since she didn't slam the door in his face.

"How is everything, sis?" he casually asked her as he stood awkwardly in the middle of her bedroom.

Jessica glared at him. "Same as the last time you were here. Why are you here now? I figured you would stay away longer this time."

Even though he was trying to maintain a positive attitude, it was obvious she wasn't going to make it easy. "Can I sit with you?" he asked her. She agreed, and he took a seat on her bed. "I know I haven't been around here much. I plan to change that. I haven't totally avoided the whole situation, although I'm sure you think I have. I had lunch with Dad yesterday to see how things are going for him." It was partially true. He had gone to lunch with their dad, but it was to ask for money instead of wanting to know about his life.

"Did he tell you about his girlfriend?" Jessica asked in a slightly friendlier tone. "Did he tell you how old she is?"

With a chuckle, Alex responded, "Yes, he did. I didn't take it too well either."

Jessica smiled a little. "I didn't either. What else did he tell you?"

"There wasn't much. He said he was happy. I guess that's good for him, but I'm worried about you and Mom."

She shrugged and looked down at the floor. "I'll be okay, but I worry about Mom, too. She puts up a good front, but I don't buy into it as other people do. Everyone thinks she is being so strong through everything. I know better though. I heard her crying in her bedroom the other day. She doesn't know I heard her."

Alex wrapped his arm around his little sister and asked, "What can I do to help out more? How can I be supportive of you and Mom?"

Jessica looked deep into her brother's eyes and said, "You could always move back in with us." Her suggestion was obviously a surprise to Alex. When he didn't offer a response, she continued, "I know it would make Mom happy, and I wouldn't mind having you around again. I hated it when you left after the accident. I'm sure you could benefit from it, too."

"I don't know about all that, Jess," Alex said, removing his arm from her. This was definitely not on his list of things to accomplish in Jack's absence. "How would I benefit from it exactly?"

"Well," Jessica started, sounding confident in what she was going to say, "I know you haven't been working for a while now. If you move back in, you could get caught up on your bills. You could stay here rent-free through the rest of college and save some money to leave after you graduate. That sounds good, doesn't it?"

She looked so pleased with her argument that Alex didn't want to burst her bubble by flatly saying it wasn't enough to convince him to move back. "I guess that sounds like a good plan..."

"Good! We'll tell Mom over dinner!"

With that, Jessica sprang from the bed and darted out of the room. She didn't let him finish his sentence. He found himself in a real mess with no easy way out of it.

TWENTY-SEVEN

The public library was pretty busy with college students the day Detective Wynne decided to do a little side research. There was one table with four chairs that only had one occupant. Wynne sat at that table with a small stack of books in front of him. He flipped through an open book as he scanned the pages, looking for information he deemed important enough to write down on the yellow legal pad beside him. Even though the library was busy, Wynne was pleased the people were abiding by the silence rule. It allowed him to concentrate.

The books he had chosen were about Jack the Ripper. Most people in the United States had at least heard of the Jack the Ripper murders, though not many knew the facts of the cases, including Wynne. He figured it was time he learned about the subject the media had been referring to, especially since Bagster seemed to already know why people were comparing the murders. It was a well-known fact that the killer was never discovered. Wynne hoped that wouldn't be the outcome in this day and age.

As he absorbed the information each book held, Wynne noticed all the similarities between the victims of the Ripper and the victims he and Bagster had. The big difference was in the type of people the victims of this era were. The Ripper victims were mostly prostitutes, drunks, or thought to be both. Wynne wondered why the killer they were chasing was not following every detail if he was trying to copy the Ripper murders. The Ripper had supposedly sent two letters, and even organs, to the police in 1888, but none of this had been received by the police department this time around. One of the present-day victims had been missing a few organs, but nothing ever came out of that.

Even though some of the books hinted that there may have been more murders linked to Jack the Ripper than originally thought,

Wynne's detective skills weren't so sure about that. He wasn't out to prove anything about cases from the past, besides. He was only interested in the ones that matched the cases he had now. Particularly how many total murders were matched to Jack the Ripper. According to everything he read, it appeared there were five in all. Since he and Bagster had four bodies already, it was clear there would be at least one more. Wynne checked his notes to see if he could find a pattern or a clue about when the last murder might happen. Something did stand out, but he had to check his current cases to be sure he was correct.

After Wynne had gathered as much info as he could, he headed back to the station to compare his notes on the Ripper murders with the current cases. When he arrived at the station, he realized the drive there had seemed like a dream. His focus was on getting to his case files, not on the journey there. It was difficult, but Wynne managed to avoid all contact and conversation once he was inside the building. The elevator ride up to his desk on the third floor seemed longer than it ever had. When the doors finally slid open, he rushed out of the elevator and down the hall.

The office area Wynne shared with his fellow detectives was empty. He barely noticed the fact as he started to clutter his desk with case files. He pulled off his jacket, sat down in his chair, and leaned over his desk to begin comparing the past and the present. An hour had passed before he had even realized it. A familiar voice broke his deep concentration. With a glance up, he realized Bagster was sitting at his desk across from him.

"I asked what you are doing?" Bagster repeated, since he could tell Wynne hadn't heard a word he had said. He looked suspiciously at the papers and files that covered Wynne's desk.

Wynne glanced around the top of his desk and realized he had made a mess. "I'm just looking through the case files," he answered nonchalantly.

"For what?"

"For... similarities," he replied. "I went to the library this morning to learn about the Ripper murders like you suggested."

Bagster leaned forward to take a closer look at what his partner had on his desk. "Did you learn anything of use to us?"

Wynne glared at him and answered, "You know I did. You told me to learn about the Ripper murders. You knew these were copycat murders all along. Why didn't you say something earlier?"

"Actually," Bagster started as he leaned back, "I wasn't positive at first. Well, at least not a hundred percent." He paused for a moment before explaining what he meant. "When I was in college, I wrote a paper on the Ripper murders. Secretly, I hoped I would find the missing piece in my research to solve the mystery of who he was. Of course, I was young and dumb. But that was a long time ago. I had forgotten most of the details of those murders. I wasn't sure for a long time why these cases seemed so familiar until I heard a news report mention the Ripper."

"Why didn't you mention it then?" Wynne asked, still glaring at his partner.

Smiling, Bagster answered, "Because I was waiting for you to bring it up. You're the rookie here. You have to learn to think outside the box. I can't just hand everything to you."

A look of utter annoyance flashed across Wynne's face. "I'm not a rookie!" he said in a harsh tone. "I thought we were supposed to work together to solve these cases. How can we do that if you keep things from me and insist on playing games?"

Bagster shot straight up and looked Wynne dead in the eye. "I'm not playing games. I'm also not trying to hide anything from you. If I seriously thought this connection could help us catch this guy, then I would have been all over it. Did your little research project suddenly tell you who our man is?"

"No." Wynne shamefully hung his head as he said that single word. He hated when Bagster was right. "Why did you want me to learn about all of this then?"

"The more you learn about cases like this, the better you will get with your instincts." He backed off and leaned against the back of his chair. "Tell me what you learned during your trip to the library."

Scrambling to organize the mess on his desk, Wynne started, "Well, I see a lot of similarities, but only a few differences between the victims. I looked over Alicia's reports and compared the injuries from our victims to the Ripper victims. The killer has to be trying to mimic the Ripper murders, but he's not concerned with every small detail."

"How so?"

"Cuts on the faces don't match up exactly. Just little things like that. Plus, whoever the Ripper was had made contact with the police and such with letters. He had even sent part of a human organ with one of the letters. Part of a kidney I believe." Wynne started rustling through his papers, looking for something. "Now, our guy did take some organs from one of our victims, but he didn't send anything to us or the press. But there is something I want to show you once I find it." He rustled some more before pulling out a yellow paper from a legal pad. "Here it is."

"What is it?" Bagster inquired as he leaned across his desk.

Wynne leaned farther across his desk to show Bagster the paper's contents. He used his pen to point to the two sets of matching numbers on the paper as he explained what each number meant. "There's not much info on here, but as you can see, the numbers in each column match, except the last one."

"Are these dates?" Bagster asked.

"Yes," Wynne said, smiling. "The left column represents the dates each of the Ripper victims were found. The third date, of course, had two victims. The column on the right is when our victims were found. The third one had two victims."

"So, you are trying to tell me we will have our fifth and final victim on this bottom date?" Bagster couldn't believe he hadn't made that connection himself. Was his memory of the Ripper murders so cloudy? With a nod of affirmation from Wynne, Bagster stated, "That date is only a couple of weeks away."

"I know," Wynne replied with a glow on his face. He had pointed out something important that Bagster hadn't already known. He was quite proud of himself. "The only thing I'm not sure of is if this will indeed be the last murder."

"What do you mean? There were only five that could be definitely linked to the Ripper."

"You're right, but what if our guy tries to go ahead with the ones that may or may not be a part of the Ripper case?"

"I doubt he will, but I guess anything is possible." Bagster stood up. "I need some coffee. Do you want some?"

Wynne nodded again and returned his attention to his stacks of paper and files. He searched for anything that would stand out while Bagster went for coffee in the break room. Nothing seemed to be grabbing his attention. The murders were being followed closely, but everything else was being left out. Letters could betray fingerprints. Envelopes could reveal DNA. Both would be a huge help to them in finding their man. Wynne figured that was why the letters had been left out. No one knew for absolute sure they came from the Ripper anyway.

"Do you know what I think we should do?" Bagster asked, setting a coffee cup down on Wynne's desk.

"Thank you," Wynne said, accepting the coffee. "What should we do?"

"I think we should not worry about the other murders right now," he said, sitting back down in his desk chair. "I think we need to figure out a way to stop the fifth one from happening if we can."

"How do we do that?"

Reaching into his jacket, Bagster pulled out a stack of small papers and said, "We start with these. Your idea to run a video of our killer on the news has brought in a bunch of tips. Do you feel like hitting the streets for a while to check some of these out?"

With a big grin on his face, Wynne stood up and grabbed his jacket from the back of his chair. "Let's go!"

TWENTY-EIGHT

"Alex."

Alex squirmed a little in his bed. The sound of his name being called only stirred him slightly from his deep sleep. He wasn't sure if he had even heard it, or if he had dreamed it.

"Alex."

"What?" he mumbled once it was clear he had heard it. Rolling over and sitting up, he opened his eyes to see who called his name. He snapped awake when he realized he was alone. Alex plopped back down and said, "Hello, Jack. You made it back." The sarcasm in his voice couldn't be missed.

"You seem unhappy to hear from me. I told you I would return."

With a sigh, Alex slid his feet off the bed and onto the floor as he sat up. "It's not that I'm unhappy to hear from you. Since you are here, that means it must be about time to finish up our business. I just wish you could have waited a couple more hours to show up." He stood up and walked to the bathroom. When he returned, he explained, "This is my day off from work. It would have been nice to sleep in a little today."

"I apologize, Alex, but we do have business to attend to," Jack said as Alex went to the kitchen to start the coffee pot. "We only have two days until the final task. I must get you prepared to complete it."

"Get me prepared?" Alex retorted. He leaned against the kitchen counter and crossed his arms. "I suppose you want me to go cut up another deer carcass or something. I think I can skip that step now."

"Tell me, Alex, have you been able to return to your normal life in my absence?"

"Are you trying to change the subject now?" Jack was beginning to irritate him already.

"No. Tell me how things are for you now."

Alex didn't answer. Instead, he went to the living room and sat down in the spot on the couch he hadn't occupied since Jack had left. "Yes, Jack, my life is back to normal. There are a few problems here and there, but nothing I can't handle. I'm back to work. I have made amends with family and friends. I feel pretty good about my life now. I just need you gone from it."

"That time is near. I do wonder if you had the desire to continue on with your own tasks after I was gone."

"At first," he admitted. "I didn't feel the need to complete more tasks, but I did continue to seek out ideal victims."

"Did that eventually change?" Jack inquired.

"It has slowed down," he admitted. "I don't view every woman as a candidate, but I still find myself seeking 'the perfect one' from time to time."

Jack was silent for a moment. "I am pleased to hear that, Alex. I want to get you in the right mindset for the last task, but I do not want the mindset to stay with you. This last task will be different from the other ones. That is why I must prepare you. Are the problems you are having in your life going to get in the way?"

Standing up and going to the kitchen, Alex answered as he went for his first cup of coffee. "No. They won't get in the way."

"Good," Jack said, sounding pleased. "Our deal still stands. You complete this last task to my satisfaction with my instruction, and then I will go away forever. If not, I will be with you until it is done. I can be with you forever if you fail me. I can slowly drive you mad. I don't want that any more than you do. So time is of the essence. Drink your coffee and get dressed. There is much to do."

Doing as he was told, Alex took what would be his only cup of coffee to his bedroom to get ready. It was unclear what Jack had planned for him. He'd figured the last task would probably be a big one. He hadn't known he would have to be prepared for it. Regardless, as long as he could get through it, Jack would leave for good.

The previous weeks without Jack had been strange to Alex, but he had gotten used to the absence. Things had been going well. There were still some unresolved issues with Jana. She had continued to behave strangely toward him. It was almost like there was a wall between them that he hadn't been able to penetrate. They weren't spending any more time together than they had before Jack had left. Alex vowed to make things better with Jana, but it would take more of an effort than he had imagined.

Then there was the issue with his mom and Jessica. Jessica had told their mom he would be moving back. Once Alex saw his mom's excitement and saw how it matched Jessica's, he couldn't bring himself to disappoint them. Deep down he knew it would help his family if they could all be together, with the exception of his dad, but it would cost him his independence. He had managed to stall the move for a few months. He knew Jack would be back, and it would be better for Alex to be alone when he returned.

Once Alex was dressed, Jack informed him it was time to leave. The first thing on the agenda was to try to find the perfect location, and then the perfect subject for the task. Jack wanted to get Alex back in the mode of a predator. Alex had shown he had the ability to pick out good targets. This time would be different though. The last victim would have to come with certain features. He was unaware of this as he drove around waiting for Jack to instruct him where to go.

An hour had passed before Jack finally instructed Alex to pull into a parking lot outside an apartment building downtown. "I don't like being in the downtown area, Jack," Alex said as he parked the car. "The last time I was here the whole area was crawling with police."

"I agree. It was busy with the police officers at that time. You have committed two murders here, Alex. Things are different now," Jack stated.

"How are they different?"

Jack laughed slightly. "My dear boy, you made things different by committing the next two murders far away from here. I wanted you downtown, but you went elsewhere. The police have no clue where you might strike again."

The parking lot was only about half full. Alex seemed to be the only one in a vehicle. "Why are we here in this parking lot? You know it is November now. It's kind of cold. I hope we aren't going to be here long."

"Yes, I know it is November," Jack replied. "How long we will be here will depend on you and your hunting skills."

"My hunting skills? I'm not doing the task today, so what am I supposed to be hunting for?"

"The last task will involve much," Jack started to explain. "It will take more time than the previous tasks. Since you will need more time, you will also need more privacy. You need to not only find your ideal woman, but you also need to find your ideal place. My suggestion is a female that lives alone in an apartment or house. You will start here. If you are not satisfied with what we find here, then we will move on to another location."

This time Alex laughed. "So we are basically on a stakeout. This is just great. How long are we going to be doing this?"

"Until you find the right one. Time is short. The task needs to be completed tomorrow night. So, please, do not be too finicky."

"I thought I had two days!" Alex shouted.

"Yes, today and tomorrow. Tomorrow night is not included in that."

"But I have to work tomorrow!"

"Then I suggest you be quick," Jack said calmly.

Anger quickly filled Alex's body. Jack was asking too much in too little time. There was no way he could find the perfect woman and learn if she lived alone in the time frame he had been given. Jack had to be toying with him. He kept his mouth shut though. For the time being, he would play along with Jack's insane request. So, Alex waited and waited in his car in the cold November weather. As hours passed, his blood started to boil more.

"Jack, this is ridiculous!" Alex shouted. "I've been here for hours and nothing has even looked promising."

"Then we need to move on to another location," Jack suggested.

Even though his frustration with Jack was growing, Alex followed his instruction and drove to a different apartment building downtown. "I have one problem with this one, Jack."

"What is the problem?"

"There is a police station a few blocks from here."

"It will be fine," Jack assured him. "They will not be looking so close to their headquarters. This may work out perfectly."

"Maybe, but I'm still nervous about being this close to the enemy," Alex said as he looked around nervously.

"Well, well. Take a gander at the young lady entering that ground-floor apartment. She may be the one," Jack said, drawing Alex's attention to a young blonde woman.

Sitting straight up in the driver's seat, Alex frantically tried to locate the woman Jack was referring to. He spotted her just as she opened the door to the apartment. She stepped inside and shut the door. Alex hit his hands on the steering wheel. "I barely saw her!"

"It is okay, Alex. Just stay put for a while and see what happens."

An hour passed with no one else arriving at the apartment. Alex hoped this was a sign the young woman lived by herself, but he couldn't be sure just yet. Another hour passed and, still, no one else showed up. Alex could feel his eyelids growing heavy. He was getting tired from boredom. Jack had been silent during the long wait. Before he could nod off, he was snapped alert by the door to the apartment opening. He watched as the young woman stepped outside and shut the door. She locked her door and walked toward her car.

"What do you think of her?" Jack asked, finally breaking the long silence.

Alex shrugged and said, "She's okay. I think she will do. She is about average height and has a small build. That means I can handle her just fine. So far, I haven't seen anyone else go into the apartment."

"Good," Jack said. "Go get yourself something to eat. You must be starving. Afterward, we will return to keep watch for a while longer. If all goes well with our pretty young lady, we will return tomorrow night to pay her a visit."

Alex started his car and backed out of the parking spot. As he drove off, he said, "That sounds good to me, Jack. One more day and night with you, then you'll be gone. I was kind of hoping for a brunette for my last task, not a blonde. I'm not sure why though. Just a preference thing I guess."

"I think she is perfect."

"If you say so, Jack. I thought I was supposed to be the hunter, but you were the hunter this time," Alex pointed out sarcastically.

"As I said, I think she is perfect."

TWENTY-NINE

The hours seemed to tick by slower than usual at work for Alex. His mind definitely wasn't on stocking canned vegetables. Jack had said the last task would involve more than the previous ones. Originally, Alex hadn't given much thought to the statement, but now he found himself constantly wondering about what the final task entailed. Alex supposed it really didn't matter what the statement meant. His life was back on track. If he could get rid of Jack by finishing this last task that loomed over him, then he would do whatever Jack asked of him.

Alex was in the back storage area of the grocery store stacking more boxes of canned vegetables when Stacy barged in the double swinging doors.

"Alex," she called to him in her chipper voice.

A chill of irritation ran down his spine as he stood up straight to answer her. "What is it, Stacy?" he asked coldly.

She approached him and said, "Mr. Jenson wants to see you before you leave today. He wanted me to find you before I left."

"Thank you, Stacy. I'll go find him in a little bit," he replied with his tone still cold. He watched as she turned on her heel and pranced back out the swinging doors.

"Annoying, isn't she?"

The voice caught Alex off guard. He had been so caught up in his own thoughts he hadn't realized there was someone else in the storage area with him. He looked over to see a fellow employee rummaging through a stack of boxes. The man had a clipboard, so Alex assumed he was taking inventory. "Yes. She can be from time to time," he agreed with a chuckle.

Not wanting to carry on a conversation with the man, Alex took his flat cart from the storage area out into the store. As he cut open the boxes and started to stock the shelves with French-style green beans, his mind started to wander back to the plans he had for that night. He was pleased Jack had left him alone at work. That was something he hadn't done before, which usually drove Alex crazy. The time alone was much appreciated, but he knew Jack would be back as soon as work ended. He wondered if Jack would allow him some more time alone before the task so he could go to Jana's apartment.

Since he had always secluded himself and sunk into a slight depression after the previous tasks, Alex figured he had better prepare for that to happen again. The last time hadn't bothered him too badly, but some time had passed. Anything could happen after this one. With things being so rocky with Jana, he knew it would only be worse if he disappeared again for days. They already hadn't seen each other in a couple of days. It wasn't worth paying the long-term price to make that break even longer.

At the end of his shift, Alex clocked out and went on the hunt for Mr. Jenson. It took a while, but he located him in the frozen food section. He approached him and told Mr. Jenson his shift was up. "Stacy said I should find you before I left."

"Yes," Mr. Jenson said. "I'll walk you to the door."

As the two began walking through the store, Alex inquired, "Did I do something wrong, Mr. Jenson?"

Mr. Jenson laughed and patted him on the back. "No, you didn't do anything wrong. It's quite the opposite. You have been doing an excellent job since you've been back."

"Thank you," Alex said with a hint of confusion in his words.

"What I wanted to talk to you about was a head position in your area. I need someone to oversee all the stockers. Are you interested in a managerial position?"

The shock was written all over Alex's face. "I don't know. This is completely unexpected. I haven't been back that long. Are you sure I'm the one you want to be talking to? What about Stacy?"

Mr. Jenson laughed again. "Are you kidding? Stacy is after my job, remember? If I even considered her, which I wouldn't, her head would get too big for her body! She may have some sort of business degree, but that doesn't mean she can handle people. You know how things run in your position. Your coworkers seem to like you." The two men stopped by the front entrance. Mr. Jenson turned to Alex and suggested, "At least think about it for a day or two."

"I'll think about it," Alex assured him with a smile.

"Good. Now get out of here. Go enjoy your evening. We'll talk about it more later."

On the way home, Alex thought about the new position he had been offered. Things were improving for him. He felt proud that Mr. Jenson had that kind of confidence in him. Of course, the position wouldn't be a lifelong thing, but Alex felt it could be a learning experience for him. The extra money wouldn't hurt either. Maybe after he moved back home, he could save some of that extra money and finally get a decent car. Then he could start saving again to move away. Maybe a new position and the move home was just what he needed.

"Are you heading home?" Jack asked, interrupting Alex's thoughts, again.

"Yes, Jack, I am," Alex replied with a sigh. "I have something I need to take care of later, before the task. Do you think you could give me some privacy later?"

"I suppose you are going to see Jana," Jack stated. "I guess I can take leave of you for a while. Will you be long? We really need to get to our destination shortly after nightfall."

"We have plenty of time. I won't be long," Alex promised. "Thank you, Jack." There was no response, only silence.

When Alex arrived home, he took a hot shower. He put on a pair of black jeans and a pair of black work boots. Then, he put on a plain white T-shirt and tucked it into his jeans. To keep his hair contained and out of his face, he wore a low ponytail. As he fixed something to eat in the kitchen, he called for Jack. Alex felt they needed to touch on a few things before he left for Jana's apartment.

"Yes, Alex," Jack answered.

"I'm confused about something, Jack. You said you needed to get me prepared for tonight's task. So far, all we have done is pick a person and a place. What else needs to be done?" He flipped a grilled cheese sandwich out of a pan and onto a plate. Then he started rummaging through his cabinets for some potato chips.

"Well," Jack started, "I considered preparing you for tonight's activities, but I believe that will not be necessary. You just enjoy your time with Jana. I will return once you have arrived at the destination downtown."

"So that's it?" he asked while he pulled a bag of chips out of a cabinet. He took the plate and the bag and went to the living room. Once again, he sat in the usual spot on the couch.

"Yes, that is it for now. We will talk later."

"All right. Thanks again for the private time, Jack." Alex thanked him again because he wasn't sure if Jack had heard him earlier. Again, there was no response.

The night ahead really didn't cross Alex's mind as he drove to Jana's apartment. The air outside was getting colder as the sun crept closer to the horizon. There would be a couple of hours to spend with Jana before he had to be downtown. That would be enough time to spend with her. He hoped it would be anyway. She hadn't been very demanding of his time, and that actually worried him. Deep down, he knew if he disappeared for any longer than a week, she would probably be gone for good. He just wasn't willing to take that chance. She was too important to him.

He parked his car in a spot in front of her apartment. When he got out, Alex zipped up his black jacket to block the cold wind from slicing through his thin shirt. He shoved his hands into the pockets in his jeans and headed for Jana's apartment door. Her car was in the parking area, so he knew she was home. He pulled one hand out of a pocket and knocked on her door. The wind was hitting him right in the face, so he turned to shield himself as he shoved his hand back in his pocket. When Jana didn't answer, he was forced to pull out his hand again to knock.

Finally, the door opened. Alex turned toward her with a smile, but she looked very surprised to see him. His smile faded.

"Alex," she said, sounding even more surprised. "What are you doing here?"

Immediately, Alex sensed a strange vibe coming from her. They had been together for years. He knew all too well how to pick up on her vibes. This one was different from any other he had felt from her. "I wanted to see you. Can I come in for a few? It is pretty cold out here."

Jana hesitated for a moment, but she finally moved back to allow him to enter. She shut the door and said, "Alex, I don't think you should be here."

He looked at her, puzzled. Rubbing his hands together to warm them, he asked, "Why not?"

Jana backed away from him and went to stand behind a chair on the other side of the room. With a little shakiness in her voice, she said, "I've been seeing things on the news. Security camera pictures and videos."

"Okay," he said, not understanding. "What does this have to do with me being here?" He started to walk toward her but he saw her jump a little at his movement. "Are you afraid of me? Why are you so jumpy?"

Jana started to tear up. Her eyes were restless, darting from corner to corner, so she wouldn't have to look at him. "I'm guessing you haven't seen the news. They are showing the person who is a suspect in the murders that have happened." She sounded so nervous talking to him. Finally, she looked directly at Alex. "It's you, Alex. I know it's you. How could you do something like that?"

Alex felt like someone had just punched him in the gut. She knew. And, worse, she was afraid of him. She had never been afraid of him. He looked at her and was unsure of how to respond. He did need to know something though. "What makes you think it was me?"

"I know you, Alex. I know how you walk, how you carry yourself," she started. "In one video, you had that baseball cap you wear every so often. I couldn't clearly see your face, but I know it was you. It IS you!"

He wanted so badly to deny it, to deny everything. He started to go to her without saying anything. She still jumped at his movements and shook her head no. Stopping in his tracks, he started speaking: "Jana, I'm sorry. I'm sorry I am scaring you. I have never wanted that." After retreating toward the door, he turned and grabbed the door handle and stopped. He slowly turned to face her. "I'll fix this. I'll fix all of this. Everything I do is for you, Jana." He opened the door and stepped back out into the cold.

He got in his car and slammed the door shut. Quickly, he started the engine and sped away, leaving Jana's apartment behind. As Alex drove his car with no set destination in mind, he started to lose the stunned feeling. It was replaced by the worst pain he had ever felt. His heart felt like it was on the verge of an explosion. He couldn't believe he had messed up so bad and she discovered his secret. Everything he had done up to that moment had been done for her so they could have a normal life together again. Now that probably would never happen. Would she turn him in? Did anyone else know it was him? The biggest question that kept running through his mind was how was he supposed to stop the horrible ache that not only pierced through his heart but his whole body at the same time.

There were no answers to that question. Alex knew the agony would last for an eternity. He drove around for the couple of hours he had planned to spend with Jana. A few tears were shed during that time, but he refused to allow too many to fall. Desperately, he tried to bury his feelings. Jana or no Jana, he still needed to be rid of Jack. In order to complete the last task, Alex had to have a clear mind. He worked on composing himself as the time grew near. One more task, then he could spend forever in peace with his broken heart and his shame.

THIRTY

Alex couldn't remember the drive from Jana's apartment to the parking lot where he lurked downtown. There had been too many thoughts running through his mind. He just couldn't seem to grasp how he had been so careless. The shattering of his heart and soul seemed as real as anything, but his mind was trying very hard to convince him it had only been a bad dream. It didn't matter at that moment what had happened at Jana's apartment. Alex knew he needed to pull himself together to get through the night that lay ahead of him. He only needed a few minutes more before he could accomplish that.

"I am truly sorry, Alex," Jack said, trying to sound sympathetic.

"For what, Jack?" Alex asked as he cleared his throat. He fidgeted in his seat and quickly tried to act like everything was fine. After a quick glance at himself in the rearview mirror, he started to focus on the apartment he would be entering that evening.

"I am sorry about the situation with Jana," Jack replied.

Alex rubbed his face roughly with his hands then ran them through his hair. Finally, he asked, "How do you know anyway? I thought you were giving me some privacy tonight?"

"I did, as I said I would," he answered. "I can tell what you are feeling. I can tell what is going on with you. I just hope you can keep it together enough to get this last task completed tonight."

"Did you know about the cameras, Jack? Did you set me up? I thought you didn't want me to get caught!" The more Alex talked, the more aggravated he became.

"I did not know about the cameras. Nor did I want you to be found out," Jack firmly assured him. "Alex, you must put this evening and everything that has happened aside."

"I'll be fine. This will probably help keep my mind off the whole thing anyway, at least I hope." Alex wanted to forget about everything, and he wanted to forget about Jack. The task would help with both on the same night. "So, explain to me what your plan is for tonight."

"Our lady friend has not yet arrived home for the evening. We need to be patient and wait for her. Once she is home, you will wait a while longer," Jack told him. "Then you will exit your vehicle, when you feel the time is right, and approach the door. You have to gain access to her home. Do you have a plan on how to accomplish that?"

That was a problem he had hoped Jack had an answer for, so he could just go do it. Of course, that would have been too easy. "I don't know how to accomplish that. Let me think about that for a while. As you said, she isn't even home yet."

"As you wish, my dear boy. I have a plan for the rest of the night, but I want to see if you can come up with a logical plan to get inside."

The harder Alex tried to formulate a plan on how to gain access to the downstairs apartment, the more his mind wandered back to Jana and what she knew. For some reason, he felt as though she was watching, judging him, as he schemed to take the life of another woman. It seemed that every ten seconds he was forcing himself to redirect his thoughts to the task at hand. Several ideas came to him on how to get to his target, but these ideas were left uncompleted. It was going to be hard to finish his final task. But it had to be done somehow. Nothing was distracting enough to keep him from completing this last obstacle to rid himself of Jack.

Finally, Alex was forced to focus on his duties for the night. The pretty young blonde had arrived home. He had to formulate a plan. He'd thought of a few promising ideas, but those were gone now. The lower-level apartment wouldn't be easy to break into. Since it was part of a tall building, there were plenty of apartments and people nearby to catch him. It suddenly occurred to him that there were plenty of neighbors to hear her if she screamed. Handling tasks outside made him nervous, but this one was making him downright shaky. Killing her wouldn't be the problem. He was used to that part. Cutting her up didn't bother him either. The blood, the smell, and the feel of organs didn't bother him anymore. But breaking into someone's home and keeping them from screaming bothered him.

"Jack, you are going to have to help me out here," Alex said as he tucked his ponytail into the baseball cap Jana had mentioned. "I can't seem to think straight. How do I get inside? I'm drawing a blank here."

"That is why I asked you about your plans to gain access to the apartment ahead of time. Perhaps you can just knock on the door and ask her if you can come in to chat."

Alex let out a sigh as he rolled his eyes. "That's your idea? I'm sure she will be more than happy to invite me in, and maybe she will offer me a drink too!"

"Well, I doubt that Alex, but I do not think there are many other options available to you. The number of windows is limited, and I am almost positive they are locked securely. She does live alone. You will have to get her to open the door for you."

"I don't like that idea though, Jack. She's not going to let me in there."

"You are right. Once the door is open, you will have to force your way in," Jack informed him. "It is the fastest, easiest, and quietest way to accomplish your entrance. Think about that for a while. She just arrived home. We should allow her a little time to get comfortable before you approach the door."

"All right, you tell me when I should go," Alex said. "I still don't like this plan, but I can't think straight enough to come up with anything else right now."

"I know, Alex. Everything will be fine once you are inside the apartment," Jack assured him.

Time passed slowly. Before long, the lights inside the apartment went out. "Did we wait too long?" Alex asked, hoping he hadn't missed his opportunity.

Jack responded, "No. Wait just a little longer. The darkness inside will be to your advantage."

Alex started to get nervous. He wasn't nervous about performing the task, just nervous about getting inside to do the task. His gut kept telling him one thing while Jack kept telling him something else. As his mind shot through ideas of what to say when the woman opened her door, Jack instructed him to go to the door. Alex got out of his car and shut the door. Slowly, he started across the parking lot. Knots twisted inside his stomach. A couple of times, he stopped and turned to go back to his car. Jack convinced him each time to continue to the door by reminding Alex of what would happen if he didn't complete this last task. It had to be tonight.

It was tough, but Alex finally found himself standing at the door. There was no turning back now. He knocked on the door.

"Get her to her bedroom first, Alex," Jack ordered. "This will be easier for you if she is in her bedroom."

The door opened. There in front of Alex was the woman he had been watching. She wasn't too short. She wasn't too tall. This was a relief for him. For a moment, he did lose his focus. The woman was very attractive with her long blonde hair and gray eyes. He also couldn't help but notice the small baby blue shirt she was wearing with a pair of extremely short shorts. When his eyes finally made their way back up to hers, he suddenly remembered his purpose. The look she was giving him was of utter displeasure at the way he had examined her.

"Can I help you with something?" she asked sharply with one hand on the door handle and the other on her hip.

"Uh," Alex stammered. "I'm looking for a friend of mine. He said this was his apartment." He looked at the letter on the door. He pointed at it and laughed slightly. "This is so embarrassing." He flashed a big smile, but it didn't seem to faze the young woman a bit. "Maybe you know my friend. His name is Tony." It was the first name to pop into his head.

"No, I don't," she answered flatly.

"Okay. I'm sorry to have bothered you." He turned slightly like he was going to leave, but he didn't. He turned back and said, "Would it be possible for me to use your phone, just for a minute? Tony will kill me if I don't show up, but I evidently don't know where he lives."

"No. You can't use my phone. There's a pay phone about a block away," she snapped, and then she started to slam the door.

Alex quickly shoved his boot in between the door and the jamb. His friendly smile turned into an evil little smirk. It was clear by the look on her face she knew she was in trouble. The young woman stumbled back as Alex pushed his way through the door. He shut the door behind him quietly so it wouldn't draw any attention from the neighbors.

With terror filling her eyes, she asked, "What do you want?"

The apartment was dark, but the outside lights lit the room enough for him to see her eyes. This was the first time he had been face-to-face with a victim after she knew something was wrong. The woman at the nightclub had been the only other one he had talked to, but once he pulled her into the alley, he turned her away so quickly he couldn't see her reaction. This was new. His final victim looked at him in horror as she trembled from head to toe. At first, the eye-to-eye contact was strange, but he soon realized he liked the fact she was terrified of him. He suddenly felt in control, which was something he hadn't felt in a very long time.

"What do you want?" she screamed.

In response, Alex pulled his trusty knife out of his jacket. When the outside lights flashed across the blade, the woman jumped and let out a gasp. This pleased him even more. "I want you to keep quiet. Do you understand?" He showed her the knife again. When she nodded, Alex said, "Go to your bedroom." She didn't move at first. "Go!" he yelled.

The young woman jumped at the sound of his voice. She hurried to her bedroom with Alex following behind her. His grin never faltered as he followed her through the small apartment. Since he had made it inside and all was going well, he seemed to be letting his darker side take over, and he liked it. He was positive he would enjoy whatever Jack wanted him to do, but he planned to have a little fun with his newfound fun factor, being in control. Once they were both inside her bedroom, Alex continued with his mischievous thoughts as he closed the door behind him.

THIRTY-ONE

"Alex!" shouted Jack. "It is time to get to work. End this now!"

Alex chuckled as he stood at the end of his prey's bed, playing with his knife and watching her reactions. "Come on, Jack. I'm just having a little fun." The reaction on the woman's face reminded him that no one could hear Jack but him. "Don't worry. I'm not crazy. I know you can't hear Jack, but that's okay because I can. That's what's important."

The woman jumped when Alex moved quickly to the side of her bed. She tried to hurry away from him as he sat down beside her. Her twin-sized bed was squished right into the corner of the room and left her little space to get away from him. Alex placed his hand on the bed behind her. He felt her body tighten up against his arm.

He smiled down at her. "I can't let you get away. You are too important to me right now. And, I can't play around with you anymore. Jack is getting impatient with me." He placed his knife close to her throat. She winced as she pushed her head back into the pillow under her. "So, even though I hate to do this right now, I must." With those words, he quickly ripped his knife across her throat, digging it deep into her flesh. Then he watched as blood spewed from the opening he had made in her neck. He watched, and listened, to her slowly die.

"Thank you, Alex. Now we can proceed with the task at hand," said Jack in a calmer voice. "I do believe this will go well if you keep your mind on the prize."

"What prize?" Alex inquired as he stood and started to straighten out the girl's limp body on the bed.

"Us parting ways, remember?"

"Ah, yes. I remember. That is all I have to look forward to now but it's still worth it," answered Alex. "So what's first?"

"Remove all of her clothing."

With a sly smirk on his face, he agreed to do that. It didn't happen as easily as he thought it would though. Her deadweight caused problems for him. Once her lower half was bare, he decided to just cut her shirt from her body to save himself the hassle of removing it over her head and dealing with her arms. He rolled her body from side to side to remove the shirt from under her back. Then he stood up again, put his hands on his hips, and took a couple of deep breaths. Something that sounded like fun had actually turned out to be hard work.

"Very good," Jack stated. "Are you ready to begin? There is much to do."

"I think so."

Jack started to give directions to Alex as he sat back down on the bed next to the naked body. Alex worked as fast as he could while Jack told him in detail what to do. He cut open her abdomen, just like he had done before, but this time he removed the skin and tissue in three large sections and laid each piece carefully on the bed next to her. Making precise cuts as before, Alex worked hard to remove the organs from the abdominal cavity. Normally, he only removed certain things from the victim, but it appeared Jack wanted more this time. Each warm, slimy organ was removed carefully and placed in different areas around the room. It seemed to take more time than he anticipated. When Jack finally told him to stop, her abdominal cavity was empty.

"That wasn't so bad," Alex commented as he looked around the room at what he had accomplished.

Jack informed him, "You are not done, my good man. There is plenty more to do yet."

Alex stood up and removed the hat that had been holding his hair. He rubbed his arm across his forehead. "What more do you want me to do? She's basically empty."

"I told you this would be more involved than the others. Please put your hat back on, Alex."

"Fine," he said flatly as placed the hat back on his head. He didn't place his ponytail back in it though. "Can I take a break for a minute to clear my head a little?"

"Yes, you may take a short break. Be quick though. We do not know how much time we actually have."

Storming out of the bedroom, Alex went to the kitchen of the small apartment. He took a chair from a small table and went back to the bedroom. Alex placed the chair by the foot of the bed at an angle where he could sit and look upon his masterpiece. The cover on the bed was turning a deep crimson. The only part that betrayed the true color ran along the bottom of the bed just above the floor. His victim's organs were placed all around the room, surely cold by now. To Alex, these organs represented him being one step closer to freedom.

"Okay, Jack," he said as he stood and stretched. "What else do you possibly want me to do to this poor girl?"

"Is the task getting to you?"

"Not at all, which is weird. Just tell me what to do next." Nothing was bothering him about what he had done. Nothing at all. He had grown used to the sight of blood, the feel of the insides of the human body through his gloves, and even the strange smells.

Jack wasted no time giving orders to Alex once he was back on the bed. It shocked Alex to learn that he would be moving on to other parts of the body this time. This he wasn't used to, but he was sure he could handle it. The first thing Jack ordered him to do was to remove the skin from the woman's left thigh. This was a struggle for Alex. He lifted the right leg and pushed it out so the inner thigh was accessible. The left leg was also bent and pushed out to the other side so it was not in the way. He had never skinned anything in his life, but he managed to slice into the upper part of the inner thigh and work his way down with a rough sawing motion. The thick layer of skin slid off the muscle underneath once Alex reached the area above the knee. Next, Jack wanted the muscle removed from the same leg. Once again, Alex had to work at it, but in the end, he had removed most of the thigh muscle easier than the skin. Only the bone remained.

Alex returned to the chair when he was done. He started to think about what he was doing. "What is the point of all of this?"

"Time is running short, Alex. You must keep going. We will talk later," Jack told him.

After a moment, Alex returned to bed. Jack instructed him in what he wanted. "I want to see more of her bone on that left leg. Then the same on the left thigh." Alex did as he was told. He carved deep into the thigh tissue and muscle over and over again until he felt his knife hit the bone. It took a while, but Alex finally removed a large portion of meat from her right thigh in one piece. Her femur had been fully exposed. It wasn't as clean and creamy in color as expected, already stained with the girl's blood and turning a brownish color. This sight made Alex pause for a moment.

Next, he was instructed to remove both of the young woman's breasts. When he asked why, Jack explained that her heart needed to be removed, which made little sense to Alex. Removing the left one might help him access her heart, if that was what Jack wanted, but the right one had nothing to do with it. He didn't see the point in asking any more questions though. Jack would probably just yell at him, and he was getting too tired to hear it. A few hours had already passed, and Alex didn't think he was close to being done. The size of his knife wasn't helping matters either. A larger one would have been more practical for such a large job, but it was a bit late now.

Once each small breast was removed and placed on the table next to the bed, Alex carefully ran the blade of his knife along her breastbone. He used the tip of the knife to loosen the skin and tissue from the bone, just enough for him to get his fingers under the flap and start tearing it from the rib cage. One by one, he broke some of the ribs over the heart. This was not as easy as Alex thought it would be, as there was rib meat and tissue holding each rib firmly in place. After a period of time, he had managed to free the unbeating heart from its protective cage, and Jack told him to retrieve a plastic container from the kitchen for its safekeeping.

"Why do I need to keep her heart safe?" This puzzled Alex.

"It will be going with you when you leave."

Alex pretty much figured that. Why else would he need a container for it? He didn't ask why he was taking it. Taking organs from a victim had been done before on Jack's orders. These organs were now in wooded areas for the wild animals. When Alex returned to the bedroom with the container and lid, he gently placed the heart inside and sealed it. After he sat the heart by the bedroom door, Alex was ready for the next part. He knew the end had to be drawing near because there couldn't be much left for him to do to the young woman.

"What's left, Jack?" he asked. "I'm ready to get out of here."

"Good. No more breaks then," replied Jack. "Her face is the next step. Complete that, and you will be almost finished with her."

He knew he was close to losing Jack. The time had just about come to be rid of him. Alex lifted the kitchen chair and put it beside the bed as close to the woman's head as possible. He turned her face toward him. Leaning forward on his elbows, he rested his upper body on the bed. He wanted one last look at her before he finished doing whatever it was Jack would tell him to do. Her features had changed already. Over the hours, her face had started to swell and had become discolored. Her mouth was slightly open. The pinkish color of her lips had turned to a deep purple. He could see his reflection in her eyes. They had turned to glass—colorless and foggy. He couldn't remove his gaze from their mirror-like nature. He felt like he could really see himself for the first time in months, see what he had done.

"Alex," Jack called to him.

"Her eyes..." Alex whispered softly.

"Alex, I need you to focus."

"I can't do this anymore, Jack," Alex muttered.

"Yes, you can!" Jack screamed with frustration.

Alex stood up without breaking eye contact with the dead eyes on the bed. "I'm sorry, Jack, but I can't finish this." He finally broke free from the hold her eyes had on him. He went to the living room.

Jack became harsh in tone. "Do you realize the consequences of your actions?"

"I have to think for a minute," Alex whispered as he paced back and forth with his fingers on his temples. He obviously wasn't talking to Jack, but only to himself. After pacing for a moment, he went back to the bedroom to look again at the woman's eyes.

"Finish her, Alex," Jack demanded in a calm, but cold, tone. "Finish her."

"No, Jack. I'm done." With those words, Alex ripped off his hat, pulled out the hair tie from his ponytail, and unzipped his jacket. The jacket came off his body in a swoop, and the gloves followed. All was left in a pile on the bedroom floor.

Jack became furious. "What are you doing?"

"I'm done. No more." Alex then stormed out of the bedroom. Jack continued to yell as Alex left the apartment and shut the door behind him.

The sun was barely beginning to peek over the horizon behind the downtown skyline as Alex crossed the parking lot and headed up the sidewalk. Jack yelled inside his head. Alex ignored him. He'd made up his mind, and Jack couldn't talk him out of what he had planned. As he walked, Alex replayed all the horrible things he had done. Images of each task, each woman, overwhelmed him. All of it had been done for one person. That one person he lost because of what he had done. Those women died so he and Jana could be together. It wasn't right.

Jack screamed at Alex one more time as he climbed the steps to one of the buildings. "Do not do this, Alex! Finish what you started!"

Jack's voice caused a sharp pain in Alex's head for the first time. It was enough to stop him for a second, but not enough to stop him from entering the building. Once inside, he stopped the first person he saw in the busy crowd. He grabbed a man by the arm. "I'm here to turn myself in."

The police officer looked at the hand on his arm, and then back at Alex. He chuckled and asked, "What for? What is it that you could have possibly done?" Then the officer noticed blood on Alex's face and neck.

THIRTY-TWO

There was dead silence in the interview room while Alex waited for the return of the two detectives. Even though he wasn't under arrest, he still wore handcuffs. When the police officer he first encountered had failed to believe him when he'd stated he wanted to turn himself in, Alex reacted with an outburst of anger. It took that officer and another one to get him under control. Once he was placed in the room, Alex started to fall apart mentally, which he hadn't done in a long time. It was as though his world had crashed down around him.

He was left in the room for some time before anyone came to talk to him. So much ran through his exhausted mind while he sat alone. The things he had done to innocent people, Jana discovering he was a murderer, and everything he had done to the young woman's body during the long hours of the night. The hardest thing to come to terms with was the fact that killing had become a part of him. When Jack left him alone, he still thought about it. He still tried to pick out victims. He really didn't know if he would be able to stop, even if Jack did leave. With the tasks not fully complete, it was unclear what Jack would do. Jack was dead silent. With that realization, Alex withdrew further into himself and started to shut down.

When Bagster arrived back at the station, he checked in with a fellow detective that had been watching Alex on a monitor. He asked, "What's he been doing in there this whole time?"

The female detective answered, "He's just been sitting there. He hasn't moved a muscle. I'm not sure if he has even blinked."

"So what do you make of him?" asked Bagster. He stood next to her, watching the monitor. "Do you think he's 'normal'?"

"It's hard for me to say. It appears there is something wrong with him, but who knows? It could all be an act," she replied. "Where's your partner?"

Bagster started to walk away. "Wynne's still at the crime scene. He'll be back shortly." He stopped at the doorway and turned back. "When he gets here, we will be talking to Mr. Dorson again. Make sure it all gets recorded. I don't want any of it missed." After she nodded, Bagster left the room to wait for his partner at his desk.

Once Wynne arrived, he filled Bagster in on what was found at the apartment. Alex's jacket, hat, and gloves were there. The hat they recognized from the security footage, so they agreed it was time to officially place Alex Dorson under arrest and hope he would talk to them without an attorney. Neither one of them knew what to expect as they entered the interview room. They each took a deep breath before entering. Wynne shut the door, and they sat down at the table calmly. Bagster informed Alex he was under arrest for the death of the woman in her apartment. Then he read Alex his rights. Alex didn't respond to any of it. Wynne finally asked, "Alex, will you tell us what happened? Will you tell us why you did what you did to that young woman?"

With a blank stare, Alex answered, "I already told you."

"All right, Alex," Bagster said, a hint of frustration in his voice. "Start at the beginning, okay? Explain to me who Jack is and where he came from because I have my doubts that he even exists."

"Why do you doubt?" Alex asked without even a blink of his eyes.

Bagster took a breath. "Have you ever heard of Jack the Ripper?"

"Yes."

"What do you know about him?"

"He killed some women somewhere in England and got away with it. So?" Alex replied, this time with a slight shrug of his shoulders.

"We believe you know more about those murders than you are letting on," Wynne elaborated. "We have a suspicion you were trying to imitate those murders."

For the second time since being put in the interview room hours earlier, Alex sat straight up and responded fully to what he had heard. "You think I was imitating Jack the Ripper?" He sounded bewildered. "I know the news reporters had mentioned something like that, but then

Jack said I shouldn't watch the news or read the newspapers anymore. He said it would cause me to get too personally involved with the victims."

"Alex," Bagster started when he saw Alex's mood change, "you have to tell us who Jack is. You said you turned yourself in so you could be stopped, and so Jack would leave you alone. What needs to stop so Jack will leave you alone? What's to stop Jack if you don't tell us who he is?"

Alex calmly put his cuffed wrist on the table and leaned toward the two detectives. He chuckled and said, "You can't stop Jack. He's in my mind." Alex pointed to his head and grinned. "He overruns my thoughts, and when he feels the need, he takes control of my body during the murders if what I was doing wasn't correct. I stopped him from doing that by doing exactly what he wanted me to do." When Alex saw the two detectives glance at each other, he said, "I'm not crazy. You may think that I am, but I'm not."

"Okay, then, Alex," said Bagster, "you know you are under arrest for the death of the woman you sent us to find. You are not under arrest for the deaths of the other women, although you claim to be responsible for them also. Your rights were read to you. Do you understand them?"

"Yes."

"Do you understand that you do not have to talk to us? You understand that you have the right to an attorney, don't you?" Bagster wanted to make sure he understood those points since his mental state seemed questionable.

"I understand all of that."

"Good. Now then, will you tell us about Jack and about the others?"

To the relief of the two detectives, Alex agreed to share the story of all the horrible things he had done. Wynne took notes as quickly as he could as Alex started his tale with his car accident. That had, after all, been the beginning of the end for him. That was when Jack had become an overpowering force in his life. Alex made it as clear as he could to the two men just how overpowering Jack had been. He told them about the agreement with Jack. He told them about the tasks he was to complete, and that Jack was supposed to leave when they were completed. The specificity of the details he disclosed confirmed to the detectives that he was responsible for all the murders. Alex unloaded all his burdens through three hours of the official interview, but he chose to keep the most private parts, those concerning his family and Jana, to himself. He also kept to himself the reason he turned himself in instead of finishing his last task.

When the interview concluded, Alex was taken by an officer to be processed and placed in a jail cell. Bagster and Wynne went to their desks to unwind and absorb everything they had heard. Neither man spoke a word. Wynne folded his arms on his desk and laid his head on them. The office area was buzzing with people. The morning had passed them by, and so had lunch. While the noise from their coworkers didn't disturb them, Bagster's phone ringing caused them both to almost jump out of their skins.

"Bagster," he said after putting the phone to his ear. After a brief phone conversation, he hung up the phone and said, "Let's go, Wynne. Alicia has the body, and she wants us to be there when she takes a closer look at it."

Alicia was already making notes about the condition of the young woman's body when the two detectives arrived at her office. She looked up from her clipboard as they approached her. "I've seen a lot of things during my career, but this is something new to me," she said.

"I would have to agree with that," said Bagster. "So, show us what he did to her."

"Okay. The first thing is the neck area. Her throat was cut, just like the others." Bagster and Wynne leaned in from one side of the table while Alicia leaned in from the other side. "The cut is deep. I don't think he was behind her this time. The cut is pretty straight."

Wynne asked her, "Do you think she was already on the bed then?"

She nodded yes and then Bagster added, "That is what he told us happened."

Alicia walked them along the entire corpse. She continued to make notes as the three of them examined each wound on the body. Wynne was relieved to hear Alicia say the mutilations had occurred postmortem. Alex had told them he had killed her first, but it was good to hear her confirm it. Wynne still couldn't be sure what parts of Alex's story to believe. Alicia was at least confirming some of the details. Her reports on the other victims would probably confirm other parts. It was still unclear to Wynne and Bagster whether Alex Dorson was playing with a full deck or not.

"Did you get to talk to this guy?" Alicia asked the detectives when they were seated in her office after the exam.

"Yes," said Wynne, "he actually did talk to us. It was... interesting."

Bagster sat on the opposite end of the dark brown leather couch. He let Wynne have the opportunity to talk about the interview with Alex Dorson as he was still formulating his opinion about Alex and didn't want to talk about him anyway. Alicia was curious, and Wynne was more than eager to handle her questions.

Wynne carried on the conversation by saying, "Alex Dorson really doesn't look like the type of person to do things like this, but he does seem to know a lot about each murder. He claims there is a voice in his head that told him to do this."

"Really?" Alicia asked, fascinated. She changed her position in the matching leather chair across from them. "Do you buy that, or do you think he is trying for an insanity defense already?"

Smiling, he replied, "That's the ultimate question. We have a signed confession, we have his personal items he left behind, and we even have the knife, but we still can't say for sure whether he is telling the whole truth or not. It could be months before we know the whole story."

"If you ever know the whole story," she added.

"This is true," Wynne agreed. "At least we've got him. That's what counts."

This was also true. Alex was locked up, but Alicia wondered, "Would you have gotten him if he hadn't turned himself in this morning?"

The leather couch made noises as Bagster stood. Wynne and Alicia both watched him and wondered what he was doing. He answered her question this time. "I honestly don't know if we would have gotten him or not. There's no point in worrying about that now because we do have him." With that said, Bagster walked out of Alicia's office.

Wynne gave Alicia a meek little smile and said, "I guess it's time to go."

THIRTY-THREE

The days and weeks blurred as Alex sat in his jail cell alone, waiting to be charged with each murder. Thanksgiving had come and gone. He had received letters from both of his parents, and he spoke to his mom on the phone a few times. Patiently, he waited for his first visit. His mom and dad were coming, but nothing had been mentioned about Jessica. Alex wasn't sure if he wanted her to come or not. Once again, he had let her down.

The cell door clanked as it was pulled open. The guard instructed Alex to stand and place his hands behind his back. The guard cuffed him, turned him around, and directed him out of the cell. Alex was, of course, considered dangerous. There was a time he wasn't capable of hurting a fly, but that wasn't the case anymore. The extent of the murders he had been charged with so far made it mandatory for him to be cuffed when leaving his cell. Because of this, Alex spent most of his time alone in his cell with his thoughts. He looked forward to contact with someone from the outside world.

There was no one else in the visiting room when the guard escorted Alex through the doors. After the guard locked the door behind them, he took off Alex's handcuffs.

Alex peeked over his shoulder. "Where's my family?"

"It's the procedure to bring you in first," the guard replied. "The cuffs are off. Pick a table and have a seat. I'll be here by the door."

Looking around the drab room, Alex wandered over to a round table and sat on a round stool attached to it. The guard positioned himself by the door just as he said he would. Alex proceeded to look out the window at the white snow melting into the ground. Butterflies were fluttering in his stomach. He didn't know if he could face his parents. Most of their questions and concerns had already been addressed through his letters, but now he would have to look them in the eye. As the door on the other side of the room slowly opened, Alex took a deep breath and stood, ready to face them once and for all.

"Alex!" his mom cried as she entered the room, her arms wide open. Tightly she wrapped herself around him and kissed him on the cheek. His dad offered him a handshake when she finally let go of him. Jessica was with them, but she chose not to approach her brother. Instead, she sat down at a table far from the others.

The three of them settled onto their stools after the greetings. Alex glanced at his sister several times, but she continued to ignore him. His mother whispered to Alex that Jessica was still upset and in shock about everything. He decided to leave her be for a while as his parents started off with general questions about his day-to-day life in jail. There wasn't much to tell, and what he could tell wasn't overly pleasant. Though it was obvious Alex was stretching the truth for his mom's benefit, she didn't acknowledge the fact that she knew this. He knew what she wanted to hear, so that's exactly what he told her.

Alex's dad wasted little time with the small talk. As soon as he saw the opportunity to interrupt, he did. "Alex, what does your attorney think about your case so far? Have there been any updates since the last letter you sent me?"

"There hasn't been much going on lately," answered Alex. He could see the concern on his dad's face. Mr. Dorson had decided to hire a defense attorney for Alex instead of having one appointed to him. It was against Alex's wishes. He had already confessed, and he wasn't going to change his mind about it. Because of the confessions, he viewed it as a waste of his dad's money. He figured both of his parents were hoping for a miracle. Unfortunately, they wouldn't get one because Alex didn't want to be set free.

"I know things are moving slowly, but what did Mr. Caudel say during his last visit?" pressed Mr. Dorson.

The trials and the meetings with his attorney weren't subjects Alex wanted to waste time talking about, but both of his parents stared at him, intently waiting for an answer. With his mom tightly holding one of his hands in both of hers, Alex started telling them what he knew. "Mr. Caudel thinks we should try to use the insanity defense. He wants me to enter a plea of not guilty by reason of insanity. Since I already confessed, it is the only defense available to me. If I don't agree to it, then the trial is skipped, and I go straight to being sentenced."

Mrs. Dorson released Alex's hand and irritably said, "I don't know why you confessed to those horrible murders anyway."

"We've already been through this, Mom," Alex snapped. "I confessed because I did those horrible murders."

"Well, I just don't believe it. I don't think I'll ever believe it."

Alex rolled his eyes and chose not to respond to her since she was being irrational about the whole thing. Of course, no one believed he could do something like that, but the truth was he did do it. His guilt wasn't up for debate. What was up for debate was whether he should try to plead insanity or not. It was his only chance to avoid prison, and his sanity had already been questioned by everyone. Alex didn't think he was insane at any point. He would admit his life had been a bit strange for a while, but he didn't believe he was ever crazy.

"What does it take to use the insanity defense?" Mr. Dorson asked Alex.

"I have to be evaluated by a psychiatrist, which will cost more money, and be evaluated by another psychiatrist, which the state will pay for because they will want to have their own expert. There are certain criteria I have to meet to be considered legally insane, and these experts will determine if I meet those criteria."

"And if you do?"

"Then a jury will make the final decision if I am or not."

"And if you don't?" Mr. Dorson wondered.

"Then it is all a waste of time and money, which is what I believe it will be anyway."

"I think you should give it a try, Alex."

"Dad, it will be a waste of money. I'm not insane now, and I wasn't insane then."

Mr. Dorson leaned in close to his son and whispered, "When someone is insane, do they know they are insane? You may be fine now, but you could have been suffering from temporary insanity instead of depression like you told everyone. Besides, it's my money. I think you should try it."

It wasn't what Alex wanted, but he gave in to his dad. "Okay. I'll tell Mr. Caudel to set it all up when he comes tomorrow."

Both of his parents were pleased with his decision and decided to not discuss it any further. They choose not to discuss their still pending divorce either. Alex wondered where that stood, but chose not to ask, and neither parent had brought it up. Jessica hadn't talked to him over the phone or sent him any letters, so he had no clue how everything was affecting her. He watched her off and on during the short visit as his parents talked about everything and everyone they knew. Jessica appeared to be worn down. Her usually rosy complexion seemed pale, and her pretty blue eyes were undercut by dark circles. She avoided all eye contact with him. He couldn't take it anymore. Alex left the table and went to her.

Jessica turned her back to him before he could even sit down. Even though Alex wanted to be close to his sister, he thought it would be wise to leave an empty stool between them. He spoke first, trying to choose his words wisely.

"Jessica," he started softly, "I love you dearly, and I hope you can find it in your heart to forgive me for letting you down. I know I have left you to deal with everything by yourself. I just want you to know that I hadn't planned for that to happen."

She turned toward him, a fire burning in her eyes. "So you didn't think that murdering five women would have any effect on anyone? This isn't about being left alone to deal with Mom and Dad. This is about what *you've* done, Alex. I'm only here because they made me come. After today, you won't see me anymore. As far as I'm concerned, I no longer have a brother."

Alex's heart fell right into the pit of his stomach. There was nothing he could say to win her over. She was right. He had murdered five women. And they too had been someone's sister or daughter. Alex hung his head for a moment before leaving Jessica's table. To make matters worse, back at his parents' table, his mother had started crying. What had started out as a fairly pleasant visit had quickly turned sour. He had wanted contact with his family for a while, but now he just wanted to be alone again.

"Don't worry too much about it, son," Mr. Dorson said, trying to comfort Alex.

"About what, Dad?" He knew what his dad was talking about even though he let on like he didn't have a clue. He wasn't sure why he was pretending to not know. Maybe it was because he really wanted to hear something comforting from his dad.

"She will come around, eventually. Just give it some time."

"Well, Dad, time is all I have now," replied Alex glumly.

Very little else was said during their time together. When one of the guards announced that the visit was over, Alex hugged both of his parents, then he went to the door he had come in through earlier. There, the guard cuffed Alex and led him from the room. He could hear his mom's cry of pain as he was led away. Nothing passed between him and the guard during the trip back to Alex's cell. Once he was left in his cell alone, his mind replayed the visit over and over again.

Jessica had been right. Alex had not really thought about how his actions would affect everyone. All he had been concerned about was getting his life back and being with Jana. It all seemed to boil down to what he wanted. Even turning himself in had been about him. It was the right thing to do, but would it have even crossed his mind if he hadn't learned about Jana's fear of him? That question wouldn't ever have an answer. Alex knew this as he sat on his small bed with his back against the wall. He drew his legs up and rested his arms on top of his knees. As he reflected more on his sister's face and about what she had said to him, a tear streamed down his cheek.

THIRTY-FOUR

The next day, Alex met with his attorney, Mr. Caudel. The two men sat in a small private room. It was only about four weeks until Alex was to again appear before the judge. Mr. Caudel had planned to enter a plea of not guilty by reason of insanity for Alex, but that was changed by Alex when he initially appeared in front of the judge in late November. It was unusual, but the judge allowed an extension for Alex to enter a plea since the two of them couldn't agree. The current meeting between him and his attorney was strictly to determine that plea.

Before the visit with his parents, Alex had planned on sticking with a guilty plea. His dad seemed to think the insanity plea was worth a shot, but Alex felt he needed more information and started to ask questions. With a slight chuckle, Mr. Caudel said, "Let me give you some background and some information on the insanity defense before you decide. I'm thrilled you are at least considering it, but don't make up your mind just yet. Most people think of the insanity defense one way when really it is something entirely different."

"Okay," Alex said, shrugging and leaning back in his seat. "I'll listen, but the only reason I'm curious about it is because my parents like the idea."

"I understand. I agree you should at least consider it, but I don't want you or your parents to think it's a way for you to get out of this. You will have to face what you have done, no matter what. Based on what you have told me about Jack and the changes in your life and mental state when he arrived, I feel you being put in prison for the rest of your life isn't what you need." Mr. Caudel pulled a legal pad and pen from his briefcase.

Alex crossed his arms. "I know everyone believes I'm crazy because Jack was only a voice in my head, but I'm not. I don't think anyone will ever understand everything that went on with Jack."

"Maybe not, Alex, but Jack may be the key to keeping you out of prison," Mr. Caudel pointed out. "Have you ever heard of the M'Naghten Rule?"

"Not exactly," Alex replied sarcastically.

"Let me briefly tell you the story," Mr. Caudel started. Alex nodded. "M'Naughten lived in England back in the early 1800s. Long story short, he felt he was being followed, spied on I guess you could say, and he felt it all had something to do with the Prime Minister. So, he decided to take out the Prime Minister. He thought that would solve his problems. The funny part was he ended up killing the secretary to the Prime Minister by mistake. His counsel said he was innocent because he was insane, and he was obviously delusional. He was found to be insane and was acquitted. The public wasn't happy with the decision of the court. They saw it as him getting away with murder. So, England established a set of standards to determine whether someone is legally insane or not."

"Interesting story, but this isn't England, and it's not the 1800s," Alex stated. "What does this have to do with me right now?"

"Well, that standard made its way to America. Over the years, two more standards were put into place, but when it comes down to it, each state has its own criteria for what is considered legally insane. Kentucky's standard isn't much different than what I just described."

Leaning forward and placing his elbows on the table in front of him, Alex asked one question of his attorney. "Do you think I'm legally insane?"

Mr. Caudel leaned in toward Alex and answered, "That is not for me to determine. That will be up to a judge and jury to decide."

"What happens if they decide I'm legally insane?" Alex inquired as he glared at his attorney.

Leaning back in his chair, Mr. Caudel started to tap his pen on the table as he answered his client. "Well, you will be sent to the state mental institution for the criminally insane two hundred miles away.

There you will receive treatment for your illness until you are considered to be mentally fit. At that point, you will be released back into society."

"What if they never consider me mentally fit?"

"Then you stay there for the rest of your life."

Chuckling to himself, Alex tried to make sure he was understanding his options. "Let me get this straight. If I enter a plea of guilty, I will then spend the rest of my life in prison. Or, if I enter a plea of insanity, I will then spend the rest of my life in a hospital with a bunch of crazy people."

"The mental institution offers you a chance at getting your freedom back in the future. If you go to prison, that's it, you're done," Mr. Caudel explained.

Alex rubbed his hands over his head and tucked his long hair behind his ears. "What happens if the jury thinks I'm perfectly sane?"

"Then they will find you guilty, and you go to prison. You really have nothing to lose, Alex," replied Mr. Caudel.

"One more question," Alex said. "Do we only go through this once, or do we have to do this for each case?"

Sighing, Mr. Caudel sat up straight to explain things to Alex. "The judge has already decided to keep the cases separate since the detectives are still working on a couple of them. The only way that will change is for you to enter a guilty plea in each case. With the insanity defense, we will have to prove you legally insane five separate times. To be completely honest with you, Alex, the easiest way is for you to go ahead with the guilty plea. But, I would like to see you have a chance at freedom someday. I'm sure that is what your family is thinking too."

"Okay. We'll try the insanity plea and see what happens."

"Are you sure?"

"No, but yes. Let's give it a try," Alex said with a sigh.

Mr. Caudel started making notes on his legal pad while Alex sat quietly. Alex's mind should have been going over the events and the information from their meeting, but his mind was a complete blank. He didn't want to think about it anymore. He just wanted it all to end. It was far from over though.

"Okay, Alex," started Mr. Caudel. "I'll let the judge know we have agreed on a plea and see if we can move the date up to go before the court. Then you will enter a plea of not guilty by reason of insanity. The judge will then ask me to confirm your plea, and then that part will be done."

"Then what?"

Mr. Caudel started to pack up his things. "Then I will arrange for you to be evaluated. Once the prosecution hears the plea, they will do the same. After that, we wait for the trial date to be set."

"Well, then, I guess I'll see you tomorrow with an update," Alex said.

"One more thing, Alex," Mr. Caudel said before leaving the small room. "Please don't change your mind. I think the judge is already irritated with us. Don't make it any worse than it already is." Alex nodded and then watched him leave.

The next week Alex stood before the female judge with his attorney at his side.

"All right." The judge started looking at them both. "I remember the last time you stood before me, Mr. Dorson. There seemed to be some sort of misunderstanding between you and your attorney regarding how you wanted to plead to the charges."

"Yes, Your Honor," Alex replied as he stood before her in his orange jumpsuit with his hands clasped behind his back.

"Do you both have a plea for me this morning?" she asked them.

Mr. Caudel replied, "Yes, we do, Your Honor. My client would like to enter a plea of not guilty by reason of insanity."

The courtroom murmured.

"Really?" the judge asked, surprised. "Do you agree with this, Mr. Dorson?"

"Yes, Your Honor," Alex sheepishly answered. He didn't know if he really did agree with it or not, but he wasn't changing it and causing more problems.

"Do you feel your client is mentally capable to stand trial, Mr. Caudel?" the judge wondered.

"I do, Your Honor. We plan to address his mental state during the time of the crime more so than his mental state in the present," explained Mr. Caudel.

The judge turned to the prosecutor, who had been silent during the whole thing. "Do you have anything to say or to add, Counselor?"

The prosecutor replied, "The only thing I have is that the state would like to have Mr. Dorson evaluated by our own expert, Your Honor." The prosecutor was a well-dressed man in his late fifties. He had been a prosecutor for a long time, and he had a long track record of successful cases.

"Of course," she answered. "Well, then, since the plea is not guilty by reason of insanity, I guess the trial will start on the set date. You don't have much time to prepare your case, Mr. Caudel. You can file for an extension if you would like."

Alex nudged his attorney with his elbow. Mr. Caudel glanced at Alex with a harsh look on his face. Alex didn't care. He looked at him and shook his head no. Mr. Caudel nodded his head yes. Firmly, and quietly, Alex said no.

"Is there a problem?" the judge asked, interrupting them.

Mr. Caudel snapped his attention back to the bench. "No, Your Honor. I guess I won't be filing for an extension." He didn't sound pleased about it either.

"Very well. I will see you both on the morning of March 8th, then."

As the guards approached Alex to take him away, Mr. Caudel said, "We needed that extension, Alex."

His only reply was, "No, we don't."

Late that day, Alex got the chance to talk to his mom and dad. His dad had made arrangements to be with his mom at the time Alex would be allowed to call. They both had been at the courthouse that morning, but they weren't allowed to speak with Alex. He was led away quickly. Both of his parents told him they were pleased with his decision to try the insanity defense. Mr. Dorson scolded his son for not letting Mr. Caudel file for an extension. Alex just said he didn't feel like it was necessary. He asked his dad what Mr. Caudel had told them after he left. It seemed Mr. Caudel had spent some time with them explaining everything he had explained to Alex the previous day.

Before the call ended, Mr. Dorson had one thing to say. "Son, I think this was a wise decision. I'm sure it will all work out."

"Well, Dad, I'm willing to give it a try, both for you and Mom, but don't forget there will be four more trials to go through at some point. I don't see how we can win them all."

"Maybe we will, maybe we won't, but we have to try."

THIRTY-FIVE

The day of Alex's first evaluation had arrived. Alex was escorted to a small room just like the one he always had meetings in with Mr. Caudel. Again, he was cuffed at the wrist for security measures. Mr. Caudel was in the room with a woman who appeared to be in her late thirties. Since she dressed professionally with her brown hair neatly pulled back from her face, Alex assumed she was the psychiatrist. Once the cuffs were removed, Mr. Caudel stood and offered Alex his chair since there were only two. Alex sat down and smiled politely at the woman sitting across the table from him.

Mr. Caudel began to speak. "Alex, this is Ms. Pearson. She will be handling your evaluation for the defense side. I believe the prosecution's psychiatrist will be in to see you in a couple of days."

"Will you be staying with us?" asked Alex as he looked up at his attorney.

"No. It will be just the two of you," Mr. Caudel replied. "I'll return when the evaluation has concluded." He patted Alex on the back, nodded to Ms. Pearson, and left the room. The door was then locked, a guard posted outside.

"You can relax, Mr. Dorson," Ms. Pearson said with a smile.

"I'm fine. Please, call me Alex."

"All right, Alex, let me explain what is going to take place here." She pulled out a small tape recorder and a file folder from her briefcase. After placing the items on the table, she continued, "I'm going to record our session so I don't forget anything later on when I write my report on our meeting. I'm going to ask you some questions. There are no right or wrong answers, only your answers. When the interview part is over, I have a questionnaire for you to fill out. Once again, there are no right or wrong answers. The questions are pretty general, but they are important to the overall evaluation. Any questions before we get started?"

Alex shook his head. "No. Well, maybe one. How long is this going to take?"

"Unfortunately, Alex, that is one question I can't answer. We have a lot to cover, but it depends on a lot of factors and on how quickly we get started," she tried to explain. "Are you ready to start?" He nodded. "Good. Why don't you start at the beginning?"

With a deep breath, Alex went back to the car accident. There wasn't much he could tell her about the incident since he didn't remember much of it, so he told her the facts he knew, and then moved on to Jack. That was probably what she wanted to know about anyway. The insanity defense probably would rely on what he had to say about Jack. Hearing voices could be a good indication of insanity, but Alex didn't classify Jack as just a voice. Jack had to be much more. Alex wasn't sure what he was, but he was more.

Ms. Pearson directed the conversation by saying, "Alex, tell me how Jack affected your life once you acknowledged his existence."

"Jack affected every aspect of my life," Alex started clearly. "I started having problems at work, at home, with friends, and with my family. I started having problems with myself."

After looking at Alex for a moment with no expression, Ms. Pearson asked him, "Can you explain the problems you had with yourself?" That interested her the most.

Alex started to explain in an even tone. "I had no desire to do anything. I didn't want to leave my apartment. I didn't want to cook or clean. I didn't want to see anybody or talk to anybody. I knew I was the only person that could hear Jack, and I thought everyone would think I was crazy. At one point, I threw my two best friends out of my apartment, and I told my girlfriend to stay away from me for a while. Then I lost my job, and I failed to start school in the fall. I locked myself in my apartment at different times and just slept. I wouldn't even shower during those times."

"Were these behaviors continuous?" asked Ms. Pearson as she jotted down notes.

He glared at her, realizing she wasn't paying attention to his every word. "No. I just said it was at different times."

She looked up at Alex when she noticed the slight change in his tone. "What would trigger these bouts of isolation?"

"At first, it was an attempt to make him give up and go away," Alex started. "Later on, it would happen after I completed a task. I didn't know how to handle the guilt in the beginning. I would get very depressed, usually for a few days or longer."

"Explain the tasks to me. Were those the—"

"The murders I had to complete, yes," Alex finished for her without skipping a beat. "There were five in total. I didn't finish the fifth one."

The fifth murder would be addressed at the end. Ms. Pearson did want to know what made Alex stop when he was so close to finishing, but she needed to learn about the previous murders first. Alex's behaviors and thoughts were more important to the evaluation than the murders themselves. His feelings about each murder were a vital part also. All three aspects would help her determine his mental state during those critical months. She backed him up to the first murder, and Alex took her back a little further.

The first murder hadn't been the beginning. He felt she needed to know it all. Losing control of himself and his normal behaviors was only the half of it. Alex explained the deal that Jack had made with him. The fact that Jack used Jana in the deal, dangling her in front of him, clenched it for him. His thoughts of suicide were mentioned. Then, the trip to the drug store for sleeping pills along with the encounter with Jana. He even mentioned the deer carcasses in the woods. Alex explained they were used to prepare him for the murders, and then he proceeded to describe the things Jack had him do to each deer in detail. When Ms. Pearson asked him about his feelings during those trips to the woods, Alex told her he remembered the smell, and he remembered vomiting.

"You must understand," Alex said. "I didn't want to do any of that, but I wanted my life back. I wanted Jana back. I wanted Jack gone so I could have my life back."

It felt good to finally be telling every little detail to someone. The detectives had only been told about the murders and a small bit about

Jack. His attorney didn't even know everything. Ms. Pearson was getting every minute detail. She didn't glare at him like he was crazy, even though it was her job to find out if he was. She let him talk freely and asked very few questions. It took a couple of hours to lay everything out for Ms. Pearson, but once Alex felt she knew the impact Jack had made on him, he started sharing the details of the first murder with her. One by one, he shared every detail of each task until he came to the last one.

Before Alex started with the details of the last murder, he talked about the few weeks he had without Jack. He expressed the awkwardness he felt once Jack left. He discussed his urges to continue picking out victims. He also discussed the struggles of trying to get his life back. Ms. Pearson seemed confused about why Jack would want him to return to normal before the last task. There was no simple explanation, but Alex told her things didn't go as planned. Jana was the main thing he meant by that. She knew, had discovered what he had done, which then led to the final murder, the final task.

Ms. Pearson listened intently to Alex as he talked about the final murder. He hadn't revealed the real reason for stopping before the task was finished. That information would be valuable in deciding his mental status during the most horrible of all the murders. She listened as Alex described everything he did to the final victim. The tape recorder had recorded all of Alex's words up to this point, and it continued on. When he reached the point where he sat down to complete the task, Alex went quiet.

Ms. Pearson's expression changed from interest to disappointment. "Alex, you have to discuss the reason you stopped before completing what Jack wanted you to do. It is important to the evaluation."

Alex looked deep into her eyes. "Okay, I'll tell you. I sat down in the chair next to her bed, next to her body. There were a few things Jack wanted me to do to her face. I never learned what those things were. I became fixed on her eyes. They were dead eyes, but I couldn't seem to break the hold they had on me. Something about them seemed so familiar. I couldn't bring myself to finish the task. Her eyes caused pain in my heart. I knew I had to set things right."

"What was so familiar about her eyes that made you suddenly care about what you had done?" she asked him.

"They were just like Jana's eyes," Alex finally admitted. "Suddenly, in my mind, all the women I had killed and mutilated reminded me of her. I had forgotten that I was once a person that would never do anything to hurt anybody. Her eyes showed me that I had become something else."

The interview part of the evaluation ended shortly after that. Ms. Pearson gave Alex the written part, and then she left him to complete it on his own. She joined Mr. Caudel in another small room. Hours had passed, and she was certain he was probably growing impatient.

Mr. Caudel looked up from the book he was reading when the door to the small room opened. "I was beginning to wonder if I was going to finish this book before you finished the evaluation."

She smiled as she sat down across the table from him. "These things take time. You should know that."

"I do," he chuckled. "Well, what do you think? Does he have a fair chance at the insanity defense?"

"I can't answer that just yet," replied Ms. Pearson. "Some of what he told me would lead me to say that he showed signs of schizophrenia. But, some other things he said make me think you don't have a strong chance with that defense."

Mr. Caudel leaned on the table in front of him. "I'm confused."

With a sigh, she explained, "The signs of schizophrenia are there during some parts of his story. He was hearing a voice, he became antisocial, he gave up on personal hygiene, and he was suicidal. The problem is the symptoms would come and go. Now, he seems completely normal. That doesn't happen with schizophrenia. There are a number of other possible conditions to consider, but I think, at this point, temporary insanity is the best you're going to get. Even that is questionable since it wasn't a one time incident."

"What about the voice? That's not normal!"

"You're right," she agreed. "But the voice is gone. He claims the voice stopped the second he entered the police station, and it hasn't returned. The bottom line, Mr. Caudel, is that he knew what he was doing was wrong. It all was planned. You know as well as I do that one of the main issues in the insanity defense is whether the defendant knew right from wrong at the time of the crime. He did know right from wrong. All the symptoms he had, other than the voice and the delusions, can be blamed on the depression and guilt he felt after each murder. Temporary insanity might work with the first trial, but it won't work in all five trials."

He leaned back in disappointment. "That isn't exactly what I wanted to hear."

"I know it isn't, and I apologize, but there just isn't much to go on for a claim of insanity. These murders were copies of the Ripper murders. He is going to be viewed as a copycat murderer. Personally, I think there is more to it, but I can't use my personal feelings in my professional testimony."

Nodding his head, Mr. Caudel replied. "I understand. Let me know when you have reviewed everything and made your final report. Maybe something will stand out later that didn't today."

"I'll do my best, for you and for Alex. That's all I can promise."

THIRTY-SIX

A couple of days before Christmas, Alex sat on his bunk reading a book. If nothing else, imprisoned, he at least had been able to catch up on a few of the books he had always wanted to read. Unfortunately, his peace was interrupted by a bang on the cell door. Alex jumped slightly. By now, he was more than familiar with the jail's schedule, and he knew to not expect any disturbance until this evening, for dinner.

"Alex," a guard called to him from the other side of the door, "you have a visitor."

The door clanged as the lock was turned. "A visitor? Who is it?"

The door swung open. "I don't know. It's not my job to know who it is. Are you going to see who it is or not?" the guard asked as he stood in the doorway.

"I guess so," Alex replied as he put down the book on his bunk. He stood up and turned his back to the guard while placing his hands behind his back.

The guard stepped in, but he didn't cuff Alex. Instead, he put his hand on Alex's shoulder and said, "That's not necessary anymore, Alex."

Alex turned to look at the guard. "Why the sudden change?"

"Your attorney and the doctor lady used your mental evaluation to have that procedure changed for you," the guard explained. "So, from now on, you walk and we follow."

He started out of the cell with the guard close behind him. "I guess everyone knows now that I'm not insane."

"I don't know about all of that. I just know you're not being classified as a threat anymore."

A list of people ran through Alex's mind as he made his way through the jail to the visiting room. He'd had a phone conversation with his mom the day before, but she hadn't mentioned a visit. He knew it couldn't be Jessica. She would probably never forgive him. No one came to mind. Who could possibly want to see him after what he had done? Once he was secure in the visiting room, the door opened on the opposite side, and he found out who the mystery visitor was. "Jana?"

She smiled sheepishly but stayed just inside the door. "Are you surprised to see me?"

"Yeah, very surprised." He slowly made his way to the same table he had sat at with his parents. "Do you want to sit down?"

"Sure," she replied with a shrug. She went to the table and pulled off her heavy winter coat. After laying it across one of the round stools, she sat down.

Alex sat down across from her. Neither of them said a word for a moment. Alex couldn't take it. He had to ask her a question. "Why are you here, Jana?"

She looked down at her hands in her lap. "Your attorney called me the other day. He wants me to testify during your trial."

"Testify to what?" He was confused. She didn't know anything.

Finally, she looked him in the eyes. "He wants me to talk about the changes I saw in you after the accident. Things like your anger and your seclusion from everyone. He has contacted Josh and Tony, too."

Quickly, Alex turned from her on his stool. It never occurred to him that other people would have to be involved if he pleaded the insanity thing like his attorney wanted him to. That wasn't fair to them. He really didn't want to face them either. "What did you all tell him? Did you agree to do it? You don't have to, you know."

"We haven't said yes or no yet," she informed him. He turned his head to look at her as she explained. "I wanted to come here to talk to you first. Tony and Josh thought it was a good idea. They are waiting to see what I decide first."

Without moving his body, he sarcastically responded, "Well, you're here. What do you need to know to help you decide?"

Jana let out a frustrated sigh. "I don't know, Alex. I just wanted to see you. I want to hear from you that you did these horrible things because I'm still having a hard time processing it."

"Well, Jana," he started harshly as he fully turned his body toward her, "I did it. I did all of it. I'm sorry, but I did. You were right. That was me on TV."

She exhaled, her voice shaky. "Please tell me it isn't true. I tried to find the images again. To remember what I'd seen on the news. I had to have been wrong, I kept thinking. You wouldn't do that. It's not you, Alex. It's not. The Alex I know would never hurt anyone. I miss him."

Laughter filled the room. The guard had to remind Alex to keep the noise level down. "How could you possibly say that? Last time I saw you, you were scared of me!"

"I was terrified of you. How could I not be when I saw *your* hat, *your* jacket?"

"Then why are you here if you're so afraid of me?"

"I'm not anymore. You would have never hurt me, Alex. I know that now deep in my heart. But you... You killed five other women. What I want to know is why."

It suddenly dawned on Alex that life was full of irony. He had become a murderer to get rid of Jack so he could live happily ever after with Jana. When that was about to happen, he found out she no longer trusted him. With that knowledge, he went ahead with his final task but didn't finish it. He snapped back to reality and decided to set things right anyway. It didn't matter that he would be spending the rest of his life in prison or a mental institution. With Jana gone, he had nothing else to lose. Alex did rid himself of Jack, or so it seemed, since he had not heard Jack's voice since that night. And he was setting things right by facing up to what he had done, but now he was discovering he had only lost Jana for a while. He'd thought he was making the right choice by turning himself in, but he had actually made the wrong decision because he would never again be with the person that mattered the most to him.

"It doesn't matter now," Alex said. "It's in the past. There isn't anything that can be done about it now."

Jana looked at him with sad eyes. "I don't understand how someone like you could end up in here. I don't think I will ever believe you were in your right mind when you killed those women."

"Maybe you will after the trial," Alex said. "Whether you choose to believe it or not, I did murder those women, but I'm in here because I turned myself in after the last one."

"Why? Why did you do that?"

He hung his head. There was no way he could explain to her why. She would eventually learn the truth, but he couldn't bring himself to be the one to tell her. "You wouldn't understand."

"Is that why you told me to stay away? Were you afraid you would hurt me?" she pleaded again.

Quickly his head snapped back up. He grabbed her hand and replied, "No, I would never hurt you, Jana."

"I don't get it then."

"I know you don't."

A knock on the door interrupted the conversation between them. Alex turned to see who it was, but he couldn't tell with the guard standing in the way. When the door closed, the guard motioned for Alex. He went to see what was going on and left Jana at the table.

"Your attorney is here to see you," the guard told him in a whisper. "He knows you have a visitor, but he suggests you cut the visit short. He doesn't have much time."

Disappointed by the fact he would have to end his visit with Jana, Alex agreed and returned to the table, but he didn't sit back down.

"Is everything okay?" she asked, looking up at him, worried.

"Yeah," he replied, sounding regretful. "My attorney is here. I have to go, but I really don't want to."

Grabbing her coat, Jana stood. "It's okay. We'll visit another time." She hugged him with her one free arm and whispered in his ear. "Try to have a Merry Christmas."

Alex didn't want to let her go, but he forced himself to. "You have a Merry Christmas, too."

As she walked away, she turned back. "By the way, I like the short haircut."

He smiled and watched her leave the room. When she was gone, he turned and went to the guard. "Okay. Take me to my attorney."

The guard opened the door. The two of them made their way down a short hallway to a small room. Mr. Caudel was inside waiting. He wasted no time with small talk. Once Alex was in a chair, he started talking.

"I hate to rush this meeting, but I'm in a hurry. I hope you understand and don't think I'm being rude."

"I understand. Christmas is in two days. I'm sure you have family obligations," Alex replied.

Mr. Caudel stopped rummaging around in his briefcase and smiled at Alex. "I do. I didn't want to say that, under your circumstances. I know it has to be hard to be away from your family right now."

Alex shrugged. "Not really. My parents are getting divorced, and my sister despises me. I don't think it would be a happy Christmas this year anyway."

Mr. Caudel didn't respond. He paused for a moment, but then returned to his briefcase. When he didn't find what he was looking for, he shut it and pushed it to the side. "Alex, we will only have a few visits before the trial starts. The next time we meet, it will be a long visit. We will have a lot to cover. This time, I just wanted to let you know that I met with Ms. Pearson today. She doesn't think we have a case for full insanity. I think our best bet is temporary insanity. What do you think?"

"I told you I'm not insane," he responded with a chuckle.

"I know you did, but Ms. Pearson feels that you may have suffered from depression and other things off and on during those few months. I think temporary insanity is our best bet," Mr. Caudel explained.

"Okay. Whatever you think is best." Alex really didn't care. The ending would be bad either way. "Can I ask you something?"

"Sure."

"Why do you want my friends to testify?"

"They know you best," he told him. "They all knew something wasn't right with you. They saw the changes you went through after the car accident. Their observations will be a huge help in showing you weren't normal then."

He forced a smile. "I was just wondering. I really didn't want them involved."

"They haven't agreed to do it yet, but I'm hoping they do. We really could use their help on this."

"I know. It's just the fact that this is my problem, not theirs."

THIRTY-SEVEN

Alex had been prepared for a lonely holiday season. Thanksgiving had been that way, and he saw no reason for Christmas and New Year's to be any different. To his surprise, he was overwhelmed by visitors during the week from Christmas to New Year's Day. Both of his parents had visited, but separately. Jessica never returned though. That didn't surprise him. During his dad's visit, Alex did finally get to meet his dad's girlfriend. He found the visit awkward, but pleasant. The visits from his parents were followed by a return visit by Jana and a visit from Josh and Tony.

The visit from Josh and Tony had started out tense. It took a bit for the friends to loosen up with each other, but by the end of the visit, Alex hugged them goodbye and whispered something into Josh's ear. He asked his friend to look out for Jana. He felt he would never have her again, so he figured Josh would be a good pick to keep her safe and sound.

The trial was growing closer. The New Year usually symbolizes a new beginning. For Alex, it did symbolize a beginning. It was a beginning to the end. March would be the start of the first trial. There would be more to follow once the first one ended, and he wasn't looking forward to any of them. His options kept playing over and over in his head. The temporary insanity thing his attorney and psychiatrist had dreamed up was a long shot. Whether it worked or not, Alex couldn't ask his friends and family to testify on his behalf for four more trials. He planned to go along with the defense plan, but he had his mind made up that he would plead guilty to the other murders if it didn't work for the first one. That would save everyone from reliving his horrible deeds again and again. No one deserved to suffer from them except him.

There came another visit three days before the trial. When a guard came for Alex, he believed he was going to meet with his attorney. They were still supposed to have another long visit. The guard directed Alex to one of the small rooms he usually met Mr. Caudel in, but when he entered the room, he wasn't greeted by his attorney. Instead, he saw two familiar faces he hadn't seen in a long time.

"Have a seat, Mr. Dorson." Detective Bagster directed him with a wave of his hand.

Alex was immediately confused as to why the two detectives he had confessed to were there to see him. Politely, he greeted them and took a seat across from them.

Detective Wynne asked, "Alex, do you know why we are here?"

"No, sir, I don't," replied Alex respectfully. He started to worry if they were there to deliver bad news.

Bagster informed him of the purpose of their visit. "We wanted to be the ones to tell you that you are now officially charged with all five of the murders."

Alex's shoulders dropped, not in disappointment, but in relief that the news wasn't worse. "I saw that coming, gentlemen. I did confess, remember?"

"Of course we remember," Wynne answered. "We wanted to let you know that there is enough evidence to officially link you to all of them, to back up your confession. We've worked hard on each of these cases, Alex. We have had close contact with the friends and families of these victims. We wanted to see this through to the end."

Bagster interrupted and spoke harshly to Alex. "We will be there in the courtroom every day, at each trial. We heard you entered a plea of not guilty by reason of insanity for the first one. I wondered about your sanity at first, but I think that is a load of crap now!"

"Let's not get carried away," Wynne interjected. "Alex, when you confessed to us, you left a lot of information out. You didn't tell the whole story. The families of your victims would like to know why you did this. Will you tell us what you've told everyone else, for the families?"

Shaking his head no, he responded with an explanation. "I can't do that. I have told my attorney the whole story, and I have been through two psychiatric evaluations where I had to tell the whole story. The first, and maybe the last, trial is about to start. I don't think my attorney would like the idea of me telling you anything. I'm sorry. You can tell the families that it will all come out during the trial." He looked both men in the eyes, and he could see Wynne was disappointed, and Bagster wasn't happy.

"So that's it?" Bagster snapped. "The first trial is about the last victim. Is the judge allowing the other victims to be mentioned?"

Alex snapped back, "I don't know. I haven't met with my attorney yet this week. Why don't you call him and ask him?" Alex stood up. "I'm sorry I can't help you, gentlemen. If that is all, I will return to my cell now." Wynne and Bagster had nothing else. Wynne nodded his head to Alex, and then watched as he left. The small room was silent for a moment.

"Well, Bagster, I don't think that went well." Wynne started tapping his fingers on the table.

Bagster agreed. "I was hoping to shake him up a little to get him to tell us something, but the good cop, bad cop didn't work. I guess we have to wait for the trial like everyone else."

The two men stood to leave. Wynne made one more comment as they headed out the door. "It would have been nice to know the whole truth. To see if this kid actually has a chance of getting away with murder by claiming insanity."

"All I know is he looks pretty sane to me," Bagster added.

Once he was back in his cell, Alex became infuriated. It didn't make any sort of sense why two detectives would take time to meet with him and gloat about finally connecting him to all the murders. It was only obvious that would happen eventually. It also didn't make sense that they wanted more information for the victims' families. With the first trial coming up, they had to know he wouldn't tell them anything.

As he paced back and forth in his cell, Alex started to calm himself. He realized they were fishing for something. If only his attorney would show up. Maybe Mr. Caudel would have some idea of what they were trying to get at. Alex hadn't heard from him though. That bothered him more than the two detectives. Mr. Caudel said there was a lot to go over before the trial started, but he hadn't been to see Alex since before Christmas. Since there was very little to do to pass the time, Alex couldn't do anything but wonder, worry, and hope for the best.

Mr. Caudel did finally pay Alex a visit the day before the trial. The meeting between them started at nine o'clock sharp that morning. When Alex arrived once again to one of the small rooms, he saw folders and papers scattered all over the table. Mr. Caudel appeared to be worked up. Stress had started to set in on the attorney. He hadn't even noticed Alex entering the room until the door slammed shut.

He turned quickly from his pile of files and papers. "Good morning, Alex. I didn't hear you come in. Did you sleep well?"

Alex gave him a half grin and replied, "Good morning to you, too. I slept fine. What about you? You seem tense."

After the two took their seats, Mr. Caudel responded, "I am tense. Tomorrow is the start of your trial, at least one of them. Why aren't you tense?"

Alex shrugged. "The outcome is going to be bad no matter what happens. Why should I worry about it?"

Total amazement flashed across Mr. Caudel's face. "I can't believe you just said that!" Alex shrugged again. "Do you see all of this stuff piled on this table? All of this will be used to try to help with proving temporary insanity. That could be a better outcome for you."

"I'm still going to be locked away," Alex pointed out. "What does it really matter whether it is a prison or a mental hospital?"

Mr. Caudel slammed his hand down on the table. "There is a huge difference!" he yelled. "You'll never get out of prison!"

"I may never get out of the loony bin either!" Alex yelled back at him.

After a deep breath to calm himself, Mr. Caudel said, "Look, Alex, everyone has worked hard on your case, even your friends and your family. What you did was horrific, but we all truly believe you weren't yourself when you did it. No one wants to see you go away for the rest of your life. If you're not willing to fight this, then what have the rest of us been fighting for?"

Guilt can be a pretty powerful thing. Alex definitely felt it kick him in the stomach with Mr. Caudel's words. "You're right. I'm being selfish by giving up when everyone else is trying so hard to help me. What do I need to do to help?"

His attorney started rummaging through files until he found what he was looking for. "Start with this one. We need to go through all of this and make sure everything is correct and nothing is left out. You need to review written statements from your family and friends, and I want you to review police reports. I hate to rush you on all of this, but I didn't make it here a couple of days ago as I had planned."

"Speaking of a couple of days ago," Alex started as he opened the folder in his hands, "I had a couple of unexpected visitors."

"Who?" asked Mr. Caudel, sensing that the visitors probably weren't his parents.

A mischievous grin crossed Alex's face because he knew his attorney would be surprised. "I don't exactly remember their names, but my visitors were the two detectives I confessed to about the tasks."

Mr. Caudel *was* surprised. He reached across the table and pulled down the file Alex was looking through to get his full attention. "What did they say they wanted?"

"They said they wanted to tell me there was finally enough evidence to charge me with all the murders, but I think they were trying to find out why I entered the plea of not guilty by reason of insanity."

"Hmm," responded Mr. Caudel as he let go of the file and sat back in his chair. "I haven't heard about that. Either way, they shouldn't be coming here to tell you that. They must have wanted something else. What did you tell them?"

"Nothing."

"Good. I'll see what that was all about later today," Mr. Caudel assured Alex. "Now, we have a lot to cover." He picked up a file and the two began to sort through the pile to prepare for the first day of the first trial.

THIRTY-EIGHT

The courtroom was packed on the morning of the trial. This completely surprised Alex when he was escorted in. He wore a suit that his mom had dropped off at the jail earlier in the morning. The suit and his shortened hair made him look like a different person. He could have passed for part of the defense team, but the cuffs around his wrists gave him away. Once the cuffs were removed, he took a seat beside Mr. Caudel. The defense table had two other people sitting at it. Mr. Caudel introduced the other two gentlemen to Alex as his associates. He explained they had helped on the case, and they were there to continue to help as co-counsel.

The judge entered her bench promptly at nine o'clock. Everyone in the courtroom stood and waited until she told them to be seated. Alex felt like he was in the middle of a dream. None of the things going on around him seemed real.

The prosecutor gave his opening statement. Alex heard most of it, but some of it seemed to pass right by him. The prosecution accused Alex of being nothing more than a copycat murderer looking for his name to be forever connected to one of the world's most recognized unsolved cases. He described Alex as cold and malicious. The final blow came when the prosecutor said Alex should be found guilty and locked away forever.

After that, Alex blocked out the rest of the opening statement by the prosecution. He could feel himself falling into the trance-like state he used to fall victim to. When Mr. Caudel started his opening statement, Alex was already in another world. He didn't hear his attorney mention that he was a kind-hearted person, a hard worker, and a good student before the car accident. He also didn't hear Mr. Caudel talk about the depression that was deep enough to cause a mental breakdown. Nothing sunk in as he sat there with his head cocked to one side and his eyes staring off into empty space.

"Are you okay, Alex?" Mr. Caudel whispered to him when he sat back down.

Alex turned his head slightly to look at his attorney. "I guess so."

"Good. You need to pay attention to what's going on and to what is said, okay?"

"Uh-huh."

The first day lasted for an eternity—at least it did for Alex. Although he tried to pay attention, his mind kept drifting elsewhere. The prosecution presented testimonies from police officers, the coroner, the two detectives, and all kinds of experts. The one person that took the stand and caught his attention was the other psychiatrist he had met with after Ms. Pearson. Mr. Caudel had discussed Ms. Pearson's evaluation with Alex, but he hadn't heard anything from this one. Mixed emotions filled him as he listened to this psychiatrist describe him as completely sane. The prosecution's psychiatrist believed Alex had suffered from depression, but not deep enough to have any sort of mental breakdown that would cause voices or delusions. The psychiatrist concluded that the voice Alex heard was no more than a figment of his own imagination, and the voice just happened to be conveniently named Jack after Jack the Ripper. Alex felt relieved that someone called him completely sane, but he also felt furious that he was being called a liar.

Mr. Caudel did a decent job with his cross-examinations of the prosecution's witnesses, but he wanted to have a turn with his own witnesses. Alex knew from all the papers they had gone through the previous day that his attorney was well prepared. The prosecution had a steady stream of witnesses and experts to fill the whole day. The defense team was informed they would start to present their side the next day. Alex was a little relieved to be done for the day. His attorney had asked him to think about taking the stand to tell his side of the story, but Alex wasn't sure if he wanted to discuss his private thoughts and feelings, as well as the murders, in front of those he cared about the most. The fact his friends and family were in the courtroom hearing what everyone had to say about him and about what he had done was tearing at him already.

As Alex was cuffed before leaving the courtroom, Mr. Caudel assured him they would be ready to put up a good fight the next morning. He told Alex to get a good night's sleep but to think about taking the stand.

"I'll think about it," Alex assured him, "but I can't make any promises. I'll see you in the morning." He smiled at his friends and his parents before he was pulled away to return to his jail cell.

Sleep didn't come easily that night. Taking the stand in his own defense weighed heavy on his mind. It really didn't matter if he thought it was a good idea or not—he just didn't want to talk openly about it all. He didn't see where it would do any good anyway. It was the psychiatrist's place to show his mental state. How could Alex help his case when he never felt he was insane? Deep down he knew the defense wouldn't work anyway. So, as he slowly tried to sleep late that night, he decided not to take the stand and to spare his loved ones the pain and horror of hearing the graphic details come out of his own mouth.

The light of the next morning did nothing to change his mind. The task of proving he suffered from temporary insanity during those months would fall on Mr. Caudel. Alex dressed again in the same suit for court. It was all he had to use. Once again, he wore cuffs to the courtroom. The courtroom was filled with people again. The whole experience of being brought to court in cuffs was embarrassing to Alex. He had agreed to go to trial and try this defense for his parents, but now he wished he had ignored their wishes. When he looked at Jana sitting in the courtroom, he did secretly hope he would be free at some point. To be able to try to work things out with her gave him something to fight for even though his freedom was a long shot.

The first witness Mr. Caudel called was Jana. Alex wasn't ready to start the day with her taking the stand. The reality of how deeply his actions had affected her set in, and he could barely contain his emotions. It had been clear that he had hurt her, but he had no idea how bad it had been for her. He listened carefully as she talked about his drastic mood swings, not only with her but with his friends also. She then talked about how she felt when she heard about the murders. She admitted to recognizing him on the news.

"I thought I was dreaming," she said, her cheeks wet with tears. "Alex would never do those things. He isn't capable of that kind of violence. I'm still having a hard time believing it!"

One by one, Josh, Tony, and many other friends and coworkers took the stand in his defense. Eventually, his parents took the stand also. Each and every person testified to the changes in Alex's behaviors, moods, work performances, and in his overall being. One by one, the prosecutor tried to punch holes in their stories. The part that hurt the defense was that everyone admitted they never thought he was actually losing his sanity. Everyone did, however, say they thought he was suffering from depression, and they all easily bought that as an excuse for his behavior when he told them that was what had been wrong with him. The problem was that Alex had returned to his old self before he committed the last murder, which was what he was currently on trial for. The prosecution quickly made that point clear with each of the defense's witnesses. It was a hurtful blow to the case.

The one person Mr. Caudel was counting on to save the case was Ms. Pearson. She would have to convince a jury that Alex suffered from temporary insanity caused by a deep depression that started unexpectedly after the car crash. Her greatest obstacle would be his "normal" behavior before the last, most horrific, murder. Little did Alex know she had already come up with an explanation for that.

"Ms. Pearson," Mr. Caudel started after she had stated her qualifications for the jury, "explain to the jury exactly what your opinions of Alex Dorson are."

She sat in the witness chair and responded in a very professional manner. "My first impression of him was that he is a very pleasant person and very mild-mannered."

Mr. Caudel stood at the podium and continued to ask questions of her. "What did you think of him after the evaluation?"

"I still had the same impression."

"What did you discover during the evaluation?"

"During the evaluation, I began to realize Alex Dorson had gone through a period of not being so pleasant and mild-mannered. He described the car accident to me, and then we discussed his time in the hospital. It was then that he started to tell me about Jack, and about the effect Jack had on him. I firmly believe this is about the same time depression set in, and he began to change towards those around him."

"Tell us what you learned about his Jack person," instructed Mr. Caudel.

"First of all, Jack isn't a person. Jack was a voice he heard. Jack was a powerful force in everything Alex did, and Alex desperately wanted the voice to be gone. I feel the voice drove Alex deeper into the depression," she told the jury. "Simply put, the depression created Jack, a delusion, and the delusion, Jack, caused a deeper depression. It was a vicious cycle. At some point, Alex started to listen to the voice. He did what it told him to do. Alex described many things to me that could be classified as schizophrenia, but schizophrenia doesn't just go away. It can be treated with medication and such, but it doesn't go away."

Mr. Caudel left the podium and approached his expert witness. "So you don't believe Alex Dorson has an actual mental disorder?"

"No, I don't," she answered. The courtroom was filled with spectators' mumbles. After the judge quieted the courtroom, Ms. Pearson continued. "He doesn't suffer from any ongoing mental disorder that I could find, but he did have a mental breakdown for a period of time. He truly believed Jack would leave him to his life if he committed these murders."

"Can you explain his so-called 'normal' behavior right before he showed up at Taylor Bear's doorstep?"

She continued, "Alex believed he was close to committing the final task, as he called the murders, and he said Jack had told him to make things right in his life. I believe this was Alex's desire to get back to normal. He needed to make sure things that were broken could be repaired. He said, during this time, Jack was gone."

Mr. Caudel moved from Ms. Pearson's side to stand by the jury. "If Jack was gone and all was going well, what happened? Why did he continue with the final task?"

"Jack returned," she stated. Everyone in the courtroom remained quiet. It was obvious that wasn't all. Alex knew what was coming. Jana, Josh, and Tony did too. "There was another incident that set him off again."

"What was that incident, Ms. Pearson?"

"To explain that, I have to take a step back for a moment. Alex desperately wanted Jack gone because he wanted to have a normal life with his longtime girlfriend, Jana. He had wanted that more than anything. He loved her very much. As you heard in her testimony, he pushed her away and caused bad feelings. He felt it was in her best interest, but of course, she didn't know that. The night of the final task, Alex discovered Jana had realized from videos on the news that Alex was the murderer and she was very afraid of him. This was what sent him over the edge mentally one last time."

"One final question: Why do you believe Alex turned himself into the police?" asked Mr. Caudel, returning to his seat.

Ms. Pearson replied, "After he had already killed Miss Bear, he noticed something in her eyes. Her eyes reminded him of Jana. That brought him back to reality. It made him realize what he was doing. He decided to put a stop to it. He believed Jack would not leave him alone, even if he did continue to the end. The only way to stop Jack was to stop Alex. That was what he believed in his mind."

Mr. Caudel said he had no further questions. The prosecutor approached Ms. Pearson. He started his attack, and she was prepared, or so she thought.

"Ms. Pearson," he started, "I only have two questions, and they don't have anything to do with the similarities of Mr. Dorson's murders and the Ripper murders, even though they are close to exact, even down to the dates. I would like to know if you believe Alex knew the difference between right and wrong when he murdered Miss Bear."

"Yes," she answered, her expression becoming unpleasant.

"Do you think he understood the consequences of his actions?"

"Yes," she answered again regretfully.

"Nothing further, Your Honor."

THIRTY-NINE

Alex's life was left in the hands of twelve jurors. For three days, he barely ate or slept. He tried to keep his mind off the what-ifs, but all he could do was wonder why the jury needed so much time to come to a decision. By the morning of the fourth day, his wait had come to an end. Alex was taken to the courtroom to await the jury's arrival. Never before had he been so nervous and scared in his life. At the same time, he could hardly wait for it all to be over. This verdict would determine his decision on his pleas for the future trials.

Once the jury arrived, the judge instructed Alex to stand. The foreman of the jury handed the verdict to the bailiff who then passed it onto the judge. Alex held his breath, as did Mr. Caudel. No one in the courtroom was breathing either. The judge read the verdict. On the charge of first-degree murder, the jury found him guilty. That was all Alex heard. His heart sank to the pit of his stomach. That was it. His life was officially over. The courtroom became filled with many different emotions. Mrs. Dorson and Jana sobbed uncontrollably, while the family of his last victim sobbed for a different reason.

The judge announced, after the order was restored, that she was going to hand down the sentencing right then instead of waiting. The defense team knew that would happen either way the verdict went, so Alex had been prepared for it. His family and friends had also been prepared for it. Even though everyone knew what was coming, they were all still unprepared for the way the words would hit them.

"Alex Dorson," the judge stated, "you have been found guilty of first-degree murder for the death of Taylor Bear. State law is clear in the fact that first-degree murder carries a mandatory life sentence without the chance of parole. I now pass down that sentence of life in prison without the chance of parole. I do feel, Mr. Dorson, that something was going on with you during this crime, but the law is also clear on the legal insanity guidelines. Since you knew the difference between right and wrong, you knew what you were doing, and you knew the consequences of your actions, you cannot be declared legally insane under those guidelines. I guess I will see in future trials, Mr. Dorson. The court is adjourned."

The judge left the courtroom, and Alex was quickly put back in handcuffs to be taken back to jail. His mom shouted she loved him as he walked out of the courtroom. Back at the jail, he was informed the next morning he would be transported an hour away to the state maximum security prison. There would be one more meeting with Mr. Caudel at the jail. Past that, all meetings with him would be at the prison. The guard put Alex back in his cell. All of the guards had gotten the chance to know Alex during his time there. The guard told him they were all sorry things didn't turn out well for him. Alex thanked him and asked him to thank the others. At that moment, he just wanted to be left alone with his thoughts.

Mr. Caudel showed up a couple of hours later to see Alex for the last time at the jail.

"We will file an appeal, Alex," Mr. Caudel assured him. "We will keep going forward with the defense and with appeals as long as we have to. This isn't over, not by a long shot."

"No, I don't want to fight anymore," replied Alex, defeated. "I tried this because my parents wanted me to. It didn't work. I'm not going to ask my family and friends to go through trial after trial and appeal after appeal. Don't file an appeal. I'm done. I'm ready to face the consequences of my actions."

Disbelief crossed the face of Mr. Caudel. "You're just going to give up? Just like that?"

"Yes," he said flatly. "When the time comes, I want to enter a guilty plea in each of the other four cases. I know each time they will give a life sentence, but I only have one life to give. There is nothing more I can give…"

Mr. Caudel sighed heavily. "All right. I won't file an appeal just yet. You think about it once you get settled at the state prison. You might change your mind. As far as the other cases, I say we approach each one as they come at us. I don't want to take your decisions now as final. I refuse to. I think you will view things differently over time. You don't belong in prison, Alex."

"That's your opinion," he snapped.

"That's everyone's opinion," Mr. Caudel snapped back.

Alex shook his head, "Look at what I did! Look at the pictures of the women I killed! Then tell me I don't deserve to be in prison."

"That wasn't you. You weren't yourself," explained Mr. Caudel.

"It was me." Alex stood and knocked on the door of the small room. When the guard opened the door, he turned to his attorney and said, "Tell everyone I love them. I'll see you soon." He left his attorney alone in the small room to return to his cell for the night.

The next morning, Alex was placed on a prison bus with a few other men from the jail. He recognized them, but he had avoided any contact with everyone during his time in the county jail. During the trip, one man struck up a conversation with him. Even though Alex wasn't in the mood to talk, he was polite to the African American prisoner.

"My name is Terrell," the fellow prisoner introduced himself.

"I'm Alex," he replied with a forced smile.

Terrell grinned. "I know who you are. Everyone knows who you are. You're the new 'Jack the Ripper'. The only difference is you got caught."

Alex took offense to that but didn't know why. "I didn't get caught. I turned myself in to the cops. There's a big difference."

Terrell grinned wider. "I thought you were about to say you didn't do it. Do you think you really would have gotten away with it if you hadn't turned yourself in first?"

"Sure, why not?"

With a boisterous laugh, Terrell said, "No one gets away with five murders in this day and age. You're not special, my friend. You've become infamous, but not special."

Alex knew he wasn't special as he turned his back on Terrell and looked out the bus window. He felt he could have gotten away with it. Jack had wanted him to get away with it. This time, Alex would be known as the new Ripper, just as Terrell had said. If he was going to spend the rest of his life in prison, at least everyone would know why. His name would be associated with one of history's most famous cases.

Alex made a mental note to learn what he could about those cases. There would be nothing else for him to do in the years to come. So, he figured he might as well learn about the similarities between what he had done and what the original Ripper had done.

The bus pulled into the drive of the old maximum security prison. The outside grounds were surrounded by a tall stone wall that had barbed wire, two sets, running along the top of it. All of the prisoners walked as fast as they could as their shackles clanged together. The thought that he would never leave this building once he entered it hit Alex hard. He became nauseous and light-headed. Then he hit the ground hard as everything went black.

—⚒—

"Alex, wake up."

Alex barely heard the words but recognized the voice, the accent. He didn't open his eyes. He was sure he was dreaming until the voice repeated itself. Then he opened his eyes and looked around. He sat up and remembered where he was. It was dark, but there was enough moonlight coming through a window that he could see the inside of the prison cell. The last thing he remembered was being outside while the sun was shining. Now, he found himself sitting on the bottom bunk. Unlike the heavy door of his jail cell, this one had iron bars. He was amazed at how quiet it was at the moment.

"Are you fully awake now, Alex?" the voice asked.

"Jack?" Alex whispered, not sure if he was fully awake.

"Yes, Alex, it is I."

Alex dropped his head. "I thought you were gone. At least I hoped you were gone."

"Look up, Alex. Look out of the bars that contain you," Jack instructed.

When Alex looked up, he saw a figure of a man leaning his shoulder against the bars of his cell on the outside. His arms were crossed, and he leaned all his weight on one ankle. The man's hair was neatly combed, and he wore a black suit with a white shirt and a dark tie. He grinned mischievously at Alex, but none of that was what stood out the most. The most important detail was the fact that the moonlight passed through him. There was no shadow on the floor outside of the cell. It was like he was staring at a ghost. Alex looked at the man in disbelief.

"You have never seen me before, Alex. I can understand your confusion," Jack said.

Alex *was* confused. He was having a hard time comprehending what he was seeing. "Who are you? What are you?"

Jack chuckled but didn't change his position. "You know me as Jack. That is fine. You can continue to call me Jack. What I am is not so easily explained. Let me just say I am more than a voice in your head, much more."

"I always felt you were more," Alex acknowledged. It suddenly occurred to him that someone might be on the top bunk. Quietly, he stood up and peeked over the edge of the bunk.

"You are alone, Alex," assured Jack. Alex sat back down, relieved. "I do not know how you managed a cell to yourself, but I am sure it will not be that way for long."

He continued to whisper as he talked to Jack, remaining on his bunk. Alex figured no one else could hear or see Jack. He still was trying to wrap his mind around the fact that he could now see him. "Do you know how I got in here? I don't remember anything past getting off the bus."

"You fainted. Two guards brought you to your cell and left you," explained Jack.

"I guess that explains the lapse in my memory," he quipped. "Why are you here, Jack? I can't do anything else for you in here."

Jack put both feet flat on the floor and stepped through the bars. He sat down on the metal chair at a small writing desk in the cell. After he crossed his legs, Jack crossed his arms again. "You are right, Alex. You are of no use to me in here. I did not come here for anything other than a brief conversation before we part ways for the last time."

So Jack really would be gone for good. Despite everything. "Can I ask you a question?" inquired Alex.

"I believe you just asked one."

Alex rolled his eyes. It had been a while since he had to endure Jack's sarcasm. "That's not exactly what I had in mind. I want to know many things. First, why me? Of all the people in the world, why did you pick me? Second, what was the purpose of it all? And, lastly, did you really want me to succeed? Or is this what you wanted all along? You never told me any of this before when I would ask. Will you tell me now?"

"That is quite a few questions, but I will answer them as best as I can," Jack said. "To answer your first question, I will say you were chosen at random. I had no real reason to pick you at all. After your accident, your mind and body was working on healing. This allowed an opening for me to step into your life."

"I thought maybe you picked me because I had so much to lose, like Jana," Alex said, still trying to whisper.

Jack laughed. "Everyone has something to lose whether they know it or not. You are not special." That was the second time he had been told that. "I was at the hospital when you arrived. You seemed younger and stronger than most of the patients there, despite your injuries. That is all. The feelings you had for Jana just worked to my advantage. I could use them to manipulate you and to keep you alive."

"Why did you care what happened to me? Again, what was the purpose of it all?"

"Let me tell you a story, Alex," Jack started. "There was a young man that lived many years ago in 1888. He was facing a promising future in his chosen profession. I encountered this young man on the street one day. I wondered what he would be willing to do to protect his future. I started to make a plan. He quickly gave in to my demands, much quicker than you. Of course, people were treated horribly if they were thought to be insane back then. He was more eager to be rid of me than you. You were in denial of me much longer. That is one part where Jana came in handy."

"Let me guess, he didn't have a girlfriend or wife."

"No. He only cared for his own well-being and his future career," Jack explained. "Now, let me continue. He had some knowledge of human anatomy, so I allowed him to control many aspects of the tasks. I'm not sure how he knew the human body so well, but he did. Things did not bother him as much as they did you. He became a little more daring and a little more aggressive each time. I merely watched him perform. The two victims in one night were completely by mistake. He was almost caught that night," Jack said with a chuckle. "He then started sending letters to the police to taunt them. I enjoyed it very much. So much that I wanted him to get away with it, and to keep getting away with it—for as long as he could. Alas, someone started to suspect him in the murders after the last one. I had planned on more, but he knew his life would be over if he was discovered. He would be committed to an insane asylum in that time period. He would have been used for many experiments until he died. Unfortunately for him, his madness led him to being committed for something completely unrelated. As it turned out, he did get away with it," Jack said with a chuckle.

"So that's what happened to Jack the Ripper," Alex muttered. "Was his name really Jack?"

"No, Alex, it was not. It is not mine either," Jack assured him. "I cannot tell you that information. It always has been a secret, and it will always remain a secret. Although many people believe they know who he is, no one knows for absolute certainty. I can assure you of that."

"Then who are you? *What* are you?" Alex asked. "Your eyes are as black as night. Are you… Are you some kind of demon? That's what I first thought, but now that I finally see you, you look like a person. But you are not the Ripper. He was just a random person. Like me."

Jack was silent.

Alex stood, chuckled, and began to pace back and forth. "I see we're doing the silent treatment again. Okay, let me get straight the facts I *do* know. You had no real reason to pick me. I was just in the wrong place at the wrong time. There is nothing more to any of this than it all being a mere game to you. You only wished to see if the same crimes could be gotten away with a century later, in another country, by a different puppet. Am I right so far?" Alex stopped and stared at the transparent figure in the chair.

"Yes," Jack replied. "And you failed me. I still don't have my answer. And that is why I must move on from you, Alex. I won't be a prisoner with you."

Alex felt a bitterness rise inside him. He'd been used, his life and future upended, all for Jack to abandon him. To walk away free. To move on to the next victim. The cycle would continue. And there was nothing he could do to stop it. "So that's it? Nothing more?"

"Nothing more," Jack answered as he stood. "Now, Alex, I will take my leave of you. We will not meet again, here on Earth anyway. Sometimes I can see into the future, sometimes I cannot. We may cross paths in a different realm, depending on you. I am sorry things turned out this way, but you have to realize your decisions brought you here. I did not force you to do anything per se, only helped you when needed." Jack stepped back through the bars. He turned to look back at Alex. "It has been a pleasure, Alex Dorson." Jack bowed, and then he turned and walked down the catwalk.

Alex watched Jack through the bars. Before his eyes, Jack transformed into something not human. What was once a male figure morphed down on all fours like an animal. The clothes he had been wearing faded away to show a hairless, muscular body covered with tight, dingy grey skin. Pointy horns grew from the sides of his head. The dog-like creature looked back once at Alex. Alex could barely see its eyes but could swear they were black as coal—that was the only feature that remained the same. With a slight growl, Jack turned and ran, and then he vanished into thin air. Alex stood at the bars of his cell, numb and dumbstruck. Minutes passed before Alex could break his grasp on the bars. He sat back down on the bunk and stared at the chair Jack had occupied. Maybe Alex *was* insane. What he had just seen could not be real, could it?

No matter what Jack was exactly, Jack had been right. Alex was realizing that. Jack had not really made Alex do anything. He had made the decision to do what Jack wanted him to do. He chose to stalk the victims. He chose to murder those victims. He chose to turn himself in to the police. He was responsible for ending up where he was, and he had the rest of his life to contemplate those facts, alone.